PEACEFUL JENKINS

Center Point
Large Print

Also by William Colt MacDonald and available from Center Point Large Print:

Cartridge Carnival
Gunsight Range
Lightning Swift
Ghost-Town Gold

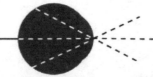

**This Large Print Book carries the
Seal of Approval of N.A.V.H.**

PEACEFUL JENKINS

WILLIAM COLT MacDONALD

CENTER POINT LARGE PRINT
THORNDIKE, MAINE

This Center Point Large Print edition
is published in the year 2020 by arrangement with
Golden West Literary Agency.

Originally published in the US
by Doubleday, Doran & Co.
Originally published in the UK
by Hodder & Stoughton.

The text of this Large Print edition is unabridged.
In other aspects, this book may vary
from the original edition.
Printed in the United States of America
on permanent paper.
Set in 16-point Times New Roman type.

ISBN: 978-1-64358-712-7 (hardcover)
ISBN: 978-1-64358-716-5 (paperback)

The Library of Congress has cataloged this record under
Library of Congress Control Number: 2020942183

To Arthur and Madge Bayliss

PEACEFUL JENKINS

1

"STOP THAT BANDIT!"

MORNING sun broiled down on Spanish Wells' main street, intensifying the shadow between buildings and causing pitch to simmer up from the new pine-plank sidewalks on either side of the unpaved, dusty roadway. It was too hot for many to be abroad; most of the town's citizens were remaining within doors, enjoying the relatively cool interiors. Heat waves shimmered and danced above roof tops. The leaves of the cottonwoods at one end of town hung drooping and listless. There didn't seem to be a breath of air stirring, and even the flies buzzing about the few horses, tethered at the unbroken line of hitch racks along either side, went at their business in a sort of desultory fashion.

Beneath the wooden awning that stretched above the sidewalk three men sat rather tensely on the porch of the Oasis Saloon. One of them, Handsome Jake Tracy, pulled out a large silver watch and consulted its face.

"Five minutes to ten now," he announced.

"You sure Dawes will go through with it as

planned?" asked the second man, named Scott Heffner. Heffner was a wiry individual, somewhere in his thirties. He wore two guns.

Handsome Jake smiled thinly. "He'll go through with it—or suffer the consequences."

The third man stirred restlessly in his chair. He was a hard-featured fellow, with tight lips and a pugnacious jaw. Pinned to his open vest was a deputy sheriff's badge of office. A holstered forty-five hung at his right thigh. Behind him, resting against the front wall of the Oasis, stood a thirty-thirty Winchester rifle. He said slowly, "There shouldn't be any hitch."

Conversation languished for the moment. The eyes of the three men kept straying diagonally across the street, where the Spanish Wells Savings Bank stood on the corner of Main and Saddlehorn streets. It was a two-story brick building, the second story having been but recently added to keep step with the sudden boom that had descended on Spanish Wells. There were three windows across the face of that second story, one of which, at present, was raised, presumably to admit more air to the interior of the building.

Across Saddlehorn Street, on the same side as the bank, a rider emerged from the Red Star Livery. He pulled his pony to a halt before the bank, dismounted, tossed reins over the hitch rack, then walked slowly away around the corner of the bank, leaving the pony to swelter beneath the blazing morning sun.

Jake Tracy, from his observation point on the Oasis porch, noticed the man and nodded with satisfaction.

"Dawes is on schedule," he murmured.

The other two didn't reply. Back of them the swinging doors of the saloon burst apart and a burly man in cowpuncher togs stepped out to the porch.

"Y'ain't seen Hugo, have you?" he asked.

Tracy, without turning his head, replied coldly, "No, we haven't. Nick, you'd better fork your bronc and get back to the ranch. Hugo Randle don't like his men wasting time when they should be working, and if he sees you in town—"

"Cripes!" Nick Corvall protested. "It was so danged hot I just had to ride in for a beer. Hugo would understand—"

"Will you shut up!" Tracy twisted savagely around in his chair, eyes blazing. "Either fork that bronc"—pointing to one of a pair of ponies standing at the Oasis hitch rack—"and get back to the ranch, or get inside and pour more beer down your gullet. But don't let me see your face around here again!"

"Sure, Jake, sure." Corvall seemed mystified at Tracy's sudden, uncalled-for anger. Then he smiled slyly. "If Hugo sees me inside I'll tell him you told me to stay here and drink more

11

beer—at the expense of the Wolf Head outfit."

"Just get out, that's all," Tracy snarled.

Corvall withdrew to the bar. Deputy Sheriff Herb Vaughn said scornfully, "Getting edgy, ain't you, Jake? Always did figure you might have a streak of yeller behind that handsome mug of yours."

"That's whatever," Tracy said sullenly.

Scott Heffner spoke. "Here comes Drake now."

The elderly owner of the JD outfit, Jabez Drake, was just riding into town. He slowed his pony to a walk as it approached the Oasis and nodded cordially to the men on the porch.

Deputy Vaughn raised his voice: "Hey, Jabez, you'd better light and wash some of the dust outten your throat."

Jabez Drake nodded. "That's an idea, Herb. I got some business at the bank first. I'll join you right after. Hot, ain't it?"

"Not near so hot as it's going to be," Vaughn returned, with an ugly chuckle that didn't carry to Drake's ears.

They watched with narrowed eyes while Jabez Drake passed on and then pulled his pony to a halt before the Spanish Wells Savings Bank. Dismounting, Drake stooped to pass under the hitch rack, crossed the sidewalk, then mounted the flight of three stone steps to pass through the open doorway of the bank.

Five minutes passed, then ten. The tenseness

of the three men on the Oasis porch seemed to spread along the street. Even the deputy's horse at the Oasis hitch rack had ceased its continual switching at flies and stood, head drooping under the blazing sun glare. A definite hush had settled through the town. Then things commenced to happen all at once:

Jabez Drake emerged from the open doorway of the savings bank and descended the stone steps, carrying in his right hand a small canvas money sack that bulged on the sides. As he reached the sidewalk the man who had left the pony before the bank but a short time before suddenly appeared around the corner from Saddlehorn Street. But this time the man was wearing a bandanna, in lieu of a mask, stretched across the lower half of his face. He leaped into sudden view before Drake, brandishing a long-barrelled six-shooter.

Drake stopped short, left hand clutching the money sack, right hand starting toward the gun at his hip. A six-shooter thundered violently in the hushed street. Drake staggered back, clutching at his shoulder, the money sack dropping from his hand. For a brief instant the hold-up man wavered, staring dumbly at the gun in his hand. The watchers on the Oasis porch could see, even at that distance, the wave of astonishment that crossed the hold-up man's gaze above the mask-like bandanna.

However, even as Drake crumpled to the sidewalk, the bandit recovered himself. Stooping swiftly, he scooped up the money sack, vaulted over the hitch rack, and leaped to his pony's back. In an instant he had turned the animal and was racing east along Main Street.

The noise of the shot had brought heads popping from windows. Doors banged; men and a few women appeared all along the street. An outcry rose. Somebody yelled, "Stop that bandit!"

The voice came from the Oasis porch. Tracy, Heffner, and Deputy Vaughn were on their feet now. By this time the roadway was swarming with men, gazing in the direction of the rapidly departing hold-up man. So far, no one had given a thought to Jabez Drake, sprawled silently on the sidewalk in front of the bank.

Deputy Vaughn turned, seized his rifle from its resting place against the saloon wall, and moved lightly down the steps to the middle of the road. Jerking the weapon to his shoulder, he sighted and swiftly pulled the trigger. When the powder smoke cleared away the bandit was still going, riding hard. Again Vaughn pulled the trigger. The hammer fell with a dull click. Vaughn cursed, lowered the rifle, and levered another cartridge into its chamber. He sighted once more, hesitated but a brief second before his finger curved tightly about the trigger. The Winchester spoke sharply, like the cracking of a whip, but once more the deputy had missed. By this time the bandit had disappeared around a curve in the street at the far end of town.

"Dammit! I never miss!" Vaughn exclaimed angrily.

"You did that time," came Tracy's scornful reply. "I reckon we'd better gather a posse and—"

"Posse be damned!" Vaughn said wrathfully. "I can get that dirty sidewinder without any help."

Brushing aside the knot of curious people who had gathered at his back, he turned and ran toward his horse, waiting at the Oasis hitch rack. Seizing the reins, he vaulted into the saddle and jabbed spurs against the animal's sides. The horse wheeled, then darted off like an arrow shot from a bow. "I'll get the dirty son!" floated back in angry tones over the deputy's shoulder.

People crowding into the street pressed back to make way for the horse to pass. Riding hard, the deputy soon reached the curve in the road at the end of town and swept from view in a cloud of dust. Only then did those on the street give a thought to the victim of the bandit, still stretched prone on the sidewalk before the bank.

Now sudden cries for a doctor filled the air. A few men ran for horses to take up the deputy's trail, but after following the well-worn road that ran east of Spanish Wells for a few miles they gave up and turned back. It was too hot to ride

15

far that day. Besides, chasing bandits was Deputy Vaughn's job.

And Deputy Vaughn was still on the job. A few miles out of town he had pulled his pony to a steady, even, ground-devouring gait. Fresh hoofmarks along the way made the trail easy to follow. He rode steadily while the sun passed the meridian and started its westward trek. Twice during the afternoon he stopped to rest the horse, then pushed on again.

By four that afternoon he was getting into the foothills of the Crazy Snake Mountains. By this time both horse and man were streaked with dust and perspiration. The trail curved between hills dotted with mesquite and cacti. There was a great deal of loose rock on either side. Another half-hour would bring Vaughn to the entrance of Surcingle Canyon where it cut through the Crazy Snakes. Ten miles beyond the other end of the canyon was located the town of Surcingle, county seat of Los Padres County. Vaughn mopped his brow with an already damp bandanna and pulled his pony to a walk. The tired beast was beyond a faster gait by this time. "I sure hope," Vaughn muttered angrily, "that damn Dawes ain't going to make me chase him clear to Surcingle."

A hail from one side caught his ear. Shifting in his saddle, Vaughn gazed up a slight rise to a live-oak tree growing from the hillside. A horse stood beneath the tree, and beside it was Dawes, the bandit, the money sack still clutched in his hand.

Vaughn looked swiftly back over his shoulder, then directed the pony up the slope. "What in hell's the idea of dragging me clear off here?" Vaughn demanded angrily.

"Wanted to make sure nobody else was following," came the reply. "Say, look here, there's something I don't understand—"

"There's a hell of a lot you don't understand, Dawes," Vaughn cut in with a short laugh. By this time, unnoticed by Dawes, the deputy had drawn his six-shooter. "Yep," Vaughn repeated, "a hell of a lot!" And with that he triggered a shot from his six-shooter.

Even as Dawes fell Vaughn pumped a second leaden slug into the man's body. Then he spurred his pony closer and gazed down at the silent form on the earth.

"Dammit!" Vaughn laughed harshly, "I never miss."

Without leaving his saddle he swung down, reached to the money sack that had fallen from Dawes's hand, then straightened up again. After a moment he directed his pony back toward the trail.

It was after midnight by the time Vaughn once more rode his weary pony along the main street of Spanish Wells. There was more life in the town now than there had been that morning. A crowd quickly gathered around the deputy as he dismounted stiffly at the Oasis hitch rack, everyone asking the same question.

"Sure I got him," Vaughn said boastfully. "Left his carcass for the coyotes, over near the entrance to Surcingle Canyon. Damn such sidewinders! What news of Jabez Drake?"

"He's over at Doc Hamilton's," a new voice put in. "Don't know whether he'll live or not. His daughter's with him. Did you bring back the money, Herb?" The speaker, Tarpaulin Thompson, was a lean, grizzled son of the range and foreman on Jabez Drake's JD Ranch. "It'll shore finish Jabez if that money is gone."

"Oh, it's you, Tarp." Vaughn squinted at the elderly cowman in the light from the Oasis windows. "Yeah, here's the sack. I reckon as Jabez' rod you're the man to take charge of it." He passed the canvas sack to Thompson.

"You reckon it's all here, all right?" Thompson said eagerly. "There should be five thousand dollars in this sack."

"Certain it's there," Vaughn said confidently. "I didn't stop to count it—didn't even open the sack, as a matter of fact. I was in too much of a hurry to get back here. Maybe you'd better take a look, Tarp."

"I figure to," Thompson replied. He jerked open the sack after untying the strings that held it closed, reached in, and produced an oblong pack

18

of cut newspapers shaped to resemble a package of greenbacks.

"What the hell is this!" Thompson exclaimed. He moved swiftly to the better light of the Oasis porch and upended the sack. More packages tumbled out, but like the first, they were cut from old newspapers. There wasn't a bank bill in the lot.

Old Tarp held his voice as steady as possible. "There's something for you to explain here, Vaughn. What became of the five thousand dollars—?"

Vaughan gulped, shook his head. For a moment he seemed unable to speak. "God!" he finally exclaimed hoarsely. "Don't blame me, Tarp. I've been a fool, that's what, a blasted fool. Dawes must have had a confederate waiting outside town. They changed sacks. And like a damned idiot I spent my time chasing Dawes while the confederate made his getaway." A look of anger swept across his face. "But nobody's going to run a whizzer like that on Herb Vaughn and get away with it. Just as soon as I can get me a fresh bronc I'm hitting the trail again. And this time I'll bring back that five thousand or know the reason why!"

He brushed past the stunned Thompson and ran swiftly in the direction of the livery stable. Others, with the thought that somewhere along the trail might be found a money sack con-

19

taining five thousand dollars, also rushed for horses. But a close scrutiny of the trail, all the way to Surcingle Canyon, failed to produce the missing sack of money. What was stranger still, even Dawes's body and the bandit's horse had disappeared by the time the searchers arrived.

2

FIVE ACES

FOUR weeks later two riders rode slowly along the trail leading to Spanish Wells. One of them, mounted on a sorrel gelding, was lean and rangy, with bright brick-coloured hair beneath his well-worn Stetson. He wore corduroy pants, cuffed ankle-high, over his high-heeled riding boots. A Bull Durham tag dangled from one pocket of his green-and-black-plaid woollen shirt. A cartridge belt supported a holstered Colt forty-five at his right thigh. His nose was somewhat aquiline; his jaw sinewy. His grey eyes were crowfooted with tiny laugh wrinkles. His name was Jenkins; to his intimates he was known as Peaceful. His age appeared to be in the vicinity of twenty-six or -seven.

Jenkins' companion, Applejack Peters, was considerably older. There were streaks of iron grey in his dark hair. His features were lined and brown. There was something of the appearance of well-weathered rawhide in his lengthy makeup. He was clad in woollen shirt and faded denims. His black sombrero was considerably battered and thick with dust. He rode a buckskin pony with a long creamy tail, and there was a six-shooter at his right hip. Both men carried Winchesters in rifle boots.

The two had pulled their alkali-streaked mounts to a walk as they headed up a slight rise bordered on either side with sage and mesquite. Overhead, the late morning sun burned down from a sky of vivid blue. There wasn't a cloud in sight.

Applejack Peters mopped at his forehead. "Cripes a'mighty! Ain't we ever going to reach Spanish Wells? It can't be more'n two-three miles farther."

Peaceful Jenkins grinned. "You've been saying that for the last ten miles, pardner." His speech was slow and drawly and carried a humorous overtone.

"And I've been plumb thirsty for the last ten miles," Applejack grumbled.

Peaceful said dryly, "Underestimating some, aren't you, pard? I never rcmember the time when you weren't thirsty."

"You're just like an elephant that never for-gets," Applejack growled. He paused. "My gosh, it gets hot in this country. Not like Texas, where a man can breathe—"

"I've seen it just this hot in Texas—and hotter," Peaceful put in.

"Mebbeso," Applejack conceded. "But you've got to admit the sluicing spots aren't so far apart.

I wish we were back there right now. I don't know why I'm such an idiot as to be always letting you pull me off on trips like this. Reckon it's just my paternal attitude makes me go against my better judgment. If I wasn't along to help pull you out of messes—"

"I never get into messes," the other said gravely. "I'm Peaceful."

"If that name ain't a misnomer, I never saw one," Applejack said irritatedly. "Peaceful—pshaw!—just like a catamount!"

Peaceful grinned. "Well, you might as well make up your mind to it pard. From all I hear of Spanish Wells, the town is booming and you know the sort of crowd a boomtown draws."

"Say, that's right." Applejack's leathery features brightened. "There'll be plenty of drinking places, won't there?"

They rode on for another half-hour, at the end of which time, topping a rise of ground, they found themselves gazing at the first buildings on the outskirts of Spanish Wells. The buildings—most of them—were of new, unplaned lumber. There were several tents with wooden floors. Many dobe houses were in process of construction. Just before they entered the town Applejack and Peaceful drew their ponies to one side off the road to allow the passage of the noonday coach. The stage swept past, its six horses running furiously under the whip-cracking commands of its driver, in a swirl of dust and flying gravel.

When the dust had settled the riders pushed on into the town. Main Street seethed with people. On all sides fresh buildings were being erected. Near the centre of Spanish Wells the structures looked older, more mature. As the ponies proceeded at a slow walk Peaceful noticed a two-story brick hotel, a livery stable, the savings bank, the first of a pair of general stores. Many of the buildings had high false fronts; from most of them wooden awnings stretched out above the sidewalk. Ponies and wagons lined the hitching rails before stores and saloons. On the older buildings the paint was sun-blistered and cracked. In the case of many painted signs dust storms had eaten the wood away from the painted letters, leaving the letters to stand forth in bold relief.

Applejack said suddenly, "Oasis Saloon! Let's stop, pard."

Peaceful eyed the building in question. "You know," he drawled meditatively, "I'll bet seventy-five per cent of the saloons in the West are named the Oasis."

"Meaning what?" Applejack asked curiously.

"Meaning that the owner hasn't any originality. Lack of originality means he hasn't any ambition. Lack of ambition means he might not be too clean in washing his glasses. Let's ride on."

Applejack sighed. "Every time you start philosophizing I lose out. All right, pick me a better place. It doesn't make any difference. The first few drinks will just be blotted up on my tongue anyway. That's how parched I am."

They pushed on, swerving aside now and then to allow the passage of teams and other riders. Peaceful noticed a huge frame building with the words HUGO RANDLE'S SPANISH DAGGER— DANCE & CHANCE EMPORIUM painted across its front wall in vivid crimson paint.

"Drinks, too, probably." Applejack looked hopefully at his redheaded pardner. "That's a right big honky-tonk, Peaceful."

Peaceful sized up the place, shaking his head. "I'll bet they'd steal your eyeteeth in that joint. Nope, it's not for us. Look yonderly, the Demijohn Saloon. Now I'm ready to stop."

They reined their ponies diagonally across the street from the Spanish Dagger, dismounted, and flipped reins over the Demijohn tie rail. Peaceful gazed around. Directly opposite the Demijohn was a building bearing a sign which proclaimed it to be Sam Purdy's General Store. Peaceful said, pointing across the street, "Applejack, there's the store where Dawes worked."

Applejack was already heading toward the saloon. "I'll look at it later." He kept going.

Peaceful grinned. "All right, go ahead. I'll join you in a couple of minutes. I'm going across and make *habla* with Sam Purdy if he's in."

Peaceful threaded his way across the street, moving leisurely between riders and pedestrians, mounted to the broad porch that fronted Purdy's establishment, and entered. There were several people in the store. It was the sort of place at which could be purchased anything from a forty-five cartridge to a mowing machine. Shelves of canned goods lined the walls. A showcase held needles, thread, and dress goods. There were racks of hardware and guns. Barrels and boxes stood about at various points on the wide stretch of flooring. There was a mingled odour of camphor and cheese in the big room. Sam Purdy himself was the only clerk on duty at the moment. He was a tall, gangling man with spectacles set rakishly on a long red nose. His grey hair was sparse and he spoke with a distinct down-East twang. Peaceful knew he was Purdy, as he heard several of the customers address him by name.

In time the last of the customers had been taken care of and Purdy approached the point at the counter at which Peaceful stood waiting. "Sorry to keep ye waitin', young feller," Purdy said genially, "but I don't usual git sech a rush of business come noontime. My clerk, he's out to his dinner, and I bin busier'n tomcat on a tin roof. Whut can I do for ye?"

"I'm looking for a pack of cards—playing cards," Peaceful said. "Me and my pard like to play high-low-jack-and-the-game come evenings."

"Playing cards? Got a prime stock, I have." Purdy turned to a shelf back of him, then tossed a pack of cards on the counter. "Bicycle Brand. Best made. Dollar an' a half the deck."

Peaceful assumed a look of surprise. "Didn't figure to pay so much. Buck-fifty is a lot of money for a man who isn't working. Haven't got any second-hand decks around, have you?"

Purdy shook his head. "Don't carry second-hand stock, young feller. Yeah, if ye ain't workin' dollar-fifty seems high. But Spanish Wells is on the boom. Prices have gone up. Ye'd be surprised if I told ye how much it costs me to get supplies freighted in here. It'll be mighty different when the railroad comes. That road will be a blessin'—" He paused suddenly. "Wait a minute. Second-hand cards, ye say? Might I can fix ye up." He rummaged in his stock back of the counter, then, turning once more, tossed a soiled cardboard case of cards before his customer. "I can let ye have those for four bits. Trouble is, they belonged to a dead bandit. Hope ye ain't squeamish none."

"Dead bandit, eh?" Peaceful looked only slightly interested.

"Yissir! Feller named Dawes. Lunger. Out here for his health. I give him a job in my store. Liked him right well. Then, sudden, for no reason at all, he went bad. Shot one of our foremost cowmen

27

and ran off with five thousand dollars. Dawes used to have his sleepin' quarters back of this here store. Shock to me, 'twas, when he turned bad."

"And he's dead now, eh?" Peaceful asked.

"Deader'n a doornail. Our deputy, Herb Vaughn, killed him."

"And got the money back, I suppose."

"No sir. Thet money never was recovered. Funny thing, Dawes's body disappeared too. Ye see, Vaughn had chased him nigh to Surcingle—"

Peaceful yawned. "Sorry I haven't time to hear the story, Mr. Purdy. I reckon these cards will do." He placed fifty cents on the counter. "Reckon I'm lucky to find a deck so cheap."

"Only for Willie Horton, ye wouldn't have," Purdy said. "Willie, he's a boy works for me. Opens the store in the mornin' and redds up the place, runs errands, and so on. Right now Willie is up to Nevady, visitin' his folks. He left a few days arter this bandit was killed. Romantic like, Willie is. Before he left he put Dawes's pack of cards out for sale, thinkin' mebbe folks would pay a good price for such a souvenir. But I reckon folks wasn't impressed, or they was too squeamish, or somethin'. Anyway, nobody cared to buy. Most of Dawes's effects were sent up to his relatives, up in Montany someplace, but I figured it was best not to send a deck of cards. It's bad enough for relatives to learn someone what's dear to 'em is a bandit 'thout them findin' out he plays cards too. Not that Louie Dawes was a gambler. Nope! Never knew him to gamble. But he'd sit him down with that there very pack of cards and play solitaire by the hour—"

"Yep, I reckon I know how it is." Peaceful cut short the long-winded narrative. "Well, I'm not squeamish. I reckon these cards are just what I want. I'm obliged to you."

"No thanks necessary. Drop in again if ye stay here. I'm Mayor of Spanish Wells, so I can probably give ye information on nigh any subject pertainin' to the town."

"Well, thanks. Good-bye, Mayor Purdy."

Peaceful shoved the newly purchased deck of cards in a hip pocket and strode outside. As he hesitated on the store porch, before descending the steps to the sidewalk, a tall, broad-shouldered man dressed rather flashily, with a canary-yellow neckerchief and a couple of cheap rings on his hands, nearly bumped into Peaceful in his rush to enter the general store. The man was handsome in a rather cheap, actorish fashion. His dark hair curled at the back of his loud plaid shirt collar. His fawn-coloured sombrero was equipped with a beaded hatband of many colours. The man muttered something and pushed on into the store. Peaceful continued down to the sidewalk and stood there a moment, gazing at the people streaming past.

A minute later the man was back, tugging at Peaceful's shirt sleeve. He seemed vastly excited about something. Peaceful turned to face him.

The man said, "You just bought a deck of cards in Purdy's store."

"Yeah, I did," Peaceful said quietly. "Any law against it?"

"Hell, no!" the other exploded. "Look, you don't get me. Maybe I'd better introduce myself. I don't want to make you any trouble. I'm Jake Tracy—Handsome Jake, my friends call me," he added with a smirk.

"I'm Peaceful—"

"Hell! I told you I didn't aim to make any trouble—"

"—Jenkins," Peaceful finished. He made no move to shake hands.

"Oh, it's a name—your name. Peaceful Jenkins. I see. Well, look, Jenkins. I want those cards that Purdy just sold you."

"Why?" Peaceful asked gravely.

"I just want 'em, that's all," Tracy snapped irritatedly. "For a souvenir. The feller that owned 'em was a friend—"

"I understood he was a bandit." Peaceful smiled gravely.

"You don't understand," Tracy half snarled. "How was I to know he'd turn bad? He was all right before that. But that ain't here nor there. I want those cards. Purdy says you paid

30

half a buck for 'em. I'll give you twice that."

"Ain't interested," Peaceful refused.

"Look, feller"—Tracy's tones were turning ugly—"I don't want any argument with you—"

"Takes two to make an argument," Peaceful drawled. "I'm not starting one."

"I'll give you five dollars for those cards."

"Ten would be higher," Peaceful pointed out.

"All right," Tracy said eagerly. "Ten it is. Give me the cards."

Peaceful chuckled. "I didn't say I'd sell for ten. I merely mentioned ten was higher than five."

Tracy's face grew red. "You trying to make a fool of me?"

Peaceful shook his head. "I figure I arrived in Spanish Wells too late for that," he drawled.

Tracy shook with rage. "Look here, you red-headed—" and he called Peaceful a name. "I want those cards and I'm going to have 'em!"

Peaceful's eyes narrowed, but the thin smile still played around his lips. "You know," he said genially, "that's not a nice name to call a man. I admit I baited you some, so I'll overlook it this time, being I'm peaceful and not inclined to trouble. But don't repeat it."

Tracy threw caution to the winds. "I'll repeat it and keep on repeating it"—and he did—"until you pass over every card in that deck, you—"

Peaceful scrutinized his hand. "There's five aces in this hand," he mused, half aloud. "Some folks call 'em knuckles, but aces is good enough for me. Now if you really want some aces, Tracy, just keep on the way you've been talking."

Tracy ripped out a curse and closed in on Peaceful, fists flailing the air. Peaceful laughed softly, took one quick side step. His right fist flashed through the air and landed against the side of Tracy's head. Tracy staggered back; his heels flew into the air, and he landed heavily on the plank sidewalk.

For a minute he lay stunned; then slowly he roused himself to motion. Climbing to his feet, he stood looking savagely at Peaceful for a moment, blood trickling from a cut on his cheek-bone. By this time there were yells along the street and a crowd started to collect. Peaceful drawled quietly, "Still want those cards?"

Tracy nodded. "You asked for it," he snarled and made a lightning movement toward the gun at his hip. Then he stopped short, mouth dropping open, in amazement. As though by magic, a gun had appeared in Peaceful's hand, and Peaceful had him covered.

"You're the one who's asking for it," Peaceful was saying quietly. "Now it's up to you. Do you want to finish that draw or don't you? Think fast, Tracy, my patience is getting short!"

And then Peaceful stiffened as he felt a gun

barrel jabbed violently against his spine and heard a voice say, "Put that gun away, redhead, before I let daylight through your innards. Move pronto!"

3

"YOU'RE BOTH COVERED!"

THERE was nothing else to do. Cautiously Peaceful shoved the gun back in his holster and raised both hands in the air. Then he cast a glance over one shoulder to meet the ugly-visaged glance of a man wearing a deputy badge. "Oh, it's the law that speaks, eh?" Peaceful remarked lightly.

"Damn right it's the law," came the reply. "You fellers come to Spanish Wells and think because it's a boomtown you can fight and kill any way you like. Well, Herb Vaughn is still enforcing the law here, and we aim to keep this town quiet. Now what's all this ruckus about?"

Tracy had his gun out by this time, covering Peaceful. There was an evil smile on the man's face. "Ain't much to tell you, Herb," Tracy said. "This redheaded hombre had a deck of cards I wanted. I offered him a good price for 'em. Suddenly he got abusive and hit me—"

"Liar!" Peaceful spoke the word coolly.

"Now look here, young feller," Vaughn said wrathfully. "I don't want none of your lip. For two cents I'd let Jake go ahead and bore you after such talk."

Peaceful smiled. "I figure the two scents are already here," he drawled. "You both smell bad."

There was a roar of laughter from the crowd that had gathered. Vaughn's face grew crimson. "All right," he snarled, "I've had enough of this talk. Either hand over those cards or—"

"There's too much talk all round," came a new voice, that of Applejack Peters. "Too damn much talk and not enough shooting. You two, holding them guns. Put 'em away! You're both covered!"

"Nice work, Applejack," Peaceful murmured appreciatively, lowering his arms. "Keep 'em covered until we learn what's what."

Tracy started a protest, but Herb Vaughn had the louder voice. "You can't do this to me," Vaughn raged. "I'm a legally empowered officer of the law. By the authority invested in me by the county of Los Padres—"

"Oh, for gosh sakes, shut up," Applejack said wearily. "You're not running for office now, Deputy. No political speeches, please. What's this all about?"

"By geez! You'll find out!" Vaughn snorted. "You can't defy the law. I suppose you're a pard to this redhead here. I'll shove you both in the cooler—"

"You'll shove nothing nowhere," Applejack said flatly. "Now what's the trouble?"

35

Vaughn cooled down somewhat, though the grinning faces in the crowd didn't help his temper to any extent. He forced himself to hold his voice steady. "This redheaded troublemaker has a pack of cards that belonged to a hombre named Dawes—"

"The said Dawes, Applejack," Peaceful put in, "being an ex-bandit. In fact he is very ex at present."

"Right," Vaughn continued, red-faced. "That bandit case isn't closed yet. I just learned that Dawes's deck of cards was still in existence. I sent Jake Tracy to get 'em. This redhead already had 'em, and he refused to give 'em up to Jake. First thing Jake knows, the redhead pulls a gun. I just arrived in time to avoid a murder—"

"Oh, it was *you* wanted the cards," Peaceful drawled.

"Certain," Vaughn said sullenly. "So long as that case remains open the cards should be in possession of the state. Maybe they'll be evidence before this case is closed—"

"Gosh, why didn't you say so?" Peaceful said cheerfully. "You can have the cards, Deputy."

"Now wait a minute, Peaceful," Applejack protested. "Don't let this law officer bluff you into anything—"

"He's not bluffing me," Peaceful said blandly. "I'm peaceful and I don't like trouble. Providing Deputy Vaughn is willing to call it quits and not make any more trouble, I'm willing to let him have the cards. He's got law on his side, remember."

"But, Peaceful—" Applejack commenced again.

"You'd better be willing to call it quits, feller," Vaughn said to Applejack. "Your pard takes the sensible view. Sure, give me them cards, and we'll say no more. Fact is, we might have a drink together—"

"This is once I don't drink," Applejack said sourly, casting a puzzled look at Peaceful.

"You feel sick, pard?" Peaceful grinned.

"I feel plenty sick," Applejack groaned. "Damn if I can understand you."

"I'm just peaceful, that's all," Jenkins said piously. "I just can't abide trouble. Here, Deputy Vaughn"—he reached into a hip pocket—"here's the deck of cards. Take 'em and welcome."

Vaughn snatched eagerly at the packaged deck and thrust it into a pants pocket. Some of his confidence returned. "All right," he growled. "I'll forget it this time, but don't make any more trouble while you're in Spanish Wells. And maybe you'd better not stay here too long, neither." He turned and walked away.

By this time Applejack had put his gun away and was shaking his head disgustedly at Peaceful. Jake Tracy glowered at Peaceful. "Mebbe the deputy can forget this business," he said threateningly, "but you and me still got a score to even, redhead. I won't be forgetting."

"Start now if you like," Peaceful invited easily. "But I warn you, I don't like fighting. Fact is, I hate fighting so much, I always get it over with as soon as possible. It saves time."

Tracy flung out an angry curse and hurried after the sheriff. The crowd commenced to break up. Peaceful, grinning, flung one hand over his pardner's shoulder. "Don't take it too hard, Applejack."

"Hard, hell!" Applejack growled disgruntledly. "It makes me boil clear through to see you give in like that. You're too blasted peaceful to suit me sometimes. After all the trouble you take to get that deck of cards, you hand 'em over meek as Mary's little lamb to that tinhorn deputy. If he isn't a crook, I never saw one." They started across the street toward the Demijohn Saloon.

Peaceful grinned. "Mary's little lamb, eh? Maybe I could make up a song. Listen:

> *"Peaceful had a little deck*
> *Whose cards might hold a clue;*
> *And everywhere that Peaceful went*
> *Those cards were sure to go—"*

Peaceful broke off. "That's a rotten rhyme. Clue and go. Let me see. Maybe I could change it—"

"Hey!" Applejack exclaimed. "You mean you still got that deck of cards?"

Peaceful's grin widened. "Certain, you cantankerous old mossback. Do I look simple?"

"But—but—" Applejack was bewildered. "I distinctly saw you give that deck to Deputy Vaughn."

Peaceful shook his head. "No, you didn't. You saw me give Vaughn that old deck that you and me play seven-up with every evening. That deck was in my pocket too. Vaughn will never know the difference, or if he does he won't be able to make head nor tail of the business."

"You redheaded devil!" Applejack exclaimed admiringly. "Thinking fast, just like always. Come on, we'll get that drink now. You'll like the Demijohn and the pint-sized hombre that runs the place."

Laughing, they walked around the end of the Demijohn tie rail and made their way through the swinging doors of the saloon. Inside the atmosphere was cool and clean. Fresh sawdust covered the floor, and behind the long mahogany bar, to their right as they entered, an undersized individual with neatly combed greying hair and twinking elfish eyes was serving several customers. At the rear of the Demijohn Saloon a door opened on to an alley. Across from the bar were some round-topped wooden tables and straight-backed chairs. The walls were decorated with pictures of racehorses, burlesque actresses, and prize-fighters clipped from a certain pink-sheeted magazine popular in those days. The glasses on the back bar were clean and polished, the bottles stacked in orderly array. Across the top of the mirror, printed in soap with many flourishes and curlicues, were the words DRINK HEARTY.

Peaceful and Applejack found a vacant spot at one end of the bar, and within a few minutes the diminutive barkeep came down to serve them. "What'll it be, gents?"

"Johnny," Applejack said, "shake hands with my pard, Peaceful Jenkins. This is Johnny Small, proprietor of the Demijohn."

"Small by name and small by nature," the barkeep chuckled.

"But only physically," Applejack put in. "Peaceful, Johnny is plumb bighearted. So help me, when I was in here before I bought just one drink, then Johnny bought one."

"So you're two drinks ahead of me." Peaceful laughed. "What do you recommend, Applejack?"

"The beer, by all means," Peters said fervently. "It's downright cool."

"Beer it is." Peaceful nodded. Johnny Small set out two bottles and glasses, then said, "I understand you had a little trouble with our deputy. I couldn't leave my bar to see what was going on, but Applejack, here, sudden let out a yell and departed like a bat out of hell. He didn't even finish his drink."

Peaceful grinned. "Applejack really must have been excited when anything like that happens. Anyway, he got there in time. I had a pack of cards that Jake Tracy wanted. Tracy got tough about the matter, and I had to knock him down. Then Vaughn arrived and got the drop on me. Applejack got there in time to square matters. Me, I'm peaceful. I handed the deputy the deck of cards and we called it quits. It didn't amount to much."

Johnny Small nodded seriously. "A month or so ago it might have. Vaughn has been known to be plumb quick on the trigger in the past. Howsomever, the past few weeks he's gentled down quite a heap. I reckon Sheriff Kimball took a few tucks in his sails."

"I'd like to hear about that," Applejack said, "but you'd better give me another beer first. That's sure good brew on a hot day. Johnny, it really gets hot over here in your country."

"This is one of our cool days," Johnny said, eyes twinkling. "Fact is, I changed back to my winter underwear this morning."

Applejack said genially, "You go to hell, Johnny."

"Joking aside," Johnny went on, setting another bottle in front of Applejack, "we really had a hot spell about a month back. I never see

41

the like. There's a boom on in Spanish Wells—I expect you noticed the building going on. The town started growing just the instant word came through that the T.N.&A.S. was laying rails to Spanish Wells. On top of that, silver was struck just across the Mexican border—that's only twelve miles from here—and we get a lot of miners' business on pay nights, not to mention the mineowners coming here for supplies. Real-estate men have been doing a land-office business, and the boom has brought in a lot of folks—though I can't say they're all the right sort of citizens."

Peaceful nodded. "We noticed the construction gangs laying rails, 'bout twenty miles east of here, when we were coming through. The railroad will mean a lot to this town."

"It sure will." Johnny nodded enthusiastically. "I just hope we don't get any more hot spells like I was telling you about. Gosh! Even with the boom on, nobody would work after nine in the morning. Laid off until three in the afternoon every day. I did a good business though, those days. It was so hot you could fry eggs on the heat waves. The barbershops didn't do any business though. Fellers would start out to get a shave, and before they could get there their whiskers would be singed off."

Peaceful nodded seriously. "Reminds me of that hot spell we had over in Texas last year.

The Rio Grande boiled under that terrible heat. I was fishing at the time, and every fish I caught was already cooked when I pulled it out. Fishing was right good too. Seems like the fish just took to those barbecued worms I was baiting with. I had to quit though after the sun melted the hooks right off'n my line."

"I give up," Johnny chuckled. "I recognize my master when I see him."

"That heat spell you mention," Peaceful continued when the grins had died away, "must have took place just about the time you had the Dawes hold-up here, didn't it?"

Johnny nodded. "I always claimed Dawes would never have got away with that, only for the sun keeping so many people off the streets. Main Street was plumb deserted. You heard about that hold-up, eh?"

"There was quite a bit in one of the Texas papers," Applejack put in. "We read about it there. Whatever happened to that money? Did they ever locate it?"

Johnny shook his head. "Deputy Vaughn took up the trail. He was gone three days. When he returned he claimed he had followed the trail of Dawes's confederate down into Mexico, where the feller had disappeared."

Peaceful smiled scornfully. "Does anybody believe that? I figure the matter rests squarely on Vaughn's shoulders. He claims he killed the

43

hold-up man and took the money sack. When he returns here the sack is full of useless paper. If you asked me, I'd say the deputy switched sacks."

"You're not the only one thinks that." Johnny lowered his voice. "But Vaughn's word is as good as the next man's and nobody can prove different from what he says. Sheriff Kimball came over from the county seat at Surcingle and bawled the living daylights out of Vaughn, accusing him of gross negligence. We expected to see Vaughn removed from office, but Hugo Randle interceded for him—Hugo has a pull with some of the politicians in this state—and Kimball consented to let Vaughn stay. But Vaughn has quieted down a heap compared to what he used to be. At that, he always did a pretty good job at the law-and-order business, though sometimes I think he lets Randle go too far."

"Who's Randle?" Peaceful asked.

"Hugo Randle. He'd like to be the big boss in this town, and I reckon he's well on his way, but don't say I said so. I wouldn't want Hugo for an enemy. He runs the Wolf Head Ranch and owns, besides, the Spanish Dagger honky-tonk and Oasis Saloon. Owns a lot of other properties too. Me, I don't say much, but I don't like his gang. And don't quote me on that either."

"We don't talk too much," Peaceful replied. "How about that feller Dawes robbed and shot—Jabez Drake, I think his name was?"

"You're right." Johnny nodded. "Drake is out to his ranch, recovering slowly from the wound. It was a narrow squeak. He may recover from the wound, but not from the loss of his money. I figure he'll lose his outfit, though Lord knows Judy—that's Judith Drake, his daughter—has done her best to hold the place together."

"What's she doing?" Peaceful asked.

"Right now she's singing in Randle's Spanish Dagger," Johnny said with a grimace of distaste. "That's no place for a nice girl. I don't just understand it. You know, one of the funniest things about the whole hold-up business was the disappearance of Dawes's body and his horse. Oh, there was 'signs'—blood on the ground and tracks and so forth—to back up what Vaughn said about killing him, but where did the body go?"

"I haven't the least idea." Peaceful yawned. He suddenly appeared to have lost interest in the matter. "Reckon I'll go out and stroll around. Coming, Applejack?"

Applejack shook his head. "Wild horses couldn't drag me away from this beer. The more Johnny talks about the heat, the thirstier I get. I'll be here when you get back."

"See you later then." Peaceful tossed some money on the bar and sauntered toward the door. "*Adios, amigos!*"

4

DEADLOCK

LEAVING the Demijohn Saloon, Peaceful strolled across the street and entered the Spanish Dagger. It was a huge, barn-like place, with a long bar stretching near one wall. Against the opposite wall were the games of chance—roulette, chuck-a-luck, dice tables, faro layouts—they were all there, though at present, due to the earliness of the hour, the tables and other equipment were covered with black oilcloth. At the rear of the big room was a small stage, where an orchestra sat to provide music; a roped-off square in the centre of the room was meant for dancing. Tables and chairs were scattered about, the surfaces of the former being covered with circular stains from countless liquor glasses.

At one side of the stage a flight of wooden steps ascended to a railed balcony that ran around three sides of the room. Ranged along the balcony were a series of rooms, whose doors were at present closed. Peaceful surmised that the doors opened on to rooms of the dance-hall girls; probably one of the rooms provided a private office for Hugo

Randle. At present none of the girls was in sight, nor was Randle. There were only a few customers at the bar, most of them newly-arrived citizens of the town. Two bartenders waited behind the long counter. Neither appeared to be particularly busy.

Peaceful's gaze flitted swiftly about the room, then narrowed a trifle. At a far corner a girl sat at a table alone, engrossed in a recent newspaper. Light entered a window near her shoulder and picked out tiny yellow glints in her blonde hair. Her eyes were dark, her chin firm and determined beneath the full-lipped mouth. Peaceful caught his breath in surprise; the girl was more than merely pretty; what is more, she looked like a lady in the exact meaning of that word. What she wore Peaceful wasn't sure: some sort of full skirt of brownish material, with a tight bodice above, and above that a touch of lace at her creamy-skinned throat. There were bits of lace at her wrists too. It came as something of a shock, seeing such a girl in a place like the Spanish Dagger. Instinctively Peaceful knew this must be Jabez Drake's daughter Judith.

As he crossed the room the girl's eyes lifted momentarily to meet Peaceful's gaze. Her eyes were level, impersonal, on his for a moment, before they again dropped to the newspaper spread on the table before her. Peaceful smiled slightly, touched fingers to the brim of his Stetson, and started toward the bar with the intention of buying a cigar. Halfway there he changed his mind and continued on toward the girl, eventually seating himself at the table next to hers. The girl glanced at him again as he seated himself, nodded in friendly fashion, and once more resumed her perusal of the news.

A beetle-browed bartender came shuffling around the corner of the bar and approached Peaceful's table. "What's yours, pardner?"

Peaceful considered. Finally he said, "Reckon I'll have a steak and fixin's and plenty of coffee."

The bartender stared, then frowned. "Look here," he growled, "this ain't no restaurant. I can fix you up with anything to drink, or furnish you tobacco, but if you want food you can go next door to the Bon-Ton Restaurant."

The bartender's reply didn't surprise Peaceful, though he assumed a look of surprise. "Sorry, my mistake," he said quietly. "I thought I could get a bait here." He started to rise.

"Wait a minute." It was the girl at the next table who spoke. "Mike, I don't think we should turn down a customer."

The barkeep shuffled uneasily, "But, Miss Judy, we don't never serve food."

"Don't be ridiculous, Mike." The girl's voice was firm. "Of course we serve food here when it is required. I've often seen you bring in trays for Mr. Randle or one of the girls—"

"That's different," the man protested. "That's—"

"Let's have no more talk about it." Judith Drake's words were quiet, but her chin lifted determinedly as she spoke. "This gentleman asked for steak and coffee, I believe—"

"But, Miss Judy," the barkeep commenced, "I'm afraid Mr. Randle won't like it if—"

"You'd better start moving, Mike." The tones were dangerously soft now. "Don't forget that I'm in charge here when your boss is out."

That settled it. Within the instant the man moved toward the doorway. Peaceful thanked the girl. She nodded coolly and again bent to the newsprint. Peaceful meditated. What sort of situation was this? A girl like Judy Drake working in a honky-tonk—even acting as manager—owned by Hugo Randle. Mentally Peaceful shook his head. It was beyond him. Well, with the food as an excuse, he could stay longer and perhaps get into a conversation with Judith Drake.

Mike returned within ten minutes or so, bearing a steaming tray of food. In rather ungracious fashion he slammed the dishes before Peaceful. Peaceful put down a bill and told him to keep the change. Mike's countenance brightened somewhat. Peaceful commenced eating; the food was surprisingly tasteful. When he had finished Mike brought him a cigar, "with the compliments of the house," and cleared away the dishes.

Peaceful puffed on his cigar and wondered how to start a conversation with the girl. Finally he said, "That was sure a good dinner. I'm obliged to you, ma'am. My name is Jenkins. Peaceful Jenkins."

"I'm glad to know you, Mr. Jenkins," the girl replied impersonally, scarcely glancing up from her newspaper. "I'm Judith Drake."

"I figured that much. You see—I—well, I'd heard about your father's hard luck—the robbery and everything."

The girl's smile was hard. "I guess most everybody has. I'm afraid there's nothing much to be done about it now."

Peaceful hesitated a moment. "I wouldn't give up hope was I you, Miss Judith."

He heard the girl's sharp intake of breath. Now she was giving him her full attention. "What do you mean by that?"

Peaceful shrugged. "I don't know—yet," he drawled.

"Nor does anybody else," the girl said shortly. Peaceful sensed the disappointment in her tones, as though his words had suddenly snatched from her a brief vision of hope. Again the girl returned to her newspaper, but this time Peaceful knew she wasn't reading. He didn't say anything more, allowing his words to sink in, nor did the girl reopen the conversation. Ten minutes passed with neither speaking. Peaceful sat smoking in silence, watching the blue smoke from his cigar spiral lazily toward the raftered ceiling of the big room. At the bar the few customers carried on a desultory conversation with the two bartenders, though once or twice Peaceful caught Mike looking curiously at him.

Abruptly Peaceful remembered the deck of cards he had purchased from Sam Purdy that morning. He drew the packet from his pocket, opened the case, and shook the cards out into his hand. He spread the cards slightly and found inserted in the middle of the deck a folded sheet of letter paper. He started to unfold the sheet, then paused and glanced around the room. The bartender, Mike, was watching him intently now. Maybe it was only idle curiosity, but Peaceful wasn't taking any chances. He slipped the folded sheet of paper into a side pocket and commenced to spread the cards on the table before him in a solitaire layout. For the next five minutes he picked up cards, placed them in small bunches, choosing carefully each time, as though the game of solitaire was the only thought he had in the world.

Behind him he heard the rustle of a newspaper, then the scraping of a chair leg as the girl pushed back her seat and arose. He heard her light footstep and felt her presence at his right shoulder as she stood there, apparently watching him at his game. Once she raised her voice, saying coolly, "I think you made a mistake in placing that nine spot there."

"It's likely," Peaceful said quietly. "I've made plenty of mistakes in my time. Right now I'm thinking hard. I don't want to make a mistake now. I don't want to believe in appearances. But what are you doing in a place like this?"

He hadn't raised his face toward hers while he talked. If anyone were watching at the bar, the man and girl were engrossed solely in Peaceful's game of solitaire. After a moment he heard the girl's soft voice: "You're right not to believe in appearances. Look, Mr. Jenkins—Peaceful, what did you mean a while back when you said not to give up hope? Why are you here? Do you know something—?" She broke off suddenly, then added, "I'm leaving now. I'll be here again to-night, or you can see me at the hotel." The final words were spoken low as the girl left his side and hastened toward the door.

Peaceful glanced at the three men who had just entered. One of them was Handsome Jake Tracy. The second man—a wiry, hard-bitten individual wearing two guns—Peaceful recognized instantly as Scott Heffner, a professional gunman who had left Texas only a few years before, a few short jumps ahead of a pursuing posse. Heffner paused as his gaze lighted on Peaceful, then spoke a few quick words to the third man, who was big and broad-shouldered, with eyebrows that met in a straight line above his beady black eyes. This third man wore a white shirt and flowing black bow tie; his unbuttoned fancy vest fitted loosely, and black broadcloth trousers were tucked into polished boot tops. A stiff-brimmed sombrero was slanted atop his straight black hair; a six-shooter hung at one hip. Peaceful guessed rightly that this was Black Hugo Randle.

As Judith Drake swept past on her way to the street Randle sought to detain her, but the girl spoke only a few quick words and kept going. Randle and his two companions came directly to Peaceful's table. Scott Heffner spoke first, coldly hostile, "Hi-yuh, Jenkins! Still moochin' with the Texas Rangers?"

Peaceful smiled lazily. "I resigned some years ago. After we'd run you over the border line things were some quieter down Santone way. Too bad you had to leave so sudden, Heffner. A lot of us craved to keep you with us—permanently."

Heffner flushed angrily, at a loss for a retort. Randle glared down at Peaceful. Peaceful eyed him calmly. Randle said, "We don't like Rangers in Spanish Wells. What do you want? You've got no authority way over here."

"Have I claimed any?" Peaceful drawled. "Besides, you just heard me tell Heffner I'm no longer a Ranger. Anyway"—the voice was still level, unperturbed—"what in hell right you got questioning me? Don't bite off more than you can chew, mister."

The thin black moustache on Randle's upper lip

lifted in a snarl. "I'm Hugo Randle. You may not know it, Jenkins, but I'm by way of being boss in this town. What I say goes."

Peaceful laughed softly. "Don't mention my name then, 'cause I'm intending to stay."

"What for? What you doing here?" Randle snapped.

"Playing solitaire, until you interrupted," Peaceful said easily. He glanced at Jake Tracy, saw that individual's gaze resting excitedly on the backs of some of the playing cards. Tracy started to speak agitated words, but Peaceful cut him short with a lazy drawl. "You've guessed it, Tracy. I made a mistake this morning and gave you the wrong deck of cards. Here, you can have 'em." Swiftly he gathered the cards, shoved them into their cardboard case, and tossed the packaged deck across the table. He leaned back in his chair, crossing his arms unconcernedly behind his head while he eyed the three glowering above him.

Tracy said angrily, "I had a hunch something was wrong, chief. Sam Purdy never has anything but Bicycle Brand in his stock. Those cards that Jenkins gave Herb Vaughn was a different brand—"

"Hush up, Jake," Randle said shortly. "I'll do the talking." He signalled the other two. As though pre-arranged, the three men drew out chairs and sat down at the table. Jenkins again leaned forward, eyes bright with sudden interest.

Across from him was Hugo Randle; on his left was Tracy, and on his right, Scott Heffner.

Randle said, "Jenkins, you knocked Jake down to-day."

"He asked for it," Peaceful replied quietly.

"That's whatever," Randle snapped. "Nobody hits a friend of mine and gets away with it. We'll take that up later. Right now I want to know what you found in that deck."

Peaceful looked puzzled. "What I found? I don't get you. There were fifty-two cards, the regulation number of aces, and so forth. Oh yes, and the joker—"

"One joker here is enough," Randle grated savagely. "Don't stall, Jenkins. I asked a question and I'm going to get an answer, or by the living God, I'll—"

"You'll what?" Peaceful asked quietly. "Don't make threats you can't carry out, Randle."

"This is no idle threat, Jenkins," Randle's voice was cold, deadly. "Right now I've got you covered under the table. You ready to talk up?"

Peaceful slowly shook his head. "I still don't get what you're driving at. And you wouldn't dare kill me—here—in sight of—"

"That's where you make a mistake," Randle snarled. "This is my place. What I say goes here. If I say an accident happened folks will take my word for it. Now use your head. Remember, I've got you covered."

Peaceful laughed softly. "That's what you'd call a coincidence. I've got you covered under the table too. I've had you covered ever since you sat down. I reckon it's a deadlock."

Randle stiffened slightly, then relaxed. His voice was still ugly as he said, "It's no deadlock in your favour, Jenkins. You fail to realize that all three of us have our guns trained on you under this table top. So you'd better talk fast and sudden, Ranger man, fast and sudden!"

5

PEACEFUL BREAKS A DEADLOCK

BY this time the men at the bar had turned to see what was happening. Behind the bar the two bartenders made a great show of bustling activity of a sudden. They invited the customers to "have one on the house" and lashed themselves into a flurry of ambition, setting out bottles and glasses and making swift conversation.

The four men at the table sat as before, rigid as granite statues, though that careless, confident smile still played about Peaceful's lips. If he was concerned about his predicament there was nothing in his features to betray the fact.

Randle repeated, "You'd better talk fast and sudden, Ranger man. My patience won't last for ever."

Peaceful grinned suddenly. "Maybe nothing concerning you will last, Randle. You sort of overlook the fact that I hold the best hand in this deal."

"Don't bluff, Jenkins," Randle snapped. "You're in a tight spot and you know it. There's three guns covering you. You'd better get ready to spill a lot of talk. I'm asking for the last time, what was in that deck of cards?"

"A lot of good poker hands probably," Peaceful chuckled, "but I didn't have a chance to prove it. You fellers didn't even give me time to finish my game of solitaire—"

"Cut it, Jenkins!" Scott Heffner spoke, his tones those of a killer. "The boss has asked a question. He ain't used to dilly-dallyin' with folks—especially hombres like you. Now you'd better get some sense in that red head of yours before you get carried out of here feet first. Just make up your mind, that's all. And I don't much care one way or the other."

"That's the talk, Scott," Tracy put in. "Fact is, I'd sort of like to bore this Texas man. Never did like Texas—"

"Don't run off at the head, Jake," Randle advised irritatedly. He faced Peaceful again. "The layout's in front of you, Jenkins. Make your play!"

"I'll do just that," came the unexpected reply, "but not the way you expect. You see, I'm plumb peaceful and—"

"Get down to cases, Jenkins," Randle jerked out.

"Right." Peaceful nodded good-humouredly. "To begin with, you three got me cornered—you think."

"No think about it," Randle interposed. "We've

58

got you dead to rights with three gun barrels pointing at your middle."

"I sure hate to disillusion you," Peaceful chuckled, "but the advantage is all on my side."

"T'hell you say!" Tracy blurted. "How you figuring?"

"It's like this," Peaceful went on easily. "It's true you three got me covered. But don't forget, my gun is out too. Now the question arises, which of you three am I covering? That will really puzzle you if you give it some thought. I had Randle covered when you all first sat down, but I've shifted my aim some since—and I figure to keep on shifting it. One of you three is covered every minute. You know, it's like the pea-under-three-shells game. You never guess right about that goldarn pea, now, do you? I can tell by the looks on your faces that you don't. Same situation here. It's going to be up to you three to guess which way my gun is pointing. Do you see the point?"

"Cut out the talk, Jenkins," Randle snapped. "You fool, you can't stop what we've got planned for you. Your gun may be out, but that won't prevent us from shooting you."

"Exactly the point I'm making." Peaceful smiled blandly. "What's going to happen if you shoot me? Why, just the shock of being shot would cause me to pull trigger. Such action would be involuntary. I couldn't help myself. And none of you three could stop me. And now we're back to the old pea-under-the-shells game again. The question is, at which of you three—Randle, Heffner, or Tracy—will my gun be pointing when it goes off? Now do you see the point? I may be rubbed out, but one of you is sure to go with me. Nice gambling prospect, isn't it? Ready to give the word to shoot, Randle? I still haven't done any talking, you know—and I don't intend to!"

Randle's face worked angrily, but he didn't say anything. Tracy's features had gone a shade paler. Heffner's eyes burned red with a sort of insane rage. But none of the three spoke. A deathly hush had settled over the big room. At the bar the customers were frozen into inaction as they stared at the scene being enacted against the opposite wall of the building.

"Come, come, men." Peaceful's good-humoured drawl broke the silence at last. "You're not giving up now, surely. Won't any of you take a chance? Lost your nerve, or have your gambling instincts plumb took wing? Look, it's three against one. I can only get one of you—but which one? That's the question. Like to know, wouldn't you? Fact is, I'm not certain, myself. I keep that gun barrel shifting so continuously from one to the other, y'understand. We might lay a bet on it. You could collect the money from my pocket if you won. Only two of you would be left to split the proceeds though. You understand that, don't you?"

Still no one answered. The three just stared at Peaceful, hate darting from their eyes—and now a trace of fear too.

Peaceful laughed softly at the three. "Reminds me," he chuckled, "of the feller that caught the bear by the tail and didn't dast let go. Remember that one?"

None of the three replied. Only their heavy breathing broke the silence in the intervals between what had become Peaceful's one-sided conversation. Peaceful moved a trifle in his chair and his holster rasped against the wood. At the sudden sound Jake Tracy jumped nervously.

Peaceful said seriously, "Gosh, I mustn't do that again. You might have shot me. It happens I had my gun on you at that minute too—no, Heffner, don't get ideas. I've shifted my aim again. I keep on shifting it, you know, back and forth. But I would like to get up a little bet as to which I shoot when you fellers pull trigger. Tracy, I'll lay a little bet that it's you. I'll give you odds, in fact. What do you say?"

"You—go—to—hell," Tracy gasped with an effort. His nerve was commencing to break. Beads of perspiration stood out on his pale forehead.

"Bet I take you with me if I do," Peaceful

drawled. He turned to the other two. "How about you, Randle—Heffner—want a bet at odds?"

Randle didn't reply. Heffner's head moved slowly from side to side. His nerve was commencing to slip too. His tongue moved spasmodically along his parched lips.

"What, won't anybody bet with me?" A sudden trace of irritation crept into Peaceful's tones. "This is what I call nerve-racking. I'd like to get this over with. Randle, why don't you give the word to shoot? I'm so shaky now I can hardly hold my trigger finger still. It'd be hell if I was to shoot first after all, wouldn't it? And I still think it would be Tracy took my slug—"

A low moan burst from Tracy's lips. He spoke shakily: "Let's talk this over, chief."

"Shut your mouth," Randle rasped, but his voice was none too steady under the strain of waiting.

"Yep, it's the old pea-under-shells game," Peaceful continued. "I sure wish the shooting would start. I'm getting nervouser and nervouser. Right then, Tracy, I almost pulled trigger on you."

That ended Jake Tracy. "I quit, I quit," he gasped brokenly.

"Shove your gun out here on the table," Peaceful snapped swiftly. "Butt toward me. Quick!"

The sudden change in his tones acted as an electric shock on Tracy. The next instant he had brought his gun up and shoved it across the table toward Peaceful. "I know when I'm licked," he said hoarsely and commenced to shove his chair back from the table.

"Stay right where you are," Peaceful ordered. "I can still shoot through the table top if necessary."

Tracy fell silent, frozen with fear.

Peaceful's eyes went to Scott Heffner. "You're next," Peaceful jerked out. "Move fast, Heffner. Both your guns!"

Heffner whispered hoarsely, "You redheaded devil!" and shoved a brace of six-shooters, one at a time, butts toward Peaceful, across the table. "You didn't scare me though," Heffner continued. "I just got too much sense to take a chance."

"Sit where you are and you won't be taking any," Peaceful advised coldly. His eyes were boring steadily into Hugo Randle's now.

Randle stared back, holding his gaze steady as long as possible. Then his eyes wavered, first to Tracy and then to Heffner. "You yellow bustards," he grated furiously.

"Calling names won't help your case, Randle," Peaceful said, his tones icy. "It's between you and me now. I'll shoot any time you say the word— or do you figure to jump the gun on me. Now it's your turn to think fast, hombre!"

Randle relaxed in his chair, shrugged his shoulders. "I ain't a complete damn fool," he snarled. "Why should I shoot when you've got a gun on me? There's other ways of getting you."

He shrugged again, brought his gun into sight, and slid it across to join the others in front of Peaceful. "And now, if you think you've heard the last of this—" Randle commenced.

"Just a minute, Randle," Peaceful interrupted, picking up with his left hand one of the guns on the table and directing it toward the boss of the Spanish Dagger, "let's not forget that underarm gun of yours. Toss it out here."

Randle cursed, put one hand inside his white shirt, under his open vest, and produced an ugly-looking derringer, which he dropped on the table.

"Well, well," Peaceful chuckled, "that was a right good guess on my part. I wasn't sure if you carried an underarm weapon or not. Figured to use it on me too, didn't you? I reckon this must be my lucky day." As though he really felt that way, Peaceful emitted a long sigh of relief.

At that moment Applejack Peters came barging into the Spanish Dagger. A look of astonishment spread over his face as he saw his pardner seated at a table holding several guns, apparently the property of the other three angry-looking men seated at the same table. He hurried across the room, one hand on gun butt, exclaiming, "What's up, Peaceful? You had some trouble?"

"Not any I couldn't handle," Peaceful said, smiling gravely. "But I sure got taught a lesson in carelessness."

"Carelessness?" from Applejack. "What do you mean?"

Peaceful explained ruefully, "I was sitting tilted back in this chair when these three hombres sat down and covered me under the table. I leaned forward but shifted too much to one side. My gun butt got jammed against the back of the chair and I couldn't make my draw. I sure had to talk fast to make these sidewinders believe I had them covered too."

There was an instant's silence; then the other three men at the table broke into violent cursing as they realized how Peaceful had bluffed them out. From one of the customers at the bar sounded sudden laughter. The man rushed across the room and gazed admiringly at Peaceful. "By geez! Redhead, that's the nerviest thing I ever saw in all my born days. And you couldn't even get your gun out? Well, I'll be damned!" He broke into another fit of laughter.

"You, feller!" Randle's words sounded rattlesnake-mean. "Get out of here and stay out. I don't want your trade!"

"Sure, I'll get." The man grinned insolently. "There's other bars will welcome my trade—and along with it the story of the best bluff I ever saw run on three tough guys. Haw-haw-haw!" He was still laughing as he passed through the doorway to the street.

Peaceful rose rather stiffly to his feet and

jerked his holstered forty-five a trifle nearer the front. "Yep, I sure learned me a lesson in carelessness," he drawled. "I won't ever get caught that way again." He stood looking down at the three furious individuals at the table. "You know," he continued easily, "if you three still feel belligerent, my pal and I will take you on and welcome."

Randle glared at Peaceful but refused to reply. The other two didn't speak. Peaceful laughed softly. "Haven't got your nerve back yet, eh?" Seizing the table, he gave it a quick wrench with his muscular hand, spilling the weapons it had held to the floor. Still the three sat there, without movement, not even looking to see what had happened to their guns.

Peaceful's lips spread in a slow contemptuous smile. "Come on, Applejack, let's get out of here. There's no scrap left in these coyotes—and I reckon I'd better apologize to real coyotes. They go down fighting anyway."

"I'm with you, pard. Let's get some more of that beer."

"I sure need a drink—now."

Once they'd left the Spanish Dagger, Randle rose slowly to his feet and, moving at the same deliberate pace, passed up the flight of stairs to his private office on the balcony. He didn't say a word to anyone. Immediately he was out of sight Heffner and Tracy rushed to the bar. Without a word the barkeep set out a bottle and glasses. It was some time before they did any talking too. Courage isn't always recaptured without trouble, and Heffner and Jake Tracy had been thoroughly shaken by the events of a short time before. Their only recourse was the bottle.

6

RANDLE LAUGHS IT OFF

IT was nearing seven that evening when Deputy Herb Vaughn mounted the flight of stairs to the Spanish Dagger balcony, made his way around to the door of Randle's private office, and knocked somewhat timorously on the panel. There wasn't any instant reply. Vaughn stood, uncertain whether to knock a second time or not, gazing down at the great open space below. By this time there were more men at the bar than earlier in the day. Many of the professional gamblers had arrived and were engaged in uncovering their wheels and tables. Big oil lamps, suspended from the ceiling, cast a bright light over the floor beneath. After a minute Vaughn knocked again.

A surly voice replied, "What do you want?"

"It's me, Hugo. Herb Vaughn."

Footsteps sounded within; then the door was flung open. "Come on in," Randle growled. "I'll light up in a sec." A match was scratched, and Randle touched the flame to the wick of the oil lamp on his desk. Aside from the desk, the room was furnished with a cot in one corner, several chairs, a table. Matting covered the floor. Behind the desk stood a small steel safe. Randle crossed the floor and pulled down the shade on a window overlooking the street. "Close the door, Herb," he said.

Vaughn closed the door and sat down. He seemed at a loss for a beginning. Randle stood looking down at him, a sardonic smile twisting his thin lips.

"Well, say it!" Randle broke the silence impatiently. "Tell me it's all over town."

"I reckon it is," Vaughn said, apologetically. "Couldn't believe it at first, Hugo, until I'd talked to a feller what claimed to be at the bar when it happened. For God's sake, how did it happen?"

"I slipped up, that's all," Randle replied ruefully.

"But Tracy and Heffner were with you. I can't see how Jenkins worked it. With three guns on him, and him just running a bluff—"

"I know, I know," Randle said irritatedly. "I should have gone slower. It might have been different, too, if Heffner and Tracy hadn't backed down, but—hell, I don't know—it just happened that way. I never saw the man yet that didn't lose his nerve sometime during his life. We're all entitled to one weak moment. Us three had ours all at the same time. Where are Tracy and Heffner?"

"They were down at the bar getting liquored up

when I came through—both of 'em ugly as bears with sore paws. I tried to question 'em, but they nearly took my head off. They're both boasting about what they'll do the next time they meet Jenkins."

"The goddamn fools," Randle said wrathfully. "That's just the thing they mustn't do. Get 'em up here."

Vaughn crossed the floor, opened the door, and yelled to those below. After a minute slow footsteps could be heard ascending to the balcony. Vaughn waited until Tracy and Heffner had thrust their shamefaced, red-eyed countenances into the room.

"All right, come in and shut the door," Randle snapped.

The two entered. Heffner commenced, "Look, chief, if you want that Tehanner rubbed out, just say the word—"

"Certain I want that Texan rubbed out," Randle snapped, "but not right off. I'll give the word when the time is right. You leave Jenkins to me. Meanwhile, get over feeling sorry for yourselves and sit down. I've done a lot of thinking the past coupla hours. Maybe I should be sore at you two. I ain't sure yet. So long as I ain't sure, let's forget it. I was to blame as much as you two—maybe more. I should have gone slower. But when I come in and saw him talking to Judy Drake—and just about the same time Scott told me he was a Texas Ranger—I let my temper get the best of me—especially when I realized how he'd slipped it over on us with that deck of cards—"

"But, Hugo," Tracy protested, "the story is all over town. We're the laughingstock of Spanish Wells."

"We probably are," Randle conceded coolly. "But we can laugh too."

"No getting away from it, Hugo," Vaughn said sadly, "it's a blow to your prestige. Jenkins made you three look like pretty small potatoes. You've got to face that fact. I was in the Demijohn a while back. Fellers are laughing and shaking his hand like he'd done something wonderful."

"I wouldn't be surprised if he did at that." Randle smiled wryly. "It's something to bluff out three guns like us three, and it couldn't happen again in a thousand years. I'll hand it to Jenkins. He's smart. He's got guts. I never saw a Texas Ranger without them two virtues—though I hate the sight of 'em."

"Texas Rangers haven't any authority over this way," Heffner pointed out.

"It's true, they haven't," Randle admitted. "At the same time, Jenkins didn't happen into this town by accident, I'm betting. I want to know why he was interested in those cards of Louie Dawes—in the face of what we know now."

Vaughn said, "Maybe it was just accident he got those cards. Sam Purdy told me that Jenkins come in looking for a second-hand deck—"

"Cripes! Do you believe that?" Randle snorted. "A man like Jenkins can afford new cards when he wants cards. He knows as much as we do, maybe more. That's why I'm aiming to string along with him and pretend to be friendly. I want to learn things too. When the time is right I can dispose of Mister Peaceful Jenkins, and I won't take any chances next time."

"But what are we going to do," Tracy asked, "when fellers give us the horselaugh because of what happened this afternoon?"

"Laugh with 'em. I've thought that out, Jake. We'll just laugh it off. Like it was a good joke on us. If we appear to stay mad at Jenkins folks will keep remembering—and laughing—at the way he made us back down. But if we get on friendly terms with him folks will soon forget the whole happening. We'll just laugh it off. You see, nobody will say anything after a day or two. That's the best way to handle a situation like this."

"I reckon you're right, Hugo." Heffner nodded in agreement.

"Sure he's right," Tracy chimed in.

"I ain't so sure," Vaughn said morosely. "Up to now, Hugo, you had this town eating out of your hand. Now I wouldn't be none surprised if you met some opposition. And folks are remembering again that you and I have always been right friendly. I can't afford to go too far. First thing you know, Sheriff Kimball will be appointing a new deputy here. To-day I caught one or two whispers from folks that were talking over the Dawes hold-up too. Seems like they're commencing to talk again about the chance I had to grab that money. I don't like it."

"Forget it," Randle said soothingly. "Don't let your nerves and imagination get the best of you, Herb. That can be laughed off, too, if anybody says anything more."

"I hope you're right," Vaughn said hopelessly. "Anyway, there doesn't seem to be anything else to do right now except laugh it off . . . I'd sure like to know what Jenkins found in that deck of cards though. I'd feel a heap easier."

"Sure, we all would," Randle admitted. "That's why we've got to go slow and get friendly with Jenkins. We'll learn things yet. Maybe he didn't find anything in that deck. That may all have been the raving of a dying man. You know, a feller gets delirious—"

"Anyway, we know what became of Dawes's body," Heffner put in. "That was a relief to me. I didn't know what to think."

Randle reached into a drawer of his desk and produced a box of long, thin black cigars. He passed the box around, but no one accepted one. Randle bit off the end of one of the weeds, touched flame to the other end, and inhaled deeply. "From now on we go slow until we find secure footing. You fellers just follow my lead. I'll get us across this jump, just like I've always done."

"There's just one other thing, Hugo," Vaughn said apologetically, then hesitated.

"What's on your mind, Herb?"

"Now I don't want you to get mad or anything, Hugo, but you said the sight of Jenkins talking to Judy Drake sort of made you lose your temper."

"So what if I did?" Randle said sharply, cigar poised halfway to his lips.

"Don't you get so interested in that girl that you forget the rest of us," Vaughn said. "We got our own skins to think of, Hugo, and I'd hate to think that tangling with a petticoat would mean our ruination."

Randle laughed shortly. "Don't talk like a fool, Herb. I know what I'm doing where Judy Drake is concerned. But money comes before women. We're on the road to getting money. Just ride with me and back me up and we'll all be rich."

From below came the sounds of strains of music and the noise of shuffling feet, mingled with the clinking of bottles and loud voices.

Randle rose to his feet. "The place is filling up. I've got to get below. Tracy, you and Scott come with me. Herb, you'd better wait a bit before coming down. It might not look too good, right now, if you were seen coming out of my office with me. And all of you remember what I said— keep your nerve and laugh it off."

7

A DEFINITE CLUE

THE afternoon had passed swiftly for Peaceful and Applejack Peters after they had left the Spanish Dagger. Before long the town had commenced to buzz with stories of "Jenkins' Bluff." There was a great deal of laughter at Hugo Randle's expense and speculation as to what he'd do to even matters. Total strangers clapped Peaceful on the back, introduced themselves, and wanted to buy drinks for him, all of which Peaceful refused with thanks. It was dark before he and Applejack had an opportunity to get away from the Demijohn and out to the street once more. They strode along, side by side, neither speaking for a few moments. Finally Applejack said, "You sure did something this afternoon, pard, when you bluffed out those three. It's made you a lot of friends in town. From the way folks talked, I'd say that Black Hugo Randle isn't as popular as he'd like to be. Especially among some of the cow folks that have lived here a long time and resent the way he's running things. I reckon Randle's Spanish Dagger is taking the wages of a lot of punchers from the local outfits as well as from the miners from across the Mex border and the railroad section hands."

Peaceful nodded absent-mindedly. "Boom-towns like this always seem to produce a Hugo Randle," he said quietly. "Things seem to go to pot generally for a time. Then somebody catches up with Randle and his like and the town settles down to be a peaceable, civilized community. That's the story of the West, told over and over again. Someday this whole country will be civilized, and there won't be any Hugo Randles—I hope."

"You're optimistic," Applejack said. "There'll always be Hugo Randles of one type or another—fellers who are greedy for wealth. This country may get complete civilized, but by that time the Hugo Randles will be more powerful, meaner—the type that will get their country into wars simply so they can sell more steel and other supplies. Yeah, they'll go on and on, ordering killing in one way or another. I just hope there'll always be a Peaceful Jenkins to stop 'em."

Peaceful smiled. "You're giving me qualities I never laid claim to, pard. Let's forget it and find a restaurant. We haven't had any supper yet."

"I can eat any time."

"That steak I had brought in this afternoon was right good—rather the steak Miss Drake ordered in for me," Peaceful commented. "Seems like they said that came from the Bon-Ton Restaurant. Let's look for the place."

"I know where it is. Right next door to the Spanish Dagger. Where do you figure this Drake girl fits into Hugo Randle's schemes?"

Peaceful shrugged his shoulders and frowned. "I don't know. She's not his kind. I just don't understand her being in a place like the Spanish Dagger."

Applejack nodded. "Course I haven't seen the girl, so I don't know. But I picked up some gossip in the Demijohn while you were away. From all I hear, Hugo Randle is crazy about her."

Peaceful's frown deepened. He didn't say anything though. They'd crossed Alamo Street. Across on Main the Spanish Dagger was commencing to run full blast. Next to the Spanish Dagger stood the Bon-Ton Restaurant. The two made their way across the road and entered the eating place. Inside a long counter stretched along one wall. The rest of the room was given over to tables covered with oilcloth. In the rear a pair of swinging doors opened on the kitchen. Peaceful and Applejack seated themselves on stools at the long counter and gave their orders to a Mexican waitress.

The restaurant was quite busy, and it took a little time before their order was served. The wide front window of the restaurant was clouded with steam from the kitchen, though near the bottom the glass was much clearer. Through this portion of the glass a burly man in cowpuncher togs was spying on Peaceful and Applejack. Had they turned and seen him, they would have recognized him as one of several men who had been one of Peaceful's loudest admirers that afternoon in the Demijohn. His name was Nick Corvall and he worked for Randle's Wolf Head Ranch. Corvall had always felt he was too good to be an ordinary cowpuncher; he craved a higher station in life. His hope was that some day he would accomplish something that would raise him in Randle's estimation and thus enable him to secure a better, higher-paying job. Meanwhile, Peaceful and Applejack sat waiting for their supper. Peaceful said suddenly, "I dang nigh forgot—"

"What?" Applejack asked.

"There's been so many hombres around us, ever since I left the Spanish Dagger, I didn't get a chance to tell you before. There was a letter folded in that deck of cards."

"T'hell you say! What does it have to offer?"

"I don't know yet," Peaceful said. "I haven't had a chance to look at it. We'll give a look right now."

Even while Peaceful had been speaking the man on the stool next to Applejack's finished his supper and rose from the counter. Outside Nick Corvall had been watching through the glass. Now he quickly entered the restaurant and dropped down on the unoccupied stool beside Applejack and bent an attentive ear to learn what Peaceful and his pardner were talking about. Neither of them had noticed Corvall enter and sit down.

Peaceful was groping in one pocket for the letter he had found between the cards in the dead bandit's deck. "This may give us a clue to what we're looking for, and maybe it won't," he was saying. "Howsomever, we'll give it a look-see." He unfolded the letter, while Applejack leaned close to his shoulder. The letter was dated at Spanish Wells and ran as follows:

DEAR STEVE:

I'm up against something I can't buck any longer. There's a fellow here, named Tracy, who knew me in the old days, and he's pulled me into some bad business. He put pressure on me and threatened to turn me over to the law unless I did as he said. I had to give in to the dirty sidewinder. If you hear of anything going wrong with me, inform the proper authorities, so I won't have to stand the rap alone. I don't figure there's any real danger in what I'm mixed into, but it's crooked and I don't like it. Here's what they're making me do . . .

And there the letter ended, as though the writer had been interrupted at his task. Applejack commented to that effect as Peaceful refolded and put the letter back into his pocket.

Peaceful nodded. Unconsciously they had both lowered their voices, making it impossible for the listening Corvall to catch the trend of the conversation. "Yeah," Peaceful went on, "it looks like the writer must have been interrupted. He didn't want anybody to see what he had written, so he slipped the letter in between his pack of cards, intending to finish it later."

"If it was Louie Dawes—and I figure it was—he didn't live to finish it. This Steve he was writing to, that's Steve Dawes, his brother, of course."

"That's the way I see it." Peaceful nodded. "Well, the letter doesn't say much, but it does definitely tie Jake Tracy to the job."

"What I'd like to know," Applejack said, "is how Tracy knew this letter was in the deck of cards. That's why he wanted the deck so badly, of course. But did he know what the letter had to say or didn't he? It looks to me like a leak some place."

"Looks that way," Peaceful conceded. "One thing, if Tracy is tied into the business—and now we know he is—so is Randle and his whole crew."

"But we haven't proof of that yet," Applejack

pointed out. "The actual proof against Tracy isn't too strong. Remember, that letter wasn't even signed. I'm afraid it wouldn't stand up in court."

"I'm afraid not," Peaceful admitted. "But it does give us definite knowledge, and with that to work on maybe we can learn more. Now, at least, we've got a point to concentrate on."

At that moment Applejack became conscious of the Mexican waitress's voice, sounding slightly irritated, "What's your order?"

Applejack started, "We gave you our orders—" when he realized the girl was talking to the man next to him. The fellow was so intent trying to hear the conversation between Peaceful and Applejack that he hadn't heard the waitress's reiterated query.

Nick Corvall looked up, startled, to see the frowning face of the waitress. "Oh—er—just bring me a cup cawfee," he stammered. Feeling the gaze of Applejack and Peaceful on him, he put on a bold face. "Oh, hello, fellers. How are you, Jenkins? I didn't notice you two settin' there."

"Must have been half asleep, then, weren't you?" Peaceful said dryly.

"Yeah, that's it." Corvall nodded eagerly. "Hardly keep my eyes open. It was so dang hot on the range to-day. Makes a feller sleepy after he's been workin' hard. Just dropped in for a cup of cawfee to keep me awake."

At that moment the waitress brought platters of steaming food for Peaceful and Applejack, and the conversation was dropped. A minute later the girl put a cup of coffee before Corvall. He drank the hot liquid hurriedly, slipped off the stool, said "S'long," and swiftly left the restaurant, after dropping a two-bit piece on the counter.

As the girl picked up the money Peaceful asked, "Who's that hombre?"

"Name's Nick Corvall," the girl replied. "Punches for Randle's Wolf Head rancho."

When she had left Peaceful said softly, "I wonder how much that hombre heard."

"Not too much, I figure," Applejack said. "We weren't talking loud. Luckily we didn't read that letter aloud. But he was sure interested. When I looked up he was leaning way over. 'Nother couple of inches and I'd been holding him in my lap."

"Anyway, he knows we've got a letter," Peaceful said. "I don't know, though, as it makes much difference. Randle knew I had plenty chance to go through the cards."

"What do you figure Randle's next move will be? He's got something to square with you, cowboy."

"I'm not worrying." Peaceful forked a mouthful of potatoes between his lips. "I figure Randle will go right slow for a time, until he has a chance to feel me out. He's too foxy to make an open battle of it now, until he can pile up an advantage on his side. What happened this afternoon sort of took him down a few pegs. He'll want that forgotten as soon as possible. I'm betting ten dollars against a plugged peso that Randle will pretend to be friendly with me. He's realized by this time that he has to go slow and that he can't ride rough-shod over me."

"What's your next move, then?"

Peaceful shrugged lean shoulders. "I'm not certain until I have more to go on. I'll just have to play the cards as they fall to me. Meanwhile, if you'll stow that grub away, we'll get moving."

"Where we going?"

"First we'll take our ponies down to the livery and see that they're taken care of. Then we get us rooms at the hotel. After that, the Spanish Dagger."

"The Spanish Dagger!"

Peaceful nodded. "I don't reckon it will be dangerous, pard. And Judy Drake sings there nights. I crave to hear her voice."

"You sure that's all?" Applejack looked narrowly at his pardner.

"All I have in mind at present," Peaceful drawled. "I told you I'd have to wait and see how the cards fell. C'mon, drink up that Java and let's get moving."

8

CHALLENGE

BY the time the two entered the Spanish Dagger some three-quarters of an hour later the big honky-tonk was running full blast. The long bar was lined three deep with thirsty customers. There were four bartenders on duty now, all of them working feverishly to supply the demand for various alcoholic refreshments. On the stage a Mexican string orchestra toiled earnestly, while booted men and short-skirted, berouged dance-hall girls shuffled about on the dance floor in the centre of the big room. After each dance the girls were escorted by their partners to the bar, where the girls did but little drinking, but received a commission on each drink sold. Much of the time it was the girls who proved to be the most enthusiastic escorters.

The place was filled with cowmen, miners, Mexicans, and construction hands from the railroad that was building toward Spanish Wells. There was much loud laughing and louder voices. The Spanish Dagger was a bedlam of sound and motion. Glasses clinked against bottles; now and then the shattering of a glass was heard. Through it all came the whirring of wheels, the click of poker chips, the rattle of dice, and the droning voices of croupiers. Tobacco smoke hung in a heavy pall half-way to the ceiling. Cigar and cigarette butts were underfoot. There was a mingled odour of cheap perfume, stale beer, dead tobacco smoke, and unwashed bodies heavy in the atmosphere. And plenty of noise.

"Whew! What a joint," Peaceful commented as he and Applejack shouldered their way through the crowd to the bar. A couple of dance-hall girls descended upon them. Applejack bought drinks for the girls but refused to go farther.

"On your way, my pretties." He grinned. "I don't spend easy and I never was much of a dancer. Me and my pard are just here to look on."

The girls hastened away to find new victims just as the orchestra swung into the strains of the "Blue Danube" waltz. At the bar Peaceful and Applejack purchased cigars, then moved around to watch the games. They wandered from faro layout to roulette wheel to dice tables and paused a time to watch one or two stud games. Applejack started to grin.

Peaceful said, low-voiced, "What you laughing at?"

"The crudity of these tinhorns. They aren't subtle nohow. And every game crooked as a houn'-dawg's hind leg. I got a hunch I could make me a living off some of these double-dealers, if we weren't here on business."

"Probably could," Peaceful agreed, "but you might have a tough time escaping with your winnings. Places like this aren't operated for the benefit of the customers—"

He stopped short as there came a sudden yell for quiet. On the stage Black Hugo Randle had appeared. The music died off in a discordant clashing of tones, and silence descended on the room.

"I've been wondering where Randle was," Peaceful commented. "What's he aiming to do—make a speech?"

"That's just it," Applejack muttered curiously, "but what about?"

They didn't have to wait long to learn.

"Friends, gentlemen, ladies," Randle commenced in a heavy, penetrating voice, "I've got a few words to say before I make a public apology. This afternoon, as most of you've heard, me and a couple of my boys sort of had a whizzer pulled on us. Well"—good-humouredly—"I reckon what we got we invited, so go on and have a good laugh at our expense."

The big room rang with sudden loud laughter. Peaceful said quietly to Applejack, "So that's the stand he's going to take. Just going to laugh it off, eh? I figure Hugo Randle is going to prove plenty dangerous before we get through with him."

The laughter died down as Randle raised one hand for further attention. He went on, "I'm not going to make any excuses or offer any alibis for what happened. We were just outsmarted, that's all. I lost my head for a spell. I'll tell you how that came about. It had come to my ears that a Texas Ranger was being sent here to investigate the Spanish Dagger. That made my blood boil. For two reasons. First, because the Rangers haven't any authority in this state, and second, because the Spanish Dagger doesn't need investigation. As you all know, I run the squarest games, serve the best liquors, and hire the prettiest girls in this whole state—"

Loud cheers interrupted. After a moment Randle went on, "Furthermore, I operate according to law—strictly. Deputy Herb Vaughn sees to that, watches that I close up on the dot, and so on. Herb is right hard on me at times, but he's only doing his duty, and I don't hold it against him. Spanish Wells is lucky to have such a conscientious law officer. But to get back to my story. It made me boil to see a Texas Ranger coming here. I've political enemies, and I thought they were framing me. I jumped to conclusions and regretted it later. I've learned since that my good friend, Jenkins, is no longer a Ranger and that he'd just dropped in to have a drink. So I'm more than glad to make public apology to my friend, Peaceful Jenkins—and—and—well, the drinks are on me all evening. So step up to the bar, folks, and drink to the finest fellow that ever hit Spanish Wells, Mr. Peaceful ex-Ranger Jenkins. Let's give him a cheer!"

Wild yells ascended to the roof; then there came a rush to the bar. Randle leaped, grinning, from the stage.

Applejack was shaking with anger. "The nerve of that sidewinder," he growled. "Can you imagine it? 'My friend, Jenkins!' Gesis! That hombre certainly smells!"

Peaceful grinned. "It's good for a laugh anyway. I told you he was foxy. He's got brains. And most of these nitwits here will believe every word of that speech. What happened to-day will be forgotten by all but a few, and the story of an actual eyewitness will be discredited as a vivid piece of imagination. Meanwhile, Randle builds himself up as a sincere open-hearted hombre who is too honest not to admit his mistakes. Oh, he smells, all right, but at the same time, he's smart—"

He broke off as Hugo Randle came threading through the crowd, a cordial smile on his dark features. One hand was extended in a gesture of friendship, but by that time Peaceful was busily engaged in rolling a cigarette and failed to see the hand.

"Well, you heard me, Jenkins," Randle said heartily. "I hope that squares me with you for being a damn fool this afternoon. I want to be friends with you. I don't know what you're doing here, but I figure it isn't official business, as the Rangers haven't any authority in these parts."

"I already told you I'm no longer with the Rangers," Peaceful drawled, touching a lighted match to his cigarette. "My pard, here, Applejack Peters, is an ex-Ranger too. We're just sloping around, looking over the country. That speech of yours wasn't necessary though."

Randle looked hurt. "I'm sorry you feel that way. It was the best way I could think of to make public apology. I want to be friendly with you—"

Applejack growled, "That reminds me of the feller who said to always be leery of a diamond-back when it pretends to be friendly, 'cause you can't ever trust the reptile—"

"Now look here, Peters," Randle interrupted, flushing, "I don't like that. I'm not going to take it. By God—!"

"Slow down, Randle," Peaceful cut in. "Remember what you said in your speech about jumping to hasty conclusions getting you into trouble once before to-day. Don't make the same mistake twice in twenty-four hours. That's not smart. Take my advice and cool down before you have some more regrets."

Randle's eyes narrowed. "That sounds like a challenge."

"It's meant to be," Peaceful drawled lazily. "I'm glad you recognized it. Now the next move is up to you."

There were men standing all around the three. Two or three of the nearest had been listening curiously. Randle noticed them and choked down the hot words that rose to his lips. He forced a thin smile. "All right, Jenkins," he said in injured tones. "I can see you and your pard just don't understand me. Well, I won't hold it against you. We'll get our difficulties ironed out yet, and you'll realize I'm on the square. I've got to tend to my business now. Step up to the bar and have a drink, or a smoke, on the house. I'll talk more to you later."

Red-faced, he hastened away. By this time the orchestra was playing again, and the din was terrific. Only the few men nearest had caught the drift of the conversation between Randle and Peaceful, though a few more had heard Applejack's louder reference to diamondbacks. The incident was forgotten within a short time, however, as the listeners soon lost themselves in the increased volume of Spanish Dagger activity.

Peaceful and Applejack shouldered their way through the big room, ears alert to overhear any scrap of conversation that might lend further clues to the problem that had brought them to Spanish Wells, but in this they met with no success. Peaceful was hopeful of seeing Judith

Drake again, but so far the girl hadn't put in an appearance. And then quite suddenly a hush fell over the big room, and all eyes were centred on the stage where Judith, dressed all in white, stood smiling down on the assembled crowd.

Accompanied by the now softer strains of the string orchestra, Judith sang "The Last Rose of Summer" in a throaty contralto that carried husky overtones. Then, for an encore, she swung into the lighter "O, Susanna." That last song really stirred the house. Men stamped and cheered and called for more, but by this time Judith had accepted the proffered arm of the beaming Hugo Randle and was descending from the stage. A number of men instantly surrounded her, but Randle waved them away with a sort of proprietary gesture, which action was augmented by a couple of tough-looking bouncers who cleared a path for Randle and the girl. Randle accompanied her to the flight of steps at the rear of the room, where she left him, to proceed on up to her dressing-room located off the wooden-railed balcony. The orchestra swung into another dance.

Applejack sighed deeply. "It's plain to be seen what keeps the crowd coming here. That girl can certainly sing. Those deep tones of hers sort of make chills run up and down a feller's spine."

A heavy frown had settled on Peaceful's face.

"I still don't understand a girl like Judith Drake singing in this place," he muttered.

"Better quit thinking about it," Applejack reminded. "That's not what we came here for."

"I'm not so sure," Peaceful said quietly, "but what she's connected up with the business in some way."

Applejack conceded that Peaceful might be correct in his surmise. "Eventually we may learn you're right, pard."

Peaceful smiled lazily. "Sometimes I haven't too much patience."

"Meaning what?"

"Eventually may be a long time off. I want to know now. I saw the door Miss Drake entered through. I reckon I'll slip up on that balcony and get a few words with her, if she'll listen."

"Now?" Applejack looked aghast.

"Right now," Peaceful nodded.

"You loco?" Applejack queried concernedly. "You saw those bouncers Randle keeps here. You can see Randle considers her his private property—"

"That's one of the things I don't like," Peaceful said grimly. "I aim to prove otherwise."

"Look here, pard"—Applejack frowned—"you falling for that girl?"

"I didn't say that," Peaceful evaded.

"Maybe there are some things don't need to be said," Applejack snorted. "You go messing

93

around that girl and you'll make yourself a peck of trouble."

"Maybe a corralful." Peaceful grinned. "Howsomever, I figure it's all in the course of duty. I'm heading for that balcony, pard."

"Sure, I knew you would," Applejack growled, "despite anything I might say. Go ahead. I'll be somewhere around when trouble breaks."

9

BRASS v. STEEL

NICK CORVALL had been trying all evening to get in a word privately with his employer, but Hugo Randle seemed always busy talking to someone else, buying drinks for friends at the bar, or going into still greater details, explaining to all and sundry that he wasn't entirely to blame for the part he'd played in "Jenkins's Bluff" that afternoon. Somehow, all his explanations didn't seem to ward off considerable laughter at his expense, and his own smiles weren't at all spontaneous.

But finally Corvall thought he saw his chance. For the past fifteen minutes Randle had been seated at a table at the rear end of the bar, imbibing drinks in the company of Jake Tracy and Scott Heffner. Heffner had had one drink, then left the table, leaving only Tracy with Randle. Corvall would have preferred to have talked with Randle alone, but, after all, Tracy was involved in the story he had to tell, so it wouldn't make much difference. The main thing was to make Randle realize that Corvall was ever alert to Black Hugo's interests; along that road led the way to promotion and a higher place in the councils of his chief.

Corvall approached Randle's table and slid easily into a chair between Randle and Tracy. "Evenin', boss," he said.

Randle eyed the man a moment. "About time you started back to the ranch, isn't it, Nick?"

"Past time," Nick agreed ingratiatingly, "but I had somethin' to tell you first. You've been so darned busy all evenin' that—"

"All right," Randle said shortly. "Spit it out."

"Look, Hugo, I'm always on the outlook to protect your interests, and I realize what happened this afternoon wasn't all your fault—"

"I suppose it was mine," Tracy snapped sourly.

"I didn't say that, Jake," Corvall started in aggrieved tones. "If you men would only listen to what I have to say—"

"Good cripes! I told you to talk up," Randle said irritably. "Now get going or start back to the ranch. I don't pay you cow-waddies to stay up nights so you can sleep on the job days. Spit it out, Corvall."

"I'm getting to it right now," Corvall said humbly. "You'll be plumb interested in what I'm goin' to tell you. Y'understand, of course, that I've heard a lot of talk about what happened to-day, not just here, but about that pack of cards that Jake tried to take off'n Jenkins to-day—"

"What about that pack of cards?" Randle cut in sharply.

"There was a letter in it," Corvall said. "Addressed to somebody named Steve. I think Louie Dawes wrote it."

Randle and Tracy exchanged quick glances. Randle said, "By God, Herb Vaughn was right, after all." He turned back to Corvall. "Where'd you learn about this, Nick?"

"Like I say, Hugo," Corvall went on, "I'm always lookin' out for your interests, so I sort of played detective for you to-day. I hung around Jenkins and his pard in the Demijohn after—after what happened here—and made out like I was friendly to 'em. They didn't pay much attention to me though. Then when they went to get their supper I slipped into the Bon-Ton and got a seat right next to 'em. I listened in on their talk. I couldn't get all of it—they kept their voices low—but I heard Jenkins tell his pard that he'd found a letter in that deck of cards—"

"T'hell you did!" Tracy blurted.

"What did the letter say?" Randle was very interested now.

"I don't know," Corvall said disappointedly, "except that I got a glance at the headin', and it was addressed to 'Dear Steve.' I didn't get to read the letter, but I heard Applejack Peters say that Louie Dawes had written it to his brother. I overheard Jenkins say, 'This definitely ties

Jake Tracy to the job,' or words to that effect—"

"Oh, my God!" Tracy exclaimed, white-faced.

"Don't lose your nerve, Jake," Randle said sharply. If there'd been anything really definite to go on you'd be in trouble right now. Nick, what other names were mentioned?"

Corvall replied, "I didn't hear any others. They were keepin' their voices too low. Then just as I leaned closer to try and read that letter the damn waitress butted in to get my order, and Jenkins and his pard saw me. They shut up like a clam, instanter, I got a cup of coffee and hustled out."

Randle considered the matter. Finally: "That's a good piece of work, Nick. Remind me to have ten dollars extra put in your pay envelope next payday."

"Thanks, chief. But, look, I want to do more for you. Suppose you let me get that letter from Jenkins."

"How do you figure to do that?" Randle asked curiously.

"Throw a chunk of lead into Jenkins when he isn't lookin'. Once I've downed him, I could go through his pockets—"

"Don't talk like a fool, Nick," Randle said roughly. "Jenkins is too smart for you. You run along now and leave the rest to me. Take to-morrow off if you like—"

"But, Hugo," Corvall pleaded, "I could down Jenkins if you'd just say the word."

"Forget it, Nick," Randle said shortly. "You've done a good piece of work. I'm much obliged. But stay out of it from now on."

"I figure I'll do some lead throwing myself," Jake Tracy said. "My God, Hugo! We've got to get that letter. It mentions my name." He was sick with fear, trembling all over. He started to his feet. "I'm going to plug Jenkins right now. Herb Vaughn will be able to square things."

Randle cursed and jerked the man back. "Sit down, you fool! Have you lost your head completely? Nothing's happened to you yet, and nothing's going to happen to you if you keep your senses about you. Now sit down and keep quiet."

Tracy subsided, green with fright and panting heavily. After a moment he reached out and poured a large drink from the bottle on the table. Randle leaned back in his chair, brows heavy in concentration. The other two sat waiting for him to speak. He raised his head, then paused suddenly as his gaze fell on the wooden flight of steps leading to the balcony. A sudden oath was ripped from Randle's lips.

There, ascending the staircase and nearly to the top, was Peaceful Jenkins There wasn't any doubt in Randle's mind as to where the red-headed Jenkins was headed. Randle paused for brief thought, then jerked around in his chair and called to the nearest bartender, "Where's Mitchell and Fraley? Pass the word for those bouncers! There's some fresh hombre up on the balcony annoying the girls." This despite the fact that all the dance-hall girls were revolving in the arms of pardners, on the floor, at the present moment. "Tell Mitchell and Fraley to give that hombre the works!"

The word was swiftly passed through the crowd and along the bar. A minute later two burly gorillas were seen shouldering their way through the crowd, pushing men right and left in their eagerness to get to the staircase. This was a job to their liking.

Meanwhile, Peaceful had reached the balcony and stood knocking on the door of Judith Drake's dressing room. After a moment the door opened a thin slit. When the girl saw who it was the door was swung wider. "Oh, it's you Mr. Jenkins," she said quietly. She still wore the white dress, but a shawl had been thrown across her shoulders.

"It's me, Miss Judith—Peaceful. I just wanted to tell you I enjoyed your singing and—and—"

"Thank you, Peaceful." A smile accompanied the words. "It's nice of you to come up here and tell me, but you mustn't stay. Hugo Randle won't like it—"

"I don't like Hugo Randle either." Peaceful smiled, his eyes steady on the girl's. "You're living at the hotel, aren't you? I just wanted to ask if I could see you home when you get through."

The girl hesitated dubiously. Then her chin came up. "I think I'd enjoy that—for a change," she said quietly. "I go on for my last number at midnight. I'll see you after that."

"Thank you, ma'am. I'll be waiting."

The door closed on the girl's smile, and Peaceful donned his sombrero and started back toward the staircase, extremely conscious that his heart was beating faster and that his features felt warm.

He had just reached the top of the staircase when he saw two burly hard-bitten men, with angry looks on their faces, rushing furiously up the steps, one after the other toward him.

"Come down from there, you redheaded bustard!" the foremost snarled.

"Exactly what I'm planning to do," Peaceful replied mildly. "If you'll just stand to one side I'll head down—"

"You're bloody right you will," the fellow bellowed. He put out one hamlike hand and closed it on the front of Peaceful's shirt.

Peaceful laughed softly. The next instant his gun was out and the barrel struck sharply across the man's wrist. A loud yelp of pain resounded through the room as the fellow released his grip and started back. Almost at the same instant the gun barrel again fell sharply, this time across the man's head. He swayed back and collapsed against his pardner, rushing on from behind.

The second man paused, cursing, and commenced to fit a set of brass knuckles to his right hand. Again Peaceful laughed, as though the whole situation had struck him as extremely ludicrous. He leaped past the figure of the first bouncer, reeling drunkenly against the banister, and closed in on the brass-knuckled artist. The gun barrel lifted and fell sharply twice, landing with punishing force on the head of the second bouncer. He fell back, tripped, and rolled head over heels to the bottom of the staircase, where he lay groaning. Peaceful shoved the gun back in his holster.

The music had stopped. A wild cowboy yell filled the room: "Yip-yip-yipee! Yow! Yip-pee-e-e-e!" as Applejack Peters gave joyful vent to his sentiments. Applejack stood below, grinning, his gun already out in case of emergency. Now he shoved it back into his holster. "Can you imagine it?" he bawled loudly. "Think of just sending two gorillas to tame that redheaded Texan. Folks sure make a mistake in under-estimating my pard!"

"Hush it, Applejack." Peaceful grinned, stepping over the groaning man at the bottom of the steps. "You aiming to disturb the peace of this sweet little establishment?"

Behind him the first bouncer had regained his feet and came stumbling, glassy-eyed, down the steps. He staggered past Peaceful without a word and lurched up to the bar, where he mumbled something about needing a drink.

Laughter filled the room. It was plain to be seen that the two bouncers weren't at all popular with the patrons of the place. A knot of men and girls gathered about Peaceful. Hugo Randle came striding, whitefaced with anger, through the crowd. He stopped a few yards from Peaceful, for a moment unable to find his voice. Finally the words came: "What in the devil do you think you're doing, Jenkins?"

"I'm not," Peaceful drawled.

"Not what?" Randle paused, puzzled.

"Not doing." Peaceful grinned. "I'm all through doing. These two hombres were blocking the stairway. I had to pass. I reckon they must have tripped, or something. Anyway, they didn't bar my way any more. Danged if I know what hit 'em—less'n it was some sort of inner persuasion. There I was, starting peaceful down the steps, when those two came rushing at me like a pair of wild bulls. Then, sudden-like, they just sort of faded away before my eyes."

From the balcony above came something that sounded suspiciously like a giggle, then the sound of a door closing. Randle glanced up, and his face reddened. There were titters and loud guffaws from the surrounding crowd. Randle's face went white again. He said harshly, "You

103

can't get away with this, beating up defenseless men. You had a gun in your hand—"

"Defenceless?" Peaceful smiled thinly. Stooping quickly, he jerked the brass knuckles from the hand of the groaning bouncer still sprawled at the foot of the staircase. He held out the brass weapon. "You call this being defenceless? I didn't shoot, though I could have. It was simply a case of a gun barrel against these knuckles. Probably a lot of men here will be glad to see what your bullies use to enforce your orders, Randle. But don't ever again call them defenceless. These things are murderous, and you know it."

Low growls of anger rose from several men. Randle commenced to back ground. "I hire those men to enforce order here," he lied, "but I never realized they went to this extent. I'm sorry, Jenkins, this had to happen. At the same time, you had no business on the balcony unless you were invited there. Were you?"

"I can't say I was," Peaceful drawled.

"Then my men were within their rights," Randle said triumphantly, "when they started to bring you down. Naturally, had I known it was you, this would never have happened. At the same time, if you had been hurt, it would have been your own fault."

At this moment Deputy Herb Vaughn pushed through the crowd. "What's up, Hugo? Having trouble here?"

Randle briefly explained the situation.

Vaughn darted an angry glance at Peaceful, then asked Randle, "Want I should put Jenkins under arrest, Hugo?"

Peaceful grinned. "I wouldn't try it was I you, Deputy. You might get your badge tarnished—"

"None of your lip, Jenkins," Vaughn growled. "I'm here to enforce the law and I aim to do it. Hugo, it's up to you."

"We'll forget it this time," Randle snapped.

Peaceful said dryly, "Thanks, Mr. Randle."

Applejack growled, "C'mon, pard, let's get out of this buzzards' roost. This tinhorn deputy isn't going to make any arrests. He don't even dast try it."

Peaceful nodded. "I reckon you called the turn, Applejack."

The pair moved off through the crowd of grinning faces. Looking back once, Peaceful saw Randle urging the bouncer, still on the floor, to his feet. The order was accompanied by considerable cursing. By the time Peaceful and Applejack stepped into the fresher air of the street the orchestra was in full swing again.

Applejack shook his head as he fell into step beside Peaceful. "That place sure doesn't allow anything to interrupt the festivities for very long, does it?"

"Those places never do," Peaceful replied. "Usually they keep running until somebody stops

105

'em cold—then they're stopped for good. That's the next thing on my programme I'm hoping to see."

"If you haven't anything else to do," Applejack proposed, "we might roll into the hay. Those hotel beds looked plumb soft."

Peaceful shook his head. "I've got a date at twelve, or a mite later."

"You have?" Applejack looked up sharply at his pardner, then relaxed. "I understand." And a minute later: "It just seems you do everything possible to rub Randle's fur the wrong direction. You're just daring him to start trouble."

"Yeah, I am"—Peaceful nodded—"though in this particular case I didn't consider him at all. I considered only myself."

Applejack whistled softly.

"And," Peaceful continued, "by the time I come to a consideration of Randle's fur I don't intend to stop at rubbing. I aim to do a complete skinning job. . . . Where'll we go next?"

Applejack said dryly, "I keep remembering that cold beer of Johnny Small's."

Peaceful laughed good-humouredly. "Danged if I don't believe you've got hollow legs."

"Hollow or not," Applejack chuckled, "you've got to admit they're always steady."

They headed their steps in the direction of the Demijohn Saloon.

10

A FIGHTING MARSHAL

APPLEJACK had just commenced consuming his second beer, while Peaceful was puffing a cigar and exchanging tall tales with Johnny Small, much to Applejack's delight, when a young Mexican boy entered with a note for Johnny. Johnny took the note, read it through, then glanced at Peaceful. There were a few other customers in the saloon, so he lowered his voice. "This is really your business," he said to Peaceful.

Peaceful asked, "What is it?"

Johnny explained: "It's from Sam Purdy— Purdy's mayor of Spanish Wells, you know. The town council is meeting tonight down to Purdy's General Store. I was there for the earlier part of the meeting but had to get back here to tend to business. The council wants you should come along and consult with 'em."

"Me?" Peaceful looked surprised. "What for?"

"I ain't got the least idea," Johnny replied. He reddened a trifle. "This note just says if you happen to come in here, will I please tell you that

Sam Purdy would like to see you on important business. Here, you can look at the note yourself."

Peaceful glanced through the note; it said no more than Johnny had told him. Peaceful nodded. "If a feller doesn't listen he never hears anything," he said. "Choke down that scuttle of suds, Applejack, and we'll drift along and see what the learned council has on its mind."

"It's you they want to see," Applejack pointed out, longingly eyeing his beer.

"What concerns me concerns you," Peaceful said. "No telling but what I might get in a fight before I get through."

That settled it. Applejack choked down his beer, and the two pardners departed for the street. Main Street was dark now, except for a few lights in store windows along the way. The high heels of the men clumped hollowly along the boardwalks until they had reached Sam Purdy's General Store. Shades had been drawn on the big front windows of Purdy's store, but at the edge of the frames narrow slivers of light showed. Peaceful and Applejack crossed the wide porch. Peaceful tried the door. It was locked.

Applejack muttered. "There's something funny about this. Did you notice how Johnny got red when he said he didn't know what the council wanted to see you about? Only that it was Johnny, I wouldn't trust this proceeding—"

He broke off. The door had opened suddenly.

Sam Purdy stood squinting above his spectacles into the darkness. "Oh, it's ye, is it, Mr. Jenkins? Come right in. We been waitin' and wonderin' if ye'd show up. Come in, come in."

Peaceful entered, with the distrustful Applejack at his back. Once inside, however, Applejack relaxed. It was a town council meeting, nothing more, judging from appearances. The big store was hazy with tobacco smoke. There were a number of men there, all intently surveying Peaceful and his pardner. Some of the men were nibbling on crackers and cheese—which would doubtless be charged up to the expenses of operating the city council. Some were seated on one of the long counters; others had chairs placed helter-skelter here and there.

"This is my pard, Applejack Peters, Mr. Purdy," Peaceful said.

"Glad to make your acquaintance, Mr. Peters." Purdy nodded. "I'll introduce you boys to these other men."

Applejack and Peaceful gravely shook hands with the others. Among them were Tarp Thompson, foreman of the JD Ranch; Jim Howell, owner of the Rafter-H; Connell, owner of the Crossed Keys outfit; Bigelow, who ran the 8-Bar Ranch; Hyde, owner of a mine across the Border; Perkins, who operated the other general store; Fisher of the Bon-Ton Restaurant, and several other small ranch owners and merchants.

"I expect ye're curious as to whut made us ask ye to come here, Jenkins," Sam Purdy said when the introductions had been completed and everybody had found seats.

Peaceful smiled. "Johnny Small just said there was a council meeting on. I'm sort of surprised to find a mineowner and cowmen on a city council. Mostly such things are just held down to town-folks."

"Well," Purdy responded, "this is more than just a regular council meetin'. Things reached the point where folks outside of town were affected, so we've made this a general sort of meetin', y'understand, lettin' them as is affected have their say. They've said it and have left the rest to me. Now it's up to you . . . I understand ye're a Texas Ranger."

Peaceful shook his head. "I resigned some years back; so did my pard, Applejack."

"But ye've had thet experience—I mean in enforcin' law and so on."

Applejack and Peaceful exchanged grins. "Some," Peaceful admitted.

Purdy's next question was more direct: "Whut are ye two doin' here at present?"

Peaceful evaded that to some extent. He smiled lazily. "After we left the Rangers, Applejack and I started us an outfit over Bandera way. Finest stretch of range in the country. Lately we thought of increasing our herds some, so we've been

110

riding around, looking to see if we could find any likely herds cheap. We just happened to drop into Spanish Wells."

Here Tarp Thompson put in triumphantly, "I could tell by the cut of their jib they was cowmen."

Purdy smiled icily. "I'm a-conductin' this meetin', Tarp, and I don't reckon our visitors are int'rested in your sailor lingo." He explained to Peaceful, "Ye see, Tarp once travelled from Galveston to Tampico, and vicy versy, on a sailin' vessel, and he ain't never wearied of boastin' how he was once a jolly jack-tar, or some such foolish words for sailormen—"

"Best life ever," Thompson maintained stoutly. "Only I got into this cow business by mistake and I got to stay on and rod the JD until Jabez Drake gets well, I'd be back before the mast right this minute."

This remark was met with considerable laughter. Jim Howell said, "Tarp, you've been threatening to run off to sea for many a year now, but I notice you always have some good excuse for staying in the cow country."

"I knew a cowman once that turned seaman," Peaceful said gravely. "This feller went into the fishing business, but he never could shake off the early influence of the range. All he could ever get to take his bait was sea cows and bullheads. Never could steer his bait toward any other fish,

111

'cepting some little sea horses he'd corral now and then."

More laughter. Again that icy, tight smile of Purdy's. "I can see how this meetin' would soon get out of order if I didn't take a firm hand," he said. "But we must get to business. First, Peaceful Jenkins, every man here aims to congratulate you on the way you gave Randle and his pards their comeuppance to-day. That was downright elegant."

Peaceful flushed. "Thanks. I reckon I just had a streak of luck."

Applejack cut in, "He had another streak of luck to-night when Randle set a couple of his bully boys with brass knucks on Peaceful. That was sure pretty to see." Before Peaceful could stop him Applejack had swung into a recital of the affair. There was some laughter when he had finished; then the meeting took on a graver aspect.

Hyde, the mining man, said seriously, "That's the sort of thing our miners are up against. We don't mind them coming across the Border for a bit of relaxation, but there are too many of them being seriously hurt night after night. It slows the efficiency of the job. What is worse, my pardner, Luke Secord, has been making a fool of himself nightly in the Spanish Dagger. He's drinking more than is good for him and losing more than he can afford at the games—"

"Something's got to be done to stop Randle," Connell of the Crossed Keys put in. "My punchers come into town and get rooked out of their pay—"

"And it's not only the punchers," said Bigelow of the 8-Bar. "Look at the cattle that are being run off by Randle's Wolf Head men. There isn't a ranch around here that hasn't lost money."

"That's all true." Sam Purdy nodded. "And conditions right here in town aren't good by any means. All due to Randle and his crew. We haven't a mite of proof against him, as we all well know. At the same time, there ain't a bit of doubt in anybody's mind about Randle and his gang. They're just plain bandits, every one of 'em—"

"Pirates! That's what I'd call 'em," Tarp Thompson said fiercely. "Operatin' just like in the old wild days on the sea. Marauders! Buccaneers! Randle an' his whole crew should be strung up to the yardarm and lashed with a cat-o'-nine-tails!"

For once Sam Purdy didn't josh Tarp about his sea-going lingo. The elderly storekeeper nodded terse agreement. "We've all suffered from the work of Randle and his buccaneers, as Tarp calls 'em. Conditions are right bad, both in town and out on the range. Tarp probably has a mite more call to complain than the rest of us. His boss was shot and robbed right here in town, and nothin's been done about it. The JD is close to ruin, due to cattle thieves. Somethin' must and will be done!" He switched his conversation suddenly, directly, to Peaceful. "What do ye think could be done about it, Mr. Jenkins?"

Still wondering what this was all about, Peaceful took his time in answering. "Well," he said slowly, "you have a law officer in town, Deputy Herb Vaughn. Have you complained to him?"

"Phaugh!" Purdy spat contemptuously, as did others in the room. "If Deputy Vaughn isn't in Randle's pay I'll eat a feather tick. Who had the best chance to make way with Jabez Drake's five thousand? Deputy Vaughn! Though we can't prove it against him. Who spends his time arrestin' and beatin' up poor Mexicans? Deputy Vaughn! At the same time he's never jailed a man in Randle's pay. Who is it that is always anxious to throw cowpunchers in the cooler on the slightest excuse, though no one heard of him arrestin' a Wolf Head puncher? Deputy Vaughn! Complain, ye say? Mr. Jenkins, we've all complained to Vaughn until we're black in the face, but we get no satisfaction from Herb Vaughn. We've even complained to Sheriff Ike Kimball, at the county seat, but so far he has shown no inclination to replace Vaughn. There's politics mixed into the business someplace."

Peaceful said, "Maybe it's politics that has

Kimball's hands tied. Maybe Kimball isn't to blame."

"Thet's likely enough," Purdy conceded. "Kimball always appealed to me as bein' squarish. But as to Vaughn—less than a week ago a committee appealed to him to see if conditions here couldn't be bettered. Vaughn claims he has to spend so much time ridin' on the range in search of rustlers that he can't devote much time to the town proper. That's his excuse, though he seems to be in town every day. So a bunch of us got together, and we've decided to appoint a marshal to Spanish Wells. We've got a man in mind who's shown he's not afraid of Black Hugo Randle and who has already had a heap of law-enforcin' experience. Will ye accept the job, Mr. Peaceful Jenkins?"

"Me?" Peaceful blurted in surprise. "Town marshal of Spanish Wells?"

"It was Johnny Small suggested you, earlier this evening," Purdy said.

Peaceful grinned. "Dang that Johnny for a pie-eyed liar. He swore he didn't know what this meeting was all about."

"Will you take the job?" asked Howell of the Rafter-H.

Applejack put in judiciously, "It might be a good idea to have some legal authority at that, pard."

Peaceful nodded, considering. "It would tie me

pretty close to town though. I might want to make a ride out on the range—" He broke off; then: "Yes, I'll take the job, providing you appoint my pard as deputy marshal of the town. Then one of us could always be in Spanish Wells if the other was out of town."

A silence fell over the group. Purdy said, "We like the idea fine, but ye see, we can only afford the salary of one man. That's one hundred a month and expenses."

Peaceful grinned. "I reckon Applejack and I won't have any trouble dividing a hundred a month. We've lived on a heap less more than once. Gentlemen, you've hired yourselves a marshal!"

There was applause. Several rose and shook Peaceful's and Applejack's hands. Tarp Thompson exclaimed, "Blow me down if we ain't got a fightin' marshal—a pair of fightin' marshals! If conditions don't change in Spanish Wells from now on, you can make me swab decks the rest of my briny days!"

Purdy was still smiling his cool, icy smile, but Peaceful knew he was pleased, could sense it in the tight grasp of the man's bony fingers. "We're countin' on ye a lot, son," he said a bit unsteadily. "We know we're lucky to get the right man." He stepped to a drawer behind his counter. "We had a marshal here 'bout ten years back. Lucky I've still got his badge. Here 'tis, Peaceful. Ye can start 'er new job first thing in the mornin', I hope."

Peaceful shook his head, drawled, "Not in the morning. Now! Applejack and me, we're on duty, gentlemen!"

Tarp Thompson beamed. "Well, blow me down if this fightin' marshal don't weigh anchor in a hurry. His canvas is spread and you can rate me for a sea cook if he doesn't sink a crew of buccaneers to Davy Jones' locker!"

11

CAUGHT BETWEEN FIRES

WITH the town meeting ended, the gathering broke up and the various members of the group headed for their respective beds. Timothy Hyde, the mining man from the other side of the Border, announced his intention of going to the Spanish Dagger to persuade his pardner to return to the mine with him.

"Might as well come along with us," Peaceful invited.

"We're headed back that way."

The three men strolled along the plank sidewalks. Peaceful and Applejack didn't say much. They were listening to Hyde pour out a tale of woe. "This pardner of mine, Luke Secord"— and he sighed deeply—"is certainly a trial and a tribulation. Luke is a peach of a fellow and a fine mining engineer. But he's run in tough luck all his days, until he struck it rich in the Montezuma Princess, as we named our mine. Luke had the brains; I furnished the capital. But we're just commencing to show a profit on our business. This is the first time that Luke ever had a few extra dollars, and the prosperity has sort of gone to his head. Night after night he gets drunk at the Spanish Dagger; he gambles and always loses. I've done my best to keep him straight; I just come to Spanish Wells every night so I can take him home."

"A pard like that sure tries a feller's soul sometimes," Applejack said sympathetically, "especially when it's somebody you think a heap of."

"As I do of Luke," Hyde said. "Eventually he'll get this wild streak worked out of his system, but meanwhile he sure does worry me."

Business was still running wide open when they arrived at the Spanish Dagger. If possible, it was more crowded than when Applejack and Peaceful had left, somewhat more than an hour before.

The three men shouldered their way inside the door and up to the bar, which was lined four deep. Clusters of men stood around each game of chance. The dance floor was crowded to the point where the dancers could do little more than shuffle about in one spot. The orchestra men played with perspiration streaming down their faces.

Across a sea of heads and shoulders Peaceful's eyes met Hugo Randle's. Randle's gaze hardened; he nodded slightly. He couldn't, of course, see the marshal's badge pinned to Peaceful's vest. Apparently nobody else had noticed it either. At the far end of the bar, near the rear of the room, Peaceful saw the two bouncers he had knocked out once more on the job. Their faces were ugly and sullen, and Peaceful surmised they were just itching to take out their own misfortune on some unfortunate victim when the opportunity arose.

"I sure feel sorry for the next hombre those two tangle with," Peaceful said to Applejack.

Applejack nodded. "But they won't hanker to tangle with you again."

Through a haze of smoke fog Hyde spotted his pardner standing near the bar.

"There's Luke now. I reckon I'll go talk to him and see can I persuade him to leave."

He pushed off through the crowd. Peaceful saw Secord turn at his pardner's touch. There was a foolish, vacant grin on Secord's face. It was plain to be seen that the man had been drinking heavily all evening. Hyde was, apparently, trying to talk some sense into his pardner, but Secord kept shaking his head in stubborn fashion.

Finally Hyde gave up and ploughed his way back to where Peaceful and Applejack were standing, at the edge of the dance floor. "The damn fool refuses to listen to reason," Hyde grunted disgustedly. "Says he won't leave until he hears that Drake girl sing. He hasn't done any gambling this evening, though, so I suppose I should be thankful for that much anyway."

"You won't have much longer to wait, then,"

Peaceful said. "Miss Drake goes on at midnight."

"The earlier the better," Hyde sighed. "Luke aims to buy her a bottle of wine when she finishes. I told him I didn't think she'd accept, but he's stubborn—"

"I wouldn't try it if I was your friend Luke," Peaceful cut in, eyes narrowing. "It might bring him trouble from Randle."

"Exactly what I told the fool," Hyde said hopelessly, "but he's like an ornery pack mule. I wish we could think of something to stop him."

Peaceful speculated, "I could stop him by putting him under arrest, but I sure hate to do that. After all, he's not disturbing the peace—any more than any other drunk in here. I tell you what, Mr. Hyde, you go stay with him. After Miss Drake has finished her number you hang on to him—tight. If he starts raising a rumpus then, I'll have a good excuse to cut in and take him off your hands until we can get him away from here. But I hate to arrest him now without some good reason."

"I think you've got the right idea." Hyde nodded. "I'll go stay with him now. See you later." He turned and pushed his way back toward Secord, who was still standing at the bar.

Peaceful turned back to watch the perspiring figures on the dance floor, eyeing them with a look of amusement. Handsome Jake Tracy danced past, smirking down on the woman in his arms, a chemical blonde with a double chin and scrawny neck. Tracy glanced up, saw Peaceful grinning at him. A look of hate crossed Tracy's features as he moved on around the floor.

Applejack nudged Peaceful, saying, "Remember that feller that was trying to listen in on us at supper to-night—you know, that Nick Corvall that works for Randle's Wolf Head? He's standing right behind you. Been watching you ever since we came in."

Peaceful shrugged, not even bothering to look around. "I figure Corvall as just a cheap spy, hanging around to see if he can learn anything for his boss. He doesn't bother me any."

The orchestra came to a stop after a few moments. The dancers waited where they were. Peaceful didn't notice Tracy standing just a few feet away; his eyes were on Judith Drake, just stepping to the centre of the stage. The orchestra played the opening strains of "My Old Kentucky Home," and Judith Drake's throaty tones swept through the big room. At the end she scarcely waited for her applause before swinging into the more spritely "Clementine."

At the song's conclusion sudden cheering and stamping burst forth. Judith, starting to leave the stage, was met by the smiling Randle, who assisted her down. The crowd was still yelling, begging for another encore. For an instant the girl paused, unable to pass through the crush. Then

Randle's two bouncers appeared on either side of Randle and Judith.

At that moment Peaceful, reluctantly taking his eyes from the girl, glanced towards Secord and Timothy Hyde. Hyde was fighting to restrain his pardner, but Secord broke away and, laughing, went staggering up to Judith Drake. Peaceful saw Judith half back away, force a slight smile, and shake her head. At that moment Randle lifted his arm and struck Secord across the face. Secord staggered back, then again rushed toward Randle, features contorted with righteous anger.

He never reached Randle, however. The two bouncers closed on Secord and jerked him to one side. Judith, on Randle's arm, reached the staircase that led to the balcony and left Randle there. Peaceful took one step toward the back of the room, then paused, looking above the heads of the crowd. He saw the two bouncers on either side of Secord, caught one glimpse of Secord's white face, eyes closed. Then, above Secord's head a second time, he saw a blackjack rise and fall. Secord went limp between his two assailants, and Peaceful saw them carry the man to a small door in the rear of the building. The door opened and the men passed through to the outer air, back of the Spanish Dagger.

Peaceful whirled on Applejack. "You stay here. Arrest those bouncers if they come back."

"What you aiming to do?"

"I'm going around the other way. Maybe I can catch 'em at some dirty work. Inside or outside, one of us can nab 'em."

Without waiting to say more Peaceful turned and commenced to push his way toward the street entrance. He didn't know that Nick Corvall had also turned and was following him. Nor did he know that Jake Tracy had heard his words and was hurrying toward the same rear door through which the bouncers had carried the unconscious Secord. Tracy believed this was his opportunity to get that letter which held his name, and Tracy wasn't one to overlook such a chance.

Peaceful was in a fever of impatience by the time he finally forced his way through the packed room and reached the doorway giving on Main Street. The instant he was outside he broke into a run that carried him around the side of the building and thence to the rear, where a sort of alley was formed with the backs of Main Street buildings on one side, and on the other a helter-skelter row of adobe shacks occupied by Mexicans. The alley was pitch-dark; heaps of refuse, tin cans, rubbish were piled behind each building, the rear of the Spanish Dagger being no exception to this rule.

None of the Mexican adobes showed any lights, but Peaceful could dimly make out their blocky outlines against the relatively lighter expanse of sky, though the moon was not yet up and but few stars showed. Once in the alley, groping his way cautiously along the back wall of the Spanish Dagger, Peaceful moved close to the earth, searching for Secord's body. There wasn't any sign of the two bouncers. From within the honky-tonk came the strains of dance music and the continued sounds of loud voices and laughter.

Suddenly Peaceful stumbled and fell across a soft, bulky object. He had tripped over Secord's body. "By cripes," he mused angrily, "those two gorillas work fast." He ran his hand quickly over the man's form and discovered that Secord's pockets had been turned inside out. Peaceful placed his ear close to Secord's lips and found he was still breathing, though unconscious. "Dirty skunks," was the thought that passed through Peaceful's mind. "Half kill a man, rob him, then toss him out here on a heap of rubbish. So help me, if I don't square this job—"

He stopped abruptly as the alley was momentarily brightened by the savage flash from a six-shooter. A leaden slug smashed into the heavy foundation of the building at Peaceful's side. Peaceful threw himself flat, close to Secord's body, and reached for his gun. A second shot came, this time passing high overhead, but in the light from its explosion Peaceful had located its source: his assailant was firing from behind the corner of one of the Mexican shacks, some seventy-five feet distant.

125

Peaceful's gun was out now, ready for action, but for the moment he held his fire, hoping his silence would lure the hidden gunman into the open. Then unexpectedly, from behind him, came another shattering roar of gunfire. Peaceful flung his body to one side, hugging the earth.

"Dammit," he muttered. There's two of 'em! They've got me caught between 'em!"

Cursing himself for being trapped in such fashion, Peaceful thumbed back his gun hammer, determined to take at least one of the gunmen with him when he died. From the corner of the adobe shack came a streak of orange fire and powder smoke that blended with a savage report from the opposite direction.

12

MISTAKEN IDENTITY

SCARCELY had the echoes of the shots died away when the two gunmen again opened fire. Still Peaceful lay flat, hugging the wall, head slightly raised to watch. This way, he figured, was the best; perhaps if he lay without movement he might draw one or both of the gunmen into the open. It suddenly occurred to him that those last shots hadn't come anywhere near. "Rotten shots, both of 'em," he muttered disdainfully.

For a brief minute there was silence in the alley. Peaceful surmised that both gunmen were reloading, not taking chances of being caught with partly depleted chambers. Powder smoke drifted in the air. From inside the Spanish Dagger there was no cessation of the sounds of merriment, but in the adobe shacks along the alley voices now rose, voices of frightened women. Peaceful could visualize the Mexican women terrorized, crouching low on the floors of their houses. He lay, himself hugging the earth, close to the unconscious Secord, his eyes darting

127

through the darkness in both directions. He knew one of the gunmen was standing just around the edge of that adobe house. But where, exactly, was the other one, the one who had closed in, unexpectedly, behind him?

Hoping to lure this other man into betraying his location, Peaceful groped on the earth until he had found a small chunk of broken rock. This, with a quick sidewise motion, he flipped through the gloom, behind him. The stone struck the earth, rebounded against a tin can. That brought results. From behind a heap of rubbish, fifty feet to Peaceful's rear, there came a quick flash of gunfire. Then the man behind the adobe shack cut loose. Hot lead snarled through the air, the corner of the adobe blazing with heavy reports. Instantly the rubbish heap beyond Peaceful stabbed the night with short orange flashes.

And then, quite suddenly, comprehension came to Peaceful. He relaxed, laughing weakly, silently. These two weren't firing at him but at each other! Peaceful told himself: *I should have known; those slugs were passing well beyond me. The first shots fired were meant for me all right; then while the feller that shot ducked back behind that adobe house, the second man arrived and commenced to take part. Oh, those idiots! They each think they're firing at me!*

He crouched back, a smile playing about his lips, wondering who the two men were. At that instant the man behind the rubbish heap pulled his trigger again. Peaceful heard the slug smash against the adobe wall behind which the other gunman was hidden. The man behind the adobe ripped out an ugly curse and fired two swift shots.

From the direction of the rubbish heap came a long-drawn moan of agony. A shadowy figure staggered up, then pitched to the earth. Now the gunman behind the adobe leaped into full view and rushed, past Peaceful, toward the rubbish heap. "You son of a bustard!" the man snarled and pumped two more slugs into the writhing form on the earth. In the quick flashes from the six-shooter Peaceful recognized Handsome Jake Tracy.

Peaceful rose silently to his feet. Inside the Spanish Dagger the music had ceased; there weren't so many voices now. Watching through the gloom of the alley, Peaceful saw Tracy's shadowy figure stoop low over the man he had shot; then a puzzled exclamation left Tracy's lips as he started to rise to his feet.

Peaceful took several quick steps, speaking as he moved: "Put 'em up, Tracy. I've got you covered!"

He heard Tracy's six-shooter drop on the ground and in the dim half-light he saw Tracy's arms lift in the air. Tracy said dumbly, "What the hell is this? Who are—?"

"It's me, Tracy. Peaceful Jenkins. Just stand steady—"

An insane snarl of baffled rage rose to Tracy's lips. "Jenkins! You redheaded devil. You—you—what—who is this feller—?"

Peaceful moved nearer, felt with one foot for Tracy's gun on the ground, found and kicked it far to one side. "I don't know who he is any more than you do, Tracy, but I've a hunch it's a case of mistaken identity. You thought you were shooting at me, and so did he—"

"No, no," Tracy stammered, "that's not so."

"All right, who is this feller you pumped lead into—and why did you do it?"

Tracy fell silent.

The rear door of the Spanish Dagger suddenly opened, throwing a broad yellow light across the alley. Applejack stepped into view, bawling, "Hey, Peaceful! Where are you? You all right?" Several men poured out behind him.

Peaceful and his captive stood beyond the light, half hidden in gloom. Peaceful raised his voice: "All right, Applejack," he replied. "Don't burst your lungs."

"What in hell happened? We thought we heard shooting, but it was so noisy inside we weren't sure." He came toward Peaceful, followed by a group of other men. "Who's that with you?"

Timothy Hyde spoke anxiously. "Seen anything of Luke Secord, Jenkins?"

"You just walked past him," Peaceful answered. "He's lying on that pile of rubbish, unconscious. He's been robbed, but I don't figure he's hurt serious."

"Thank God!" Hyde ejaculated fervently.

"And I've arrested the two scuts that did it," Applejack said. "Lucky Hyde had a gun. Randle aimed to get tough. Hyde backed me up. We took Deputy Vaughn's handcuffs to put on those bouncers. Him and Randle don't like it a bit. They wouldn't believe I was deputy marshal of this town. Show 'em your badge, will you?" He was nearer now. "Say, is that Tracy you're holding the gun on? What the devil! Who's that on the ground?"

"I don't know yet. Scratch a match, will you?"

Randle broke in angrily, "What in hell is this, Jenkins? You're no marshal—"

"I won't bother to show you my badge to prove it," Peaceful said coldly. "I'll just put you under arrest if you don't shut up."

Randle shut up. More men had appeared. One of them had a lantern. Randle's two bouncers stood sullen and ugly, their wrists handcuffed together.

Applejack had already scratched a match and stooped to look at the man on the ground. "This is Nick Corvall," he exclaimed. "He's dead!"

"Damn you, Jenkins!" Randle burst out. "Just

because you wear a marshal's badge is no sign you can kill my men."

"I told you once to shut up," Peaceful snapped. "I don't want to have to tell you again."

"Look here, Jenkins," Deputy Vaughn said angrily, "I don't care if you have been appointed marshal of Spanish Wells, a shooting is a shooting. I'm the law in this county. I reckon I'll have to put you under arrest."

"You'd better shut up too," Peaceful said coolly. "Did I say I'd done any shooting? Hell! I didn't have to." He stuck his gun barrel suddenly under Vaughn's nose. "Sniff that, Vaughn. Can you smell any smoke grime?"

Hastily Vaughn stepped back, pawing at the gun barrel to push it away from his nose. " 'Sall right, 'sall right," he stammered nervously. "Smells clean as a whistle."

"But what did happen, pard?" Applejack asked curiously.

Peaceful said, "Jake Tracy did the killing. Maybe we'd better ask him."

Tracy's tongue licked at his parched lips. "It— it was this way," he said jerkily. "Corvall and me had some words over one of the girls inside. Corvall called me some hard names and dared me to come out here and let our six-guns decide who was best man. Naturally I couldn't take a dare, so I shot it out with him."

"You liar," Peaceful said contemptuously.

132

"Until Applejack struck a light you didn't even know who you'd killed, though you'd figured you were shooting at me."

"No, no, that's not so—" Tracy commenced.

"You?" Applejack said. "But where does Corvall come in?"

"He comes in as a case of mistaken identity," Peaceful said. "This is how it looks to me: Tracy heard me tell you I was coming back here to see what those two gorillas did to Secord. Tracy ducked out through the rear door to wait for me, while I was going out the front. Meanwhile, Corvall had followed me to get in his licks, not knowing that Tracy was out here. Tracy didn't know Corvall was coming into the game either. I arrived here, found Secord. Tracy threw down on me, missed, and jumped back out of sight behind a building. I just stayed quiet. About the time Tracy fired his shots Corvall arrived behind me and figured Tracy's shots had been fired by me, so he cut loose. It was dark here; I reckon Tracy figured I'd shifted position. He thought that Corvall's shots were coming from my gun. From then on those two blazed at each other, each one thinking he was firing at me. Tracy, have I figured it out correct?"

"I'll be damned!" Applejack exclaimed.

"No, no, you got it wrong," Tracy put in, speaking feverishly. "I'll give it to you straight, Jenkins. Corvall was shooting at you, all right, but I was trying to stop him. I knew you'd only make it tougher for us fellers if Corvall tried to—"

"No more lies," Peaceful said sternly. "We've had enough out of you for one night, Tracy. It couldn't be you were both after a certain letter I carried, could it?"

Tracy fell silent, finally found his tongue to stammer, "I don't know anything about any letter."

Hyde rejoined the group, saying to Peaceful, "Luke is coming around all right. He's got a couple of nasty bruises on his head, but a night's sleep will fix him up, I reckon."

"Good." Peaceful nodded. "Take him along home. Tomorrow have him figure out how much money is missing from his pockets. We're putting Randle's bullies under arrest on a charge of assault and robbery. Applejack, take those two along to the gaol."

"What gaol?" Deputy Vaughn said belligerently. "My gaol is the only one in town."

"That's the one I'm talking about," Peaceful said calmly. "Refusal to let me use it will bring a charge of obstructing justice. Now it's up to you!"

"Oh, well, if you feel that way," Vaughn said weakly.

"That's exactly how I feel," Peaceful snapped. "You can go along with Applejack to unlock the cells. And give him a key. I aim to get back the money those gorillas stole, either from them or Randle."

Randle interposed hastily, "You're not going to hold me accountable for that, Jenkins."

"Oh, yes, I am," Peaceful drawled, "and a whole lot more before I get through with you, Randle. Right now I figure the Spanish Dagger has stayed open late enough. It's time to close up. Go on in and shoo out your customers—"

"Gesis!" Randle protested angrily. "It ain't the legal closing hour yet—"

"Did I say anything about legal?" Peaceful snapped. "A town marshal makes his own laws in this case. Now do as I say before I close you up for good!"

Randle turned and hastened, cursing under his breath, for the doorway of the Spanish Dagger.

Applejack said, "What you aiming to do with Tracy? You want him arrested and charged with murder?"

"That'd be the legal way, wouldn't it?" Peaceful grinned. "But I don't feel very legal to-night. So long as Tracy continues bumping off his own kind, I figure him as a benefactor of humanity. It might be he even saved my life. No, let him go, Applejack. We'll get him on another count some other time."

Without a word Tracy turned and vanished swiftly down the darkness of the alley. The cluster of men standing around commenced to drift away. Peaceful said, "Take your prisoners down to the gaol, Applejack. After Vaughn has let you in have him locate the undertaker for you. Corvall's body has to be removed. Take care of that, can't you, Vaughn?"

Vaughn muttered a sullen "I guess it can be done."

Peaceful nodded, turned, and made his way back to the Spanish Dagger. By the time he stepped inside the last of the customers were drifting through the doorway to Main Street. The musicians were packing up their instruments and the gamblers covering up their paraphernalia. Bartenders were washing glasses and replacing bottles on the back bar. Smoke and the stench of stale alcohol still hung heavy in the air. No one said anything, but many evil glances were bestowed in Peaceful's direction.

Peaceful glanced up toward the balcony, wondering if Judith Drake had already departed. At that moment Randle came running lightly down the stairway, a gleam of triumph in his beady eyes.

He reached the bottom and strode over to where Peaceful was waiting.

"Well," he said with assumed cordiality, "you won a round to-night, Jenkins, but my turn will come. Don't forget that. Just because you wear that tin marshal's badge is no sign you've got me bullied. No hard feelings, you understand. I play the cards as they come to me—"

"And never stack the deck, I suppose," Peaceful drawled.

"Not Hugo Randle," the man said lightly. "You'll learn some day, though, Jenkins, that it doesn't pay to buck me."

Peaceful smiled scornfully. "I'd buck you without pay, Randle, just for the fun I'd get out of it."

That brought an end to the exchange. Glancing up, Peaceful saw Judith just descending the stairway. He stepped forward to meet her as she reached the bottom. "Howdy, Miss Judith." He smiled, removing his sombrero. "Ready to leave, I see."

The girl eyed him coldly. "I'm sorry if there's been a misunderstanding, Mr. Jenkins. Hugo Randle will be taking me to my hotel—as usual."

She brushed coolly pasta and accepted Randle's arm. Peaceful was struck dumb for the moment. Randle said mockingly, "Good night, Mister Jenkins. I hope you've enjoyed yourself."

Puzzled, not understanding, Peaceful watched the man and girl pass out to the street. Then he slowly started for the doorway, not hearing the scornful laughter of the other men in the room, even unaware of their presence by this time.

13

A NOCTURNAL VISITOR

PEACEFUL walked slowly down Main Street, still trying to fathom the girl's suddenly changed attitude. She had been so friendly up there on the balcony, and then, later . . . "Danged if I can understand it," Peaceful mused. "When she saw I was waiting to see her to the hotel she sure turned cold of a sudden. Her voice would have froze living flame. But why? What did I do that was wrong? Or did I do anything? Maybe she felt that way right along and was just joshing me when she was so friendly. And yet it don't stand to reason, after the things I've heard about her. Oh well, it'll work out someway."

There were but a few pedestrians on the street now. With one or two scattered exceptions, no lights showed. Farther on a light burned in Deputy Vaughn's office. By the time Peaceful arrived there Applejack Peters was just coming out.

"You, Peaceful?" He squinted through the semi-gloom.

"Me, Applejack. Put your prisoners to bed?"

"Yeah. Vaughn even turned a set of keys over to me. He's plumb anxious to please all of a sudden. Mighty inquisitive, too, but I side-stepped all the questions he's been shooting at me."

"Where is he now?"

"Gone to wake up the undertaker and have him pick up Corvall's body. Pard, you had a close escape to-night, with two of 'em gunning for you."

"I'm usually pretty lucky. Those hombres must want that letter bad. I can't understand Corvall being so interested, though. He wasn't mentioned."

"Maybe he was acting on orders from Randle?"

"I don't reckon. Randle showed as much surprise as anybody when he learned it was Corvall. Besides, Corvall is just small calibre. Randle would hunt me with a bigger gun."

"Probably you're right. Say, you sure got back from the hotel quick. Did the girl have anything to say?"

Peaceful didn't reply for a moment. They stood leaning against the tie rail in front of Vaughn's office. Peaceful was concentrating on rolling a cigarette. When he had finished he passed the sack of Durham and the papers to Applejack. They scratched matches and lighted up. Peaceful inhaled deeply, exhaled, then said with a wry smile, "Yeah, she said something. She said it quick and cold, like I didn't even have any business speaking to her. She allowed as how Randle would see her to her hotel."

"T'hell she did!"

"I'm telling you. And Randle stood there grinning like a black ape. Cowboy, I came right close to getting mad about then."

"I'll bet. You know, I'd of sworn a girl that could sing like that wouldn't—"

"I know, I know." Peaceful nodded. "I'd have done some swearing myself. What bothers me, I'd figured we have her on our side. After all, it was her own father that was shot and robbed."

Applejack said philosophically, "Nobody ever knows what a woman will do. . . . Well, I reckon we better get along to the hotel and try our own beds."

They walked slowly back to the hotel without saying much and entered the small lobby. A sleepy-eyed clerk eyed them drowsily from behind his desk and offered a feeble nod. The bar to the left of the lobby was still open, though it was quiet in there. Peaceful got their keys from the clerk and mounted a flight of thinly-carpeted steps to the second floor.

"Here's your key," Peaceful said as they turned into a narrow corridor lined with closed doors on either side. "You got room 23; I've got 22. Good night, hope the bed is soft."

"You don't hope it any more than me." Apple-

140

jack yawned. "It's been a long day." He entered his room and closed the door.

Peaceful had fitted the key to his lock before he realized the door was already unlocked. That immediately struck him as queer. He drew his gun and entered cautiously, then stopped still. He could hear someone's faint breathing. Peaceful located the sound and raised his gun barrel. "All right," he said grimly, "talk or start shooting. Who is it?"

And then he heard a quick, light step and the rustle of skirts. He felt a hand rest tentatively on his arm. "Mr. Jenkins—Peaceful—I just had to—"

Peaceful didn't answer at once. He found a match and scratched it, looked about the room for the oil lamp, and touched flame to the wick. He replaced the chimney carefully, allowing his nerves an opportunity to settle. Then he turned to face the girl. She still wore the dress he had seen her in last; the shawl was still about her shoulders. She was smiling rather wistfully.

"What are you doing here?" Peaceful asked quietly. "How did you get in?"

"With the key to my own room. One key fits all these rooms, you know."

"I didn't, but it doesn't make any difference, Miss Drake. What can I do for you?"

"Peaceful"—there was a wail in the girl's

141

voice—"don't be like that. You don't understand—"

"I reckon I don't," he replied quietly. "One
time we meet and you're friendly. The next time
you scarcely know me. I believe you said you
were sorry if there'd been a misunderstanding.
All right. You're sorry! So what about it? It's
bedtime for me. Run along, lady."

"Peaceful!" She stamped one foot angrily.
"You've just got to listen to me! I've waited here
purposely for your return. I'll admit that I acted
like a—like a—well, what you probably thought
I was, but you just don't understand. Do you
think I'd really feel that way toward anyone who
bucked Hugo Randle?"

"I'm not a mind reader," Peaceful said politely.

Again that angry stamp of the foot. "I'm commencing to think you're an idiot. All right. I'll
say no more. But you've got to hear this much.
If I hadn't gone with Randle when I did you
might be dead now. There! I've told you. My
conscience is clear. What you think now doesn't
matter to me! Good night, Mr. Peaceful Numskull
Jenkins!"

She turned and flounced toward the doorway. Peaceful reached out and caught her arm,
drawing her back into the room. Her eyes looked
moist. "Let me go," she said tearfully.

"Not right away," Peaceful said softly. "I'm
going to hear what you've got to say. Maybe I

142

have been a fool. Am I to understand that Randle threatened my life if you didn't go with him to-night?"

"That's what I've been trying to tell you." Judith brushed tears from her eyes.

Peaceful laughed softly. "He wouldn't dare. He was bluffing."

"He was insane with anger when I told him you were going to see me to the hotel. He said he'd have his men shoot you down unless I did exactly as he told me. I hated to do it, Peaceful, but there seemed nothing else at the time. I had to act a part, can't you see?"

"Lady, you're a perfect actress," Peaceful said fervently.

"And then—and then I kept remembering that hurt look in your eyes, so I let myself in here to wait and explain. Now do you believe me?"

"I not only believe you, but I want to have a talk with you if you'll wait a while longer. First, why are you working in a place like the Spanish Dagger?"

"One hundred dollars a week." Judith smiled. "Randle claims that I draw trade. Maybe—"

"There's more to it than just money," Peaceful said shrewdly. "What—?" He paused.

Judith said, "What's the matter?"

"Good heavens, you can't stay in here, talking to me."

Judith smiled. "Golly, Peaceful, you're surely

143

not worrying about the reputation of a Spanish Dagger employee—"

"You get right out." Peaceful's voice was firm.

"But, Peaceful, we were going to have a talk. I'll tell you things that will explain my connection with Randle. As soon as Tarp said you'd been appointed marshal I knew you'd be on our side."

"Tarp Thompson—your foreman on the JD?"

"Blow me down if he isn't." Judith smiled. "Sure—Tarp. He's staying in town to-night, in the room next to mine, number 24. Wait, I'll get him. With him on the job as a chaperon, my reputation will be safe." She turned and knocked on a near-by door.

Peaceful grinned. "Maybe I'd better think of my own rep. I'll get Applejack for my chaperon."

A few minutes later the three men and Judith were settled in Peaceful's room. Judith occupied a chair; Peaceful stood leaning against one wall, smoking. Tarp and Applejack sat on the bed. They talked in low tones, so as not to disturb any other guests of the hotel. Both Tarp and Applejack were saying uncomplimentary things about Hugo Randle.

"I'll tell you one thing," Tarp informed the girl, "you'll weigh anchor tomorrow and set a course for your home port. Either that or I'll tell your dad the sort of ship you've signed on with."

"I've already decided to quit," Judith said. "I've

stood all I could—and it's done me no good. I've learned nothing of value."

"Didn't your dad know you were singing in the Spanish Dagger?" Peaceful asked.

Judith shook her head. "He knew I had some sort of job in town, but he didn't dream what it was. Up to the past week he's been too weak to ask for details. Tarp and the other boys have been caring for him. I've made the ride home three or four times a week."

Tarp put in:

"Jabez has been in sick bay a month now. He had a narrow squeak."

Peaceful and Applejack asked a few questions relative to the robbery and shooting of Judith's father. Finally Judith said, "Maybe it would be best for you to get the story from the start. Mother died when I was young. Dad has raised me on the JD since I was a little tyke—and Tarp has helped. Several years back Hugo Randle bought the Wolf Head Ranch that lies next to our holdings. For a time folks liked him. He used to visit us regularly. Then a lot of people noticed that the Wolf Head's herds were increasing pretty rapidly—"

"Just about as fast," Tarp put in, "as the other folks' cows was decreasin'."

"Trouble is," Judith said ruefully, "folks didn't realize that Randle was rustling—that is, most of us didn't. We had a bad couple of years, lost a lot of cattle through disease one year. Father felt we should restock our range but lacked the money. Randle offered a loan, secured by the ranch, and father borrowed five thousand dollars. Things went along pretty well for a time, and we managed to pay the interest regularly. Suddenly it dawned on a lot of people that Randle was growing wealthy too rapidly. He was buying property right and left, getting a hold here and there. He bought the Oasis Saloon. When the boom came he opened the Spanish Dagger."

"That should have opened your eyes," Applejack commented.

Judith nodded. "It opened the eyes of a lot of folks. The cattlemen suddenly realized how powerful Randle had grown. Now we all suspected his crooked activities, but we had no proof. Dad reached the point where he didn't want to owe money to such a man, so he arranged at the local bank to borrow five thousand with which to pay off Randle. You've heard what happened. A bandit named Dawes shot him and ran off with the money. We suspect Deputy Vaughn got that money, but again we have no proof, and without proof our hands are tied. So there we were. We not only owed Randle five thousand, but the local bank held Dad's note, as well, for another five thousand. Now, just to make matters worse, the bank is asking for its money. Banker Uhlmann claims money is tight and he can't wait longer.

That is something I can't understand, considering the boom that is on."

"Bankers do strange things at times." Peaceful nodded. Then: "You haven't yet explained how you happened to be singing in the Spanish Dagger."

Judith smiled wryly. "I was trying to be a detective. Randle offered me the job, and I thought if I spent some time in his place I might overhear some information that would give us the proof we needed against him. But I was unsuccessful. Oh, the money proved to be very convenient too. You see, Peaceful, we're just about broke, and while Dad was flat on his back I simply had to do all possible to raise some money. When I took the job I didn't think it would be as bad as it was. Randle told me I'd be a sort of assistant manager. He—he—well, in the long run he proved to be rather obnoxious. I won't go back again."

"You earned every cent of your pay," Tarp growled.

"I'll miss that pay every week," Judith sighed. "It's helped to keep things going. And now we'll be right up against the same blank wall again. What is more, we'll lose the JD."

"Don't give up hope yet," Peaceful said.

Judith said quickly, "What do you mean? Do you know of some proof that will involve Randle in the holdup?"

Peaceful shook his head. "Not actual proof, but I've a strong hunch. I'd like to consider the whole matter in detail before I say anything. Is your dad able to have visitors?"

Judith nodded. "He's been growing well rapidly the past week."

"I'd like to ride out to your ranch tomorrow and meet your father," Peaceful said.

"Fine!" Judith exclaimed. "You can ride out with Tarp and me when we leave. Peaceful, you haven't told us all you know about this—"

"I haven't." Peaceful smiled. "But it's getting on toward two-thirty. It's time we were in bed. So if you'll take your chaperon and get out, Judith, I'll give mine the bum's rush back to his own room. We'll talk more to-morrow."

14

A QUESTION OF MARKSMANSHIP

PEACEFUL and Applejack rose early the next morning. After they had eaten breakfast at the Bon-Ton, Peaceful dropped into one of the local barbershops for a shave, while Applejack headed for the gaol to see that his two prisoners had breakfast.

"I'll see you around town later," Peaceful said as they parted. "I'd sort of like to sashay around and get acquainted—let folks know there's a new town marshal on the job."

For an hour Peaceful wandered about Spanish Wells, making the acquaintance of many of the merchants and townspeople. On all sides he heard complaints against Randle's Spanish Dagger and requests that it be closed.

"I can't very well close it," he smiled to one questioner. "As I understand it, the city council gave him a license to operate. At the same time, I can do my dangedest to see that it is operated in a decent manner. You've my promise on that score."

He dropped into the Oasis Saloon, owned by Randle. Three of Randle's Wolf Head punchers—

149

by name, Fred Cubera, Lippy Leonard, and Gus Clark—stood at the bar talking to Scott Heffner and Magpie Bayliss, Randle's bartender. Peaceful nodded coolly to Heffner and bought a cigar. Randle's punchers were a rough-looking lot.

Heffner said insolently, "Boys, this is our new marshal. Treat him gentle or he sure gets rough."

"You should know," Peaceful said placidly.

Magpie Bayliss said, "Awe, we've had tough hombres hit this town before. They never worry Randle much."

Peaceful smiled. "This time the tough guy is wearing a law officer's badge, Bayliss. Maybe it'll be different."

Heffner said, shaking his head at Bayliss, "Sometimes you talk too much, Magpie." Apparently Heffner was in no mood for fighting this morning.

Lippy Leonard said, "We've already got one man in town wearing a badge—Deputy Herb Vaughn."

"That's his trouble," Peaceful drawled. "He just wears his badge. It doesn't mean anything else to him." He paused; then: "I can see my appointment don't meet with the approval of you boys."

"We ain't the only ones that don't like it either," Magpie burst out angrily, impulsively.

"Who, for instance?" Peaceful drawled.

"Banker Uhlmann, for one," Magpie Bayliss growled. "And there's boys making an honest living at the Spanish Dagger—"

Heffner cut in suddenly, "Magpie, close your trap and pour me a shot of bourbon." He glared hotly at Bayliss, and Bayliss fell silent. The Wolf Head punchers had also become suddenly quiet too.

Peaceful drawled, "It's no news to me that a lot of folks don't approve of me being town marshal. For your information, said folks are just the ones I don't approve of either. So govern yourself accordingly."

He turned and pushed out through the swinging doors, stood on the porch an instant, then stepped back inside again, just in time to hear Heffner saying angrily, "Magpie, you ought to be shot for dragging Banker Uhlmann's name into the talk—" He broke off abruptly upon noticing Peaceful standing inside the entrance.

Peaceful smiled. "I was wondering about that myself, Heffner."

Heffner said hastily, "Now don't get any wrong ideas about Fletcher Uhlmann. He's all right. It's just that, being a cousin to Herb Vaughn, he sort of resents an additional officer being appointed here. Uhlmann thinks a lot of Herb."

"Thanks." Peaceful smiled dryly. "I'm glad you explained."

Again he withdrew from the saloon and

sauntered along the street until he had reached Sam Purdy's General Store. Purdy was busy waiting on several customers with the aid of a lanky, pimply-faced youth with tousled straw-coloured hair. Finally, when there was only one customer remaining, and the young fellow was seeing to his needs, Sam Purdy approached Peaceful, the usual tight smile on his face and one hand outstretched.

"Congratulations to ye, Peaceful."

"On what?"

"Getting on the job so quick last night. Them two bouncers of Randle's have been a-bullyin' folks too long. Dang nigh got yerself shot up, though, didn't ye?"

"You heard about it, then?"

"Sho! The news is all over town. Ye've made a heap of friends, son."

"And some enemies too, I reckon." Peaceful smiled. "Mr. Purdy, I've heard my appointment didn't set so well with your local banker."

"Fletcher Uhlmann? Sho, son, don't let that fret ye. Just 'tween you and me, Uhlmann's an old skinflint. He jest bought that bank about three years back. Not too popular, Uhlmann. Mite too anxious to foreclose on folks when he gets the chance. That's one reason we've always voted to keep him off'n the town council—though he's worked his hardest to get on."

"I understand he's Herb Vaughn's cousin."

"That's so? That's news to me. Might be, though. They're right friendly."

"That's interesting."

"How so?"

"Vaughn, through Randle, represents a certain faction here. One faction seems to be against law and order. See what I mean?" Peaceful changed the subject. "I notice you have a clerk now."

"Huh? Oh, ye mean Willie Horton. Willie's been with me for some time. Been away recent, though, up to Nevady, visitin' his folks. Just got back this mornin'. My reg'lar clerk has started his vacation. I'm sort of breakin' Willie in to learn the stock and so on. Usual, he just sweeps up and runs errands and so on."

"Oh yes, you mentioned him yesterday. He was the one that knew Louie Dawes. I'd like to talk to him."

"Reckon there ain't no law agin it." By this time the last customer had departed, and Purdy called to Willie, "C'mere and meet our new marshal, Willie."

Peaceful shook hands with the boy. "Have a good time up in Nevada, son?"

"Yes, sir. It was right good seein' Maw and Paw again."

"I'll bet it was. By the way, you were here when Louie Dawes shot and robbed Jabez Drake, weren't you?"

The boy nodded. "That sure was a surprise to

me. I liked Louie. Never saw a pleasanter feller. He sure turned bad sudden."

"Do you remember exactly what happened that morning? I mean from the time you arrived here at the store?"

The boy's head furrowed with concentration. "I remember I skun my shin." He pulled up one pants leg to display a thin scar.

"How'd you do that?"

"It was when Jake Tracy called to me. I always arrive early and open up and sweep out. When that was done I always went back and woke up Louie Dawes. He slept in that back room, y'know," jerking one thumb toward a door at the rear of the store.

"How come Tracy called to you?"

"I was just startin' up the steps out front when Tracy yelled at me. I hadn't seen him, and it sort of surprised me. I turned sudden and stumbled. That's when I skun my shin."

"What did Tracy want?"

"He told me to get Louie out of bed if he wa'n't already up."

"Did he say why?"

"I asked him that. Tracy, he just sort of laughed and said that he'd given Louie a big order the night before and he wanted to be sure Louie wa'n't late fillin' it. Said he had some more things to add to the order and to tell Louie he wanted to see him right off, down to the Oasis Saloon."

"Where was Tracy at this time?" Peaceful asked.

"Standin' in the middle of the road. I offered to fill his order for him, but he laughed again and said only Louie Dawes could take care of it."

"Sho now, Willie," Purdy put in, "you never told me 'bout this. I wonder if Tracy ever got his order filled."

"Probably did," Willie said.

"Do you remember if it was groceries or hardware?"

Willie shook his head and thus dismissed the subject.

Peaceful suppressed a smile.

"Did you go wake up Dawes?"

Willie nodded. "But I didn't wake him up. He was already awake, shaved, and everythin'. Reckon he'd been awake for some time. I told him what Tracy had said. He sort of frowned like he didn't like it and heaved a long sigh from his innards."

"Maybe," Peaceful said, "he didn't like your interrupting at his letter writing."

"Probably that was it," Willie nodded, then paused suddenly, mouth dropping open in amazement. "Sa-a-ay, how did you know he was writing a letter?"

"Was he?" Purdy asked.

Willie nodded, eyes still wide. He scratched his head. "Y'know, I never give that a thought until

155

you mentioned it just now, Mr. Jenkins. How did you know about it?"

Peaceful smiled lazily. "Maybe I just guessed at it."

"Dang good guessin'," Willie said admiringly. "Just like a detective, or somethin'. I always thought I'd like to be a detective and snoop for clues and catch bandits."

"Maybe we can be detectives together sometime." Peaceful smiled.

Willie reddened with pleasure. "That would be great."

"I'll make another guess," Peaceful said. "When you interrupted Louie's writing he folded the letter and slipped it into his deck of cards."

Willie's eyes opened still wider. "S'help me, he did! I'd plumb forgot that. If you ain't the smartest—Sa-a-ay, we still got that deck of cards here."

"No, we ain't," Purdy put in. "Peaceful bought that deck yesteddy, Willie. And I didn't ask him but four bits for it."

"Did you get a letter out of it?" Willie asked.

Peaceful said, "That letter was intended for his brother. What happened next, Willie?"

"Louie went down to the Oasis like Tracy had asked him to, but he never did come back with that order. He told me when he was leaving, kind of reluctant-like, that he didn't know for sure if he'd be back right away. He never did come back. Next thing we knew, he'd shot and robbed Mr. Drake."

"Did you see him again after he left?" Peaceful asked.

Willie shook his head. "I went out of the store two or three times and looked down toward the Oasis, but I didn't see him again."

"Did you see Tracy?"

Willie nodded. "Yeah, later on. It must have been close to ten o'clock. I saw him sittin' with Scott Heffner and Deputy Vaughn on the Oasis porch. We wa'n't bothered much with customers that mornin'. It was durin' a hot spell, and folks weren't stirrin' much. Then, just about ten o'clock, I heard a shot down near the bank. I stepped outside and I see Deputy Vaughn run out to the middle of the road with his Winchester. He shot twice at Louie but missed both times. Then he jumped on his horse and went poundin' out of town. Lucky he had his horse there, saddled, or he never would have caught up with Louie, I'll bet."

Peaceful asked:

"Doesn't he usually keep his horse saddled and ready for any emergency?"

"Naw," Willie said. "Come to think of it, I reckon that's the first time in months that horse had been out of the Red Star Livery. I remember hearin' the liveryman saying one day that all Vaughn's horse did was eat oats and grow fat at the county's expense."

"But Vaughn always keeps his rifle handy, doesn't he?"

Willie scratched his head. "I don't reckon. That's the first time I've seen him use a rifle since one time on Fourth of July we had a target-shootin' contest."

"Who won the contest?" Peaceful asked.

"Herb Vaughn," Willie said promptly. "Gosh, he can sure handle a Winchester. He beat everybody all hollow—and we got some pretty good shots around here too. He got the bull's-eye every time, and then afterward there was tin cans throwed in the air, and Vaughn plugged every one of 'em."

"And yet," Peaceful pointed out, "he had two chances at Louie Dawes and missed both shots."

"By cripes!" Willie exclaimed. "That's so."

Sam Purdy pointed out, "Shootin' at targets and tin cans is a heap different from shootin' at a livin' human. Some folks ain't no good that way a-tall."

Peaceful smiled. "You're right. Some folks just ain't no good a-tall."

"Say, Mr. Jenkins," Willie asked, "are you aimin' to do some detectin' and find out where that money went?"

"I might," Peaceful evaded, "and I might need your help doing it. I'll think it over. Meanwhile, I'd appreciate it if you two didn't mention our talk about this."

"We sure won't," Willie said earnestly. "And just call on me when you need help."

"There won't be a word said," Purdy promised.

Peaceful said thanks and left the store in search of Applejack.

15

UHLMANN GROWS NERVOUS

AS he had expected, Peaceful found Applejack in the Demijohn Saloon, a foaming glass on the bar in front of him He was the sole customer in the place.

"At it again, eh?" Peaceful grinned.

Applejack nodded gravely. "Yep, it won't let me alone."

Peaceful directed a steady glance at Johnny Small. Johnny looked confused.

Peaceful said, "Judas!"

Johnny reddened. "Aw, gee whiz, Peaceful—"

"Benedict Arnold," Peaceful cut in.

"Shucks, Peaceful—"

"Yep," Peaceful sighed, "I done nurtured a serpent in my bosom. My young innocence has been betrayed."

"Now, looky here, Peaceful—"

"I'm ashamed of you, Johnny, lying like that," Peaceful said solemnly. "So you didn't know what the council meeting wanted to see me about last night? And it was you suggested my name."

"All right." Johnny grinned defiantly. "I'm

guilty. I was afraid you'd refuse to go if you knew they aimed to make you marshal. Say what you like, I'm glad of it, and there isn't a good citizen in Spanish Wells this morning that don't maintain the council couldn't have appointed a better man. Cowboy, you sure took hold in great shape, from all I hear—both you and Applejack. This town is sure buzzing with talk—all except those that are hissing."

Applejack said philosophically, "Reptiles always hiss." He wiped beer foam from his upper lip.

"Have a drink on the house, Peaceful?" Johnny invited.

Peaceful shook his head. "Too early in the day—for anyone except Applejack."

Johnny asked, "Which reptile's tail are you aiming to twist next, Peaceful?"

Peaceful considered. "Well, I'm not sure if they'll be next, but I'm sure aiming to twist the rattles off the reptiles that rigged that robbery scheme on Jabez Drake."

"You are?" Johnny said eagerly. "Have you learned something new?"

"Yes, but I'm asking you to keep it under your hat. Johnny, who's the best rifleshot in this neck of the range?"

"That's easy," Johnny replied promptly. "Herb Vaughn. I don't like that hombre, but I got to admit that he could shoot the eye out of snake a mile away. Why, say, last Fourth of July—"

161

"Yeah, I heard about that." Peaceful smiled. "And yet our law-abiding and -enforcing deputy missed two clean shots at Louie Dawes when Dawes was making his getaway."

"I'm not surprised any," Applejack said.

Johnny frowned; then: "You mean that Vaughn didn't even try to hit Dawes—that he wanted him to get away?"

"What do you think?"

"Why, say"—Johnny's eyes widened—"that puts Vaughn right into the job with Dawes—"

"And also," Peaceful interrupted, "Jake Tracy and Scott Heffner. They were waiting on the Oasis porch for that holdup to happen. Vaughn's shooting and so on was just pretend. Those three just staged a neat bit of acting to impress the public. And the stunt worked. Lord knows how many more we'll find that were also in on the job."

"And once we get the whole list," Applejack put in between swallows of beer, "we'll start our whittling process."

At that moment Timothy Hyde entered the Demijohn. His face lighted when he saw Applejack and Peaceful. "H'are you, gents?" He smiled. He invited them to have a drink. Peaceful accepted a cigar.

Peaceful said, "You're across the Border early this morning, Mr. Hyde. How's your pardner feeling?"

"Like taking the pledge," Hyde chuckled. "Otherwise Luke don't feel so bad, aside from a hangover. Got a couple of nasty bruises on his head. Those bouncers of Randle's sure play mean."

"We figure to take the meanness out of them," Peaceful said quietly. "Did Secord figure how much they took out of his pockets?"

Hyde nodded. "That's what I came over to tell you. He didn't know the exact amount, but he's sure he had better than two hundred dollars in his pockets when he entered the Spanish Dagger last night. He sends his thanks to you, Peaceful."

"No thanks necessary," Peaceful said. "I was just doing my job. Two hundred, eh?"

Applejack put in, "I had those two hombres unload their pockets last night before I put 'em in cells. They had a trifle over two hundred bucks on 'em. The money's in Deputy Vaughn's desk."

"I tell you what, Applejack," Peaceful suggested. "We've got a charge of assault and robbery against those two. You and Mr. Hyde go down to the gaol, talk to 'em, tell 'em we're willing to drop the robbery charge if they'll turn that money over to Mr. Hyde for his pardner. I reckon they'll be more than willing. That'll give Luke Secord back his money."

"It's a good idea," Hyde agreed. The men left the saloon, Hyde and Applejack heading toward the gaol and Peaceful starting off in the opposite direction.

Five minutes later Peaceful found Judith Drake and Tarp Thompson just emerging from the hotel dining room after finishing their breakfast. After preliminary greetings Tarp said, "You ready to ride with us to the JD, Peaceful? If so you're due to wait a spell. Judy wants to see Randle first and tell him she's jumpin' ship and won't sing no more chanteys for him. I tell her to just let that scut drag anchor and say no more about it."

Judith looked troubled. "Randle never puts in an appearance until around noon, as a rule. I hate to talk to him again."

Peaceful smiled. "Why not leave that job for me? I'd sure like to handle it for you, Miss Judith."

Judith protested it was her duty, but in the end she consented to Peaceful breaking the news. Peaceful went on, "One thing, though, I won't be able to leave for the ranch with you this morning. Those two bouncers I arrested last night are due to come up before the justice of the peace at eleven o'clock." He consulted his watch. "That's dang nigh two hours off, but I want to be there. Applejack and I are aiming to make it tough for that pair; we talked over a little plan last night. Applejack's going to talk it over with the justice this morning before the bouncers come up for appearance."

Old Tarp frowned. "I sort of wanted to get started back. Jabez wanted me to return as soon as possible, and while he's got good boys there with him, there's nobody can trim sails to Jabez' likin' the way I can."

"Unless it's Judith Drake." The girl smiled. "I tell you, Tarp. You ride on ahead and tell Dad we're coming later. Maybe by that time Peaceful will ask me to have dinner with him; then he and I can ride out."

"It's a grand idea," Peaceful said enthusiastically. "I'll come back here to the hotel lobby and meet you a mite after twelve, Miss Judith, if that's all right."

"That suits me fine," the girl replied. "And by that time you'll have seen Hugo Randle and told him I won't be back?"

"I'll take care of it," Peaceful promised. He doffed his sombrero and once more stepped out to the street.

Diagonally across from the hotel, on the opposite corner, Peaceful noticed the Spanish Wells Savings Bank. Struck by a sudden impulse, he directed his steps toward the building, musing, "It might be a good idea to get acquainted with the town banker and see what he has to offer."

Entering the bank, he saw that the room was cut in two halves: the front half was given over to a space for customers. A tall desk with pens and ink stood against one wall. A long counter faced with three grilled windows cut across the

165

centre of the room, with, at one end, a waist-high swinging gate that gave access to the bank proper. A teller stood behind one of the grilled windows; there was no one serving the other two. The teller looked up as Peaceful approached. "Anything I can do for you, sir?"

"I'd like to talk to your boss, Fletcher Uhlmann. I'm Marshal Jenkins."

"Just a minute, I'll see if he can see you."

The teller opened a door to Uhlmann's private office at the rear, entered, and returned within a few minutes. "Mr. Uhlmann will see you."

Peaceful passed through the small wooden gate and into Uhlmann's office, closing the door behind him. Uhlmann sat at a desk, smoking a fat cigar. The room was blue with smoke haze. He was a sharp-featured man, with scanty mud-coloured hair and red-rimmed eyes, in dusty-black clothing. His fingers were long and claw-like, their nails dirty. He didn't look up from the papers he'd been studying when Peaceful entered. Peaceful smiled, dropped into a chair, and started to roll a cigarette.

After a time Uhlmann glanced up, his sharp eyes boring into Peaceful's. "You wanted to see me?" His voice was harsh.

Peaceful drawled, "No use getting upset, Uhlmann. I don't want to borrow any money."

"What do you want?" Uhlmann demanded ungraciously.

Peaceful started to rise. "I don't want anything in particular. Just thought it part of my duty to get acquainted with the leading citizens of the town. If I'm taking up your valuable time I'll be running along." Peaceful scratched a match and lighted his cigarette. "But being as I was the newly appointed marshal, I thought we should get acquainted and find out why you didn't approve of my appointment."

"Who said I didn't?" sharply.

"Magpie Bayliss."

"Bayliss! What right—?" Uhlmann paused suddenly. "Magpie Bayliss? I don't know the man."

"Bartender in the Oasis Saloon."

"I never enter saloons, unless it's for a tonic or something of the sort. This Bayliss don't know what he's talking about."

"I figured that was the case. Then you do approve of me?"

"We-ell," Uhlmann hedged, "I don't know whether I do or not. Haven't anything against you personally, of course, but I didn't think we needed another law officer here. Deputy Vaughn was capable—"

"Naturally, in view of your relationship, you'd feel that way, Mr. Uhlmann."

Uhlmann looked startled. "What relationship?"

"I understand Vaughn is your cousin."

"My cousin? Oh yes, yes, quite so." A frown

had crept into Uhlmann's features. "Who was telling you about that?"

"Scott Heffner."

"Heffner? I don't think I know the man."

"You probably wouldn't," Peaceful drawled. "Heffner's a thug."

"Naturally I wouldn't, in that case," Uhlmann said stiffly. He didn't say anything more, as though he were waiting for Peaceful to depart.

Peaceful was standing nonchalantly against the door-jamb. "Nice building you got here."

"Thanks."

"The second story occupied too?"

"I have three offices up there—that is to say, the rooms were intended for offices. I'd hoped to rent to some attorney or doctor. Something of that kind. But I've had no luck renting. I have my living quarters in the corner office. I'll stay there until I find a renter."

"Nice place to live," Peaceful commented carelessly. "From your window you could look down and see who is entering or leaving your bank."

"What's that? What do you mean?" Uhlmann had gone a shade paler.

Peaceful wondered what ailed the man. "Why, you could just keep a lookout on your bank without being downstairs here," he said. "You know, in case bandits attacked the place."

"Oh yes, to be sure. Yes, yes." Plainly Uhlmann

was nervous about something. He asked, "Why are you interested in the upper story?"

"I wasn't," Peaceful said promptly, "until you mentioned you had a couple of vacant offices up there. What rent you asking?"

"One hundred dollars a month."

Peaceful whistled softly. "No wonder you haven't found renters. That's pretty steep."

"I don't believe so. The man that owned the bank before me rented for fifty a month. He could have asked more as well as not. After all, I'm a banker, I'm here to make money."

"It occurs to me," Peaceful said, "that the town marshal should have an office."

"I agree with you—though the town council may not want to pay a hundred a month. However, you seem quite popular." Uhlmann was suddenly more affable.

"I'd like to take a look at the offices," Peaceful said.

"By all means. You'll find the entrance stairway on the outside of the building. My living quarters are locked, but the remaining two offices are open for inspection. Go right on up. If the office suits you take it up with the city council. They can handle the business with me."

"Well, thanks a lot."

"You're welcome. Drop in again any time, Jenkins."

Peaceful left the bank, wondering why the

169

banker hadn't offered to accompany him in an inspection of the vacant offices. And what had made the man so nervous when Peaceful had mentioned the view from the upper window? Something funny was up. Peaceful rounded the corner of the brick building and mounted the stairway that scaled the outside of the building. At the top of the stairs an unlocked door gave entrance to a narrow hallway. Three closed doors were set in the right-hand wall of the hall.

Peaceful tried the first one, which proved to be locked.

"Uhlmann's living quarters," he surmised.

He tried the other two doors, found them both unlocked, and entered the middle one first. There wasn't anything to be seen in the room, just the single window facing on Main Street. The walls were blank, the floor covered with a thick layer of dust. There were several footprints in the dust on the floor. Peaceful studied them and came to the conclusion they had been made by the same man.

He went to the unwashed window and glanced out. Looking down on Main Street, he spied Fletcher Uhlmann just crossing toward the Oasis Saloon. Peaceful chuckled, "No wonder he didn't come along to show me the offices. Must be it was time for his tonic. Either that or he wanted to settle his relationship and learn for sure if he was Vaughn's cousin. Somebody's a blasted liar."

Peaceful watched until Uhlmann had entered the Oasis, then switched his attention back to the room. He glanced at the window sill and found the blurred marks where a hand had rested there. There were further marks, showing the window had been raised at some time in the not too distant past. The marks were covered with dust but showed plainly when compared with the thicker dust around the rest of the window.

Peaceful scrutinized the wall around the window, then moved his gaze to the floor. Suddenly he stooped and picked up a dead cigar butt about two inches long. He studied this a moment, then wrapped it in his bandanna.

He turned and slowly started toward the door, eyes intent on the floor. An instant later he again stooped down and picked up an empty shell from a forty-five six-shooter. He examined the shell closely, then placed it in the bandanna with the cigar butt. "This," he muttered, "is mebbe pure carelessness on somebody's part. On the other hand, it may not mean a thing." He grinned. "Fletch Uhlmann was maybe holding target practice up here."

He moved on to the other office after closing the door to the room he'd just left. But the remaining office had nothing to offer. An ancient calendar

171

was pinned to one wall. Dust covered everything. There wasn't the sign of a footprint or anything like it. After a few minutes Peaceful closed the door and retraced his steps to the street.

16

A HANGING JUDGE

AT eleven o'clock promptly the two Spanish Dagger bouncers, Mitchell and Fraley, were brought to the residence of Justice of the Peace Cyrus Calhoun, who held office in his home. Handcuffed together, the ugly-visaged pair were escorted in by Deputy Marshal Applejack Peters. Justice Calhoun was a stern-visaged man with an inherent sense of justice in his make-up, and lawbreakers were always known to get at least a square deal when brought before him. In this particular case Peaceful and Applejack had already held a conference with the justice, and while the proceedings may have been conducted on a rather informal basis, the appearance moved with speed and dispatch.

Deputy Sheriff Vaughn was present, as was Hugo Randle, though neither had much to say as the proceedings got under way.

Peaceful introduced Timothy Hyde to Calhoun and explained that the charge of robbery had been dropped, as, through Hyde, the stolen money was being returned to the absent Luke Secord, who was in too precarious a condition, due to the severe beating received at the hands of Mitchell and Fraley the previous night, to be present at the hearing. There were several idle spectators present.

"At any rate," Town Marshal Peaceful Jenkins stated grimly, "the charge of assault will be pressed."

Mitchell and Fraley commenced to look nervous, but Randle, standing near-by, winked at them, and they immediately felt better. After all, with Randle backing them up, nothing much could happen. Assault charges never amounted to anything serious; similar cases had brought fines of twenty or twenty-five dollars and the criminals released. Mitchell and Fraley commenced to feel better and better and smiled at a few friends standing in the room, while Peaceful was talking to the justice.

Peaceful had Hyde tell Calhoun just what had happened the night before; then Peaceful related his part in the affair. Applejack next spoke and confirmed Peaceful's words. Calhoun listened intently, as though all this was news to him, though as a matter of fact, like the rest of Spanish Wells, he had already heard the details. Randle was next called forward. He admitted the two bouncers were in his employ and that they were mighty fine men, though this once they may have forgotten themselves and gone too far.

"Too far?" Calhoun said testily. "Seems to me they would have killed Luke Secord if they went an inch farther."

Well, that wasn't exactly what he meant, Randle tried to explain. After all, Secord had created a disturbance in the Spanish Dagger and—

"Didn't think that was possible," Calhoun snorted sceptically. "Far's I can judge, the Spanish Dagger is a disturbance all its ownself. You wouldn't toss a lighted match into a volcano and term it a disturbance, would you?"

Randle admitted he wouldn't, but—but—

"Just what do you mean?" Calhoun snapped. "Are you going to stand there and tell me you condone the actions of these two men and that you feel they are blameless? Or"— sarcastically—"that I'm persecuting the poor fellows?"

"No, no, Justice Calhoun," Randle said meekly. "Undoubtedly they did commit—commit an indiscretion—but to be too severe on them at this time might ruin their whole lives—"

Calhoun cut in sarcastically, "Isn't it about time to remind me of their poor wives and little babies, Randle?"

A chorus of tittering went around the room. Calhoun looked severely around, and the room fell silent. Randle commenced to grow red. "The point I'm trying to make, Justice Calhoun," he said, "is if you'll just get this over and name the fines they're to pay, I'll pay up and this business will be finished. I promise you it won't happen again."

"Oh, it's the fines you're thinking about, eh?" Calhoun said. "Well, we'll see about that." He glared at the two prisoners. "You—Mitchell—Fraley—stand up straighter! What you got to say for yourselves?"

Fraley mumbled something that had to do with being guilty. Mitchell glanced contemptuously at his comrade. "It's this way, Calhoun—" he commenced.

"Calhoun?" the justice thundered. "Justice Calhoun to the likes of such scum as you, Mitchell. Are you guilty or aren't you? Of course I know you are, but legally you have a right to make your plea. Now speak up."

That took the wind out of Mitchell's sails. "I reckon we're guilty, Judge—Justice Calhoun. Mebbe me and Fraley got a mite too enthoosed over our work last night. Some of them drunks try a man's patience, and we might have lost our tempers."

Calhoun leaned back in his chair. His voice fairly purred now. "Oh, so that's the way it was. This drunk, as you called him, tried your patience, did he? And for that you nearly kill him. Tell me, Mitchell, what do you do when you really get mad at a man? Don't tell me you stop short of manslaughter."

"Ain't never killed anybody yet—not that I know of," Mitchell mumbled.

"You admit then," Calhoun snapped, "that you might have killed and not been aware of it? That's downright carelessness! You two are certainly a problem. What do you think I should do to you?"

By this time Mitchell was speechless, but Fraley found his voice. He had had an encouraging glance from Randle and he was now even a trifle defiant. "Look here, Justice Calhoun," he said, "you've bawled us out. All right. We admitted we were guilty. So just state our fines and let us get out of here. Mr. Randle will pay the fines—"

"Fines? Fines!" Calhoun leaped indignantly to his feet. "Who said anything about fines? Do you think the law has sunk to such degrading levels that a small fine will square your debt to society? That is an insult to the position I hold. Fines!" His voice fairly quivered with righteous indignation. He appealed to the rest of the room: "Gentlemen, I ask you to look upon this pair of depraved criminals. Have you ever gazed on such hardened faces in all your days? Fiends in human form, I call them. Monsters in the shape of men. Never, never in all my long days have I ever before beheld two such villainous creatures."

Calhoun's voice trembled with righteous wrath. "And now—now, mind you gentlemen— these two blackened scourges of civilization, after nearly killing one of our prominent mining men—and for what, mind you? For trying their patience!" Calhoun's voice dropped to a cold, savage, slashing tone. "For trying their patience." His voice rose again. "After nearly killing Luke Secord they have the unmitigated nerve to come before me and say, 'All right, let's get it over with. How much is the fine?'" Calhoun passed one hand over his eyes as though to shut out such a terrible sight. His voice choked a little. "Have you ever heard anything so brazen, so coldly calloused? No, you haven't. Nor I either!"

Randle and the prisoners were commencing to look nervous now.

Calhoun sadly shook his head. "I'm only a mere justice of the peace here. I'm not prepared to deal with crimes of such proportion. I refuse to bear such responsibility. These two blackguards—nay, the name is too mild—these two devils incarnate should be tried by a jury of twelve. It's too much to ask one man to release again upon the world, until such trial be held, two such bloodthirsty barbarians. Some other poor unfortunate might carelessly put himself in the position of 'trying their patience,' and with what result we already know to our sorrow. So is my judgment that these two men—if such they may be termed—Mitchell and Fraley, be held in gaol until the opening of the circuit court in the fall. Deputy Peters, take them away!"

No one spoke for a minute; then Applejack stepped forward. By that time Mitchell found his voice. "Hey, Justice, can't we be out on bail?" He and Fraley looked extremely ill by this time.

"Yeah," Fraley chimed in, "set bail for us."

Calhoun considered. "Not willingly would I release you on bail, but the law says you are entitled to such consideration. Therefore, I will impose the maximum. Seven hundred fifty dollars each!"

A wail ascended from the two prisoners. "But neither of us has got that much money," Mitchell protested.

Calhoun said blandly, "I suspected as much. Of course if you have friends to furnish such bail I can't refuse."

Instantly Mitchell and Fraley turned to Randle. Fraley said, "Hugo, you said you'd back us up."

"But that means fifteen hundred dollars!" Randle exclaimed.

"You'd better keep your word, Hugo," Mitchell said, and the tones sounded threatening. Doubtless he knew much of Randle's nefarious ways.

"But I haven't that much on me," Randle protested.

Calhoun said quietly:

"I believe the bank is open."

Angrily Randle half shouted, "All right, all right, I'll go to the bank and get the money. I'll send somebody back with fifteen hundred dollars. Nobody can say I don't back up my friends. But if this isn't a hold-up I never heard of one."

Calhoun chuckled in an aside to Peaceful, "Imagine the owner of the Spanish Dagger complaining of a hold-up." He turned and left his office for the next room. Peaceful followed and found Calhoun nearly bent double with laughter. "S'help me," Calhoun chuckled, "I haven't made a talk like that since my early days at the bar."

Peaceful went back to Applejack. "Deputy Marshal," he said, "you take Mitchell and Fraley down to Vaughn's office and get them their belongings—you know, what you took out of their pockets last night. Only you'd better hang on to the brass knucks and blackjacks. Then bring 'em back here. By that time, unless Randle is a liar, that fifteen hundred bail money will have arrived."

"Randle better not be a liar," Mitchell said in ugly tones as he and Fraley were herded out the door by Deputy Peters.

"And don't take those handcuffs off, Applejack," Peaceful called after them. "We haven't that fifteen hundred yet."

Applejack returned with the handcuffed bouncers ten minutes later, just as Jake Tracy was arriving with the bail money. Peaceful grinned when he saw Tracy. "What's up? Randle had enough of Justice Calhoun? You should have been here, Jake. Calhoun was making it tough for our prisoners. Yeah, you really should have been here. I got a dang good notion to keep you here."

"Now, look, Jenkins," Tracy said nervously. "I ain't got no quarrel with you."

"I see you found your gun, didn't you?" Peaceful said, eyeing the weapon in Tracy's holster. "The hurry you left in last night, I didn't think you wanted it. I wonder just what the law is on carrying weapons in this town."

"Hell, Jenkins," Tracy said feverishly, "I ain't breaking any laws. Where's Justice Calhoun? I got this bail money that Hugo said to give you. That's my only concern here; I don't want any part of this business."

Calhoun entered from his inner room. Bail papers were prepared and the money paid to Calhoun, who gave Tracy a receipt he could turn over to Randle. Tracy at once vanished to the street without waiting for further details to be settled.

A few minutes later it was all arranged, and Peaceful and Applejack accompanied the two bouncers outside. Mitchell and Fraley were so relieved at getting out on bail that for the moment they forgot their hands were still cuffed together as they walked between the two marshals.

181

Suddenly Mitchell growled, "Hey, we're free now. When you going to take these cuffs off?"

"Danged if I didn't forget those cuffs," Applejack said cordially. "I was thinking how old Calhoun treated you."

"Me too," Peaceful said sympathetically. "Gosh, he sure poured it on. I didn't think he had any call to talk the way he did. I never saw a man so vindictive. You'd think Fraley and Mitchell were murderers or something. Law's law, but there's no sense of taking out personal spite on a prisoner."

Fraley gulped.

"He sure talked like he hated us."

By this time the men were at the corner of Main and Alamo, where the Demijohn was located. Peaceful said, "I don't want you fellers to hold a grudge against me. I only did my duty. But I sure felt sorry for you when Calhoun got so hard. What did you ever do to him?"

"Never did nothing," Mitchell growled. "Say, these cuffs—"

"I may be only a town marshal," Peaceful said, "but I got feelings for a hombre in a tough spot. Right now I'll bet you two would like nothing better than a drink. Well, come on into the Demijohn. I'm buying a drink just to show there's no hard feelings over what happened last night."

Mitchell and Fraley brightened and, still handcuffed, followed Peaceful, with Applejack behind, into the Demijohn. Here at last, while Johnny was taking the orders, Applejack unlocked the handcuffs. There were only a couple of other customers in the saloon at the time.

"Yep"—Peaceful frowned—"old Calhoun acted like he had a personal grudge against you two."

"It was a shame." Applejack blew the froth from his beer and sadly shook his head. "Too bad you two fellers don't own horses. You could go riding out of town this afternoon and really feel free after spending the night in the hoosegow. I could lend you a horse."

"We got horses," Fraley said, "down to the livery stable, eating their heads off."

"That's too bad," Applejack said seriously.

"What's too bad?" Mitchell was suddenly suspicious.

Peaceful said, "Johnny, give Mitchell and Fraley another drink."

Johnny poured another round.

Fraley said, "What's too bad, Peters?"

Applejack shook his head. "I don't like to think of it. With Calhoun acting like he did, he'll be bound to influence a jury when your trial comes up next fall."

"I reckon Randle will see we get a square deal," Mitchell said.

Peaceful laughed scornfully. "Randle sure didn't help your case any to-day. You probably

183

know him better than I do, but I wouldn't expect too much of him."

Mitchell said, "He furnished bail for us, didn't he?"

Applejack said, "What's bail? He's not out anything. When you come to trial next fall he'll get his money back and you two won't be any better off. Johnny, give Fraley and Mitchell another drink."

This time the bouncers didn't say anything. They gulped down the drinks when they came.

Applejack said, "You know, Calhoun reminds me of old Hempen Roper—"

"By cripes!" Peaceful was suddenly interested. "He sure does! Same vindictive spirit, same nasty tongue. Yep, he's the spitten image of old Hemp."

"Who's this Roper you're talking about?" asked Mitchell.

Applejack said, "He was knowed as the hanging judge down Texas way, few years back. That old cuss would take a dislike to a prisoner, and he wasn't satisfied until the feller was dead. He just had a lust for blood, he did."

Peaceful said reminiscently, "Do you remember that Warbonnet case?"

"Do I?" Applejack gave a shudder. "I wish I could forget it. I wake up nights and see those mangled bodies. . . . Johnny, give me another beer. See what Mitchell and Fraley will have."

"That was pretty terrible all right." Peaceful shook his head.

Mitchell said, "What was this Warbonnet case?"

Peaceful said, "The Warbonnet was a honky-tonk, a good deal like the Spanish Dagger where you boys work. Well, there was three bouncers there, just like you two, and one night they rolled a drunk out back of the Warbonnet—"

"Just like you two," Applejack said sadly.

"Anyway, they was arrested," Peaceful went on, "and brought up before Hempen Roper. Hempen acted just like Calhoun did to-day. Gosh, the things he said! He was all for hanging right then. But these three poor fellers had friends, and bail was procured for 'em. They stepped out, free as air—"

"Just like you two," Applejack said.

"But," Peaceful went on, "they'd reckoned without Hempen Roper. Would you believe it? That feller was so plumb vindictive that he went out and aroused a mob to a bloodthirsty pitch. He had the sort of tongue that would do that. That mob just organized and got ropes and they hung those three. Even that didn't satisfy Roper. After they were dead they cut down the bodies and cut them and kicked them around, ran wild horses over 'em. . . . How about another drink, Mitchell—Fraley?"

Mitchell and Fraley were ashen-white by this time.

Applejack shuddered and closed his eyes. "What a butchery they made of those three bouncers. I can still see the eyeballs laying on Main Street when that mob was finished. And those poor fellers, Mitchell—Fraley—were just like you. Oh, it was criminal! The way a blood-thirsty brute will act when he gets a hate at somebody."

"By the way," Peaceful broke in innocently, "where did Calhoun go when we left?"

"I don't know," Applejack responded. "I heard him say he was going to the general store to get a couple of ropes and then go to give a speech to a group of close friends. . . . How about another drink, fellers?"

Mitchell gulped and shook his head. "Nope. Thanks. We got to be getting along."

Fraley looked sick. "Got—gotta go see Randle," he half gasped. Turning, they both ran out of the Demijohn.

Peaceful and Applejack exchanged smiles. "The power of suggestion," Peaceful drawled, "is plumb potent at times—particularly to an alcohol-loaded brain."

Applejack chuckled and said, "I'll go see." He turned and headed toward the street.

Johnny Small looked curiously at Peaceful. "What's the idea in that line of guff you were handing those two?"

Peaceful said, "Mebbe you'll see. If it works

186

it won't be the first time Applejack and I have pulled that stunt. I never knew it to fail yet, when worked on the right people."

Within ten minutes Applejack entered, laughing. "It worked." He grinned. "Those two went to the livery and got their horses and left town like all the devils in hell were on their tails."

"You mean," Johnny asked, "they jumped their bail?"

Peaceful nodded. "It's best all around that way. The county is saved the expense of a trial; the town treasury is fifteen hundred richer; Spanish Wells is rid of two plug-uglies, and Hugo Randle is fifteen hundred poorer. That's what will really hurt him and give him a foretaste of what's to come. We're just starting on that sidewinder!"

Johnny laughed, struck by the humour of the situation. "You two can get more done without burning gunpowder than any law officers I ever saw."

Peaceful said seriously, "Don't jump to conclusions, Johnny. There'll be plenty powder burned before Spanish Wells is cleaned up!"

17

POWDER SMOKE

IT was a trifle after twelve noon when Peaceful left the Demijohn and sauntered over to the Spanish Dagger. There weren't many customers at the bar when he entered. The games were covered and silent, as they always were during the day. Near the back of the room Hugo Randle sat at a table with Scott Heffner, Jake Tracy, and one of his Wolf Head punchers, Fred Cubera, for company. Cubera was a swarthy-complexioned individual with a mean eye and a fast trigger finger.

Randle looked up, frowning, as Peaceful came to a stop near the table. Peaceful said quietly, "Howdy, Randle, I just thought I'd drop in—"

Randle interrupted, "I don't remember inviting you here, Jenkins. Of course if you're here in course of duty that's different."

"Nothing but my duty could bring me in here," Peaceful said easily. "I just wanted to warn you of the new closing hour, Randle. The Spanish Dagger will have to be shut up by midnight."

"Now look here, Jenkins—" Randle commenced wrathfully.

Fred Cubera spat disgustedly. "Twelve o'clock. That's the hour they put infants in bed—"

"And crooks in gaol if they're not out of here by then," Peaceful cut in.

Randle said hotly, "You trying to break up my business, Jenkins?"

Peaceful smiled.

"As a matter of fact, I am, Randle. What you aiming to do about it?"

Scott Heffner swore. "Dam'd if this town isn't getting overrun with an epidemic of morals. It's a crime to make the Spanish Dagger close at midnight."

"It's a crime if it doesn't." Peaceful laughed. He switched his gaze to Jake Tracy. "Well, what you got to say, Jake? So far you haven't voiced an opinion."

Tracy dropped his eyes. "What Hugo says is good enough for me," he growled. "I'll come and go as I please."

"Yeah?" Peaceful appeared amused. "You didn't come and go as you pleased up in the Montana penitentiary."

"Huh?" Tracy turned a shade lighter. "What you—? Say, what you talking about?"

"Third offence, wasn't it?" Peaceful asked quietly. "I don't blame you for pulling out and coming to this Southwest country. They were getting wise to you up there."

"Aw-w-w," Tracy sputtered and then fell silent. No one else said anything.

Peaceful went on, "You won't have so much business to-night, anyway, Randle. You know, that pard of mine, Applejack, he's an authority on gambling games. He's aiming to watch your dealers close to-night, and the first tinhorn that pulls a crooked move goes into the hoosegow. And those gamblers of yours can't win without playing crooked, so I figure after you've warned 'em there won't many be playing. And, furthermore you might just as well pass the word around that Miss Drake won't be singing to-night."

Randle leaped up. "Now look here, Jenkins, that's going too far. You can't stop that girl from—"

"I'm not stopping her," Peaceful drawled. "She stopped herself. She's plumb fed up with you and your place, Randle. When she learned the truth last night she was plumb disgusted with your threats to have me bumped off."

"That's not true," Randle said hotly. "I didn't say—"

"Careful, Randle," Peaceful warned icily. "Miss Drake made a certain statement. I don't reckon it would be safe for you to—well, make any denials. And we won't mention her name again. Have you got that straight?"

190

Randle decided to change the subject. "When you going to release those two men of mine, Mitchell and Fraley? I know that old fool Calhoun got the bail money; I got his receipt."

Peaceful asked innocently, "Why, haven't they come here yet? Cripes! They were released three quarters of an hour ago. I figured you must have sent them out to your ranch."

"What gave you that idea?"

Peaceful shrugged. "My pardner saw them both riding their ponies out of town. He said they were sure travelling like all the devils in hell were after them. Of course they weren't travelling toward your ranch, but I couldn't think of any other place they'd be going. Say"—as though struck by a sudden idea—"you don't suppose those two jumped bail, do you?"

A lurid curse was torn from Randle's lips. His features blazed, then turned white, then red again. For a moment he couldn't find his tongue to question Peaceful. There was no need of questioning, however; Randle realized instinctively that his two bouncers had jumped their bail. The news was a body blow!

"Damn you, Jenkins!" he choked furiously. "You ran those two out of town! My money! My fifteen hundred! It's gone!"

"I reckon it is," Peaceful drawled. "But don't say I ran Mitchell and Fraley out. I couldn't do that. They know their legal rights. Nope, I reckon they just left of their own free will and accord. And if you think that the loss of your fifteen hundred is bad—Randle, that's just a beginning. Maybe if you're wise you'll get on your own horse and do some riding. It would be safest in the long run!"

And with that Peaceful turned and left the Spanish Dagger.

After a time Randle ceased cursing and dropped back in his chair to face the facts. The others remained silent, waiting for him to speak. Finally Tracy burst out, "That damned Jenkins! How did he know I'd been in the Montana pen? I figured nobody but us fellers—Hugo, you didn't let it slip, did you?"

"Don't talk like a fool, Jake," Randle said roughly. He considered a minute. "But I think Jenkins had better be stopped before he uncovers any more vital facts. Jake, it's up to you."

"Me?" Tracy exclaimed. "Me alone?"

"I'll take a hand," Scott Heffner put in.

Randle shook his head. "Not you, Scott. You've brushed with Jenkins, and he might plug you right off. I've got a better scheme. Fred"—to Cubera—"I'm going to use you. Someway we've got to manœuvre Jenkins into being at a certain spot at a certain time—said spot being across from the bank. That office next to Uhlmann's living quarters is empty. Jake, you'll take your station up there. Fred, you go up to Jenkins and start an argument. Have your gun in your hand but pretend to be very drunk. Jenkins won't shoot a drunk. I know his type. He'll figure to disarm you. You give him a struggle. While you're fighting a gun goes off. The shot gets Jenkins. When that happens quit fighting, Fred. Somebody will grab you, thinking you shot Jenkins. Deny it. Your gun will be examined. That will prove you didn't shoot. Meanwhile, Jake makes his getaway. The shooting of Jenkins goes down in history as a mystery."

"By Gawd, that sounds good," Jake Tracy exclaimed. "I'd just like a shot at Jenkins—just one is all I ask."

Fred Cubera laughed nervously. "I'd just as soon do some shooting. I think I could beat Jenkins to the draw."

"Don't get foolish ideas, Fred," Randle said.

"What bothers me," Cubera went on, "is that Jake might shoot me while I'm struggling with Jenkins. That wouldn't be so good."

"Don't worry about Jake's shooting," Randle said confidently. "There aren't any better in these parts. And, Fred, while you're struggling with Jenkins, it ought to be easy enough to shift him around so his body is between you and Jake."

"I'm for the plan," Cubera said. Tracy nodded, grinning.

Randle smiled. "I dropped fifteen hundred

bucks this morning, but I've got another fifteen hundred to pass out to the pair that rubs out Jenkins."

At that moment Deputy Sheriff Vaughn entered the Spanish Dagger. Randle told him what had happened, still keeping his voice lowered so the customers at the bar wouldn't overhear the conversation, and then of the proposed plan. "Herb," Randle concluded, "you get outside. Get a line on Jenkins' where-abouts; then we'll think of something to draw him down in front of the bank building."

"I can tell you where he is right now," Vaughn said. "I just left the hotel dining room. Jenkins and Judy Drake were going in to dinner as I came out. They'll probably be there for the next half-hour or so."

Randle's face lighted. "Luck's working our way. We couldn't ask for a better spot, with the hotel just kitty-corner across from the bank." Then his face fell. "Dammit! I don't like shooting with that girl present. It doesn't—"

"You'll have to forget that, Hugo," Heffner cut in. "This isn't any time for sentiment."

"You're right," Randle conceded. Then to Vaughn, "Herb, you get out and keep an eye on Jenkins and the girl. Let us know when they're about due to come out."

Vaughn nodded and left the Spanish Dagger. Randle turned to Tracy. "You'd better get going,

Jake, so you'll be there in plenty of time. It'll give your nerves a chance to settle. Good luck, Jake," as Tracy nodded and headed toward the doorway.

Twenty minutes passed. Twenty-five. Randle, Heffner, and Fred Cubera sat silent at the table. Once Cubera reached for the bottle before them and poured a stiff drink. Randle said, "Spill a mite of that liquor on your shirt. Remember, you've got to pretend to be very drunk, so Jenkins will just try to disarm you. And another drink won't hurt you either. . . ."

Herb Vaughn suddenly appeared at the doorway and hurried across to the table. "Jenkins and the girl are just finishing their pie. As I left the hotel the man from the Red Star Livery was tethering two ponies to the hotel tie rail. I asked some questions. Jenkins and the girl are riding when they get through dinner."

Randle nodded with satisfaction. "Get going, Fred. And remember to be very drunk. Leave all the shooting to Jake."

Cubera rose from the table, drawing his gun. He had already assumed a very realistic stagger before he passed through the doorway. . . .

There weren't many people on the street; mostly folks were eating their dinners at this hour. Diagonally across from the hotel stood the bank building. Usually the three windows on the second floor were closed. Now the centre one had been raised and a man stood a few feet back from it, eyes intent on the doorway of the hotel. In his right hand he held a six-shooter, the hammer of which was already drawn back.

Peaceful and Judith emerged from the hotel and walked, laughing and talking, out to the two ponies standing at the hitch rack. They rounded the end of the rack; then Peaceful helped Judith up to her saddle. He was just putting his own foot in stirrup, after handing her the reins, when a drunken hail reached his ears.

Looking up, he saw Fred Cubera staggering into view around the hotel corner. Cubera's hair hung down over his eyes; his hat hung precariously over one ear. In his hand he carried his six-shooter.

"Jush a min't, Marsh'l Jenkins," Cubera called thickly. "Gotta bone—pick wish you. You dirty sonuva sheepherder, you can't ride roughshod over me an' Hugo Ran'le. Gotta noshun t'plug you ri' now!"

"Darn these drunks!" A look of exasperation stole across Peaceful's features. "I'm sorry, Judith. I'll have to disarm this hombre and arrest him. It won't take but a few minutes. Wait for me in the hotel."

"I'll wait here," Judith said coolly. "But be careful."

Peaceful left his pony, rounded the end of the hitch rail, and walked directly towards

Cubera, arms swinging at his sides. "Put that gun away, Cubera." He spoke sternly. "You're under arrest!"

And then Cubera made the biggest mistake of his life—that of thinking he could be the one to kill Jenkins. Why not? Jenkins's gun was still in its holster. This was opportunity knocking, Cubera told himself; he could gain the glory that otherwise would go to Jake Tracy. With Jenkins dead, Randle could fix things easily.

"Move fast, Cubera!" Peaceful snapped. "Drop that gun!"

Abruptly all traces of drunkenness slipped from Cubera's appearance. He straightened up, lifting his six-shooter. In a flash Peaceful saw the man had been only pretending, saw that his eyes were clear, plainly speaking what was in his mind to do.

Peaceful lunged to one side, even as Cubera pulled trigger, and jerked out his own Colt gun. A burst of flame and smoke left Peaceful's right hand. The reports blended savagely; powder smoke swelled between the two men. A look of anguish contorted Cubera's features. His gun dropped from lifeless fingers; one hand clawed at his breast. Then he stiffened and pitched forward on his face.

Shrill cries of excitement sounded along Main Street. At the same instant another shot filled the roadway with thundering echoes. Peaceful heard

Judith cry frantically, "Look out, Peaceful!" before something struck him a terrific blow on the head and he went sprawling across Cubera's dead body!

18

ROARING FORTY-FIVES

JUDITH'S terrified gaze lifted quickly from the man stretched across Cubera's body to the direction from which that shot had come. She saw instantly the open window on the second floor of the bank building and, framed in the wide opening, Jake Tracy, the six-shooter in his grasp, deliberately drawing a bead for a second shot.

Again, involuntarily, Judith cried, "Look out, Peaceful!" and jabbed sudden spurs to her pony's sides. The horse leaped forward, interposing its form between Jake Tracy and the helpless Peaceful sprawled on the sidewalk, even as Tracy fired.

Judith felt her pony stagger under the powerful impact of the roaring forty-five just before the pony went to its knees. As the horse dropped Judith jerked her feet from stirrups and leaped to earth to avoid being crushed beneath the weight of the stricken pony.

The girl didn't hesitate: the instant her feet struck the ground she started toward Peaceful who, by this time, had raised to his hands and knees and was shaking his head violently to dispel the cobwebs that clouded his brain. "Peaceful," the girl cried frantically. "Up there—that bank building—in that window!"

Moving by instinct rather than reason, Peaceful rolled swiftly to one side just in time to escape a third bullet that ploughed up wood in the plank sidewalk at a point where Peaceful had been but a moment before. From his prone position on the sidewalk he thumbed two quick shots toward that upper-story window. Both missed the mark for which they were intended, but they served the purpose of driving Tracy back from the opening. A windowpane shattered and dropped two stories to the sidewalk below.

Peaceful was on his feet now, swaying uncertainly, his gaze on that upper-story window, waiting for Tracy to reappear. Judith looked wildly about. She saw Applejack Peters running toward her, six-shooter already in hand. An arm went about her waist and started to drag her away.

"Quick, Judith"—it was Hugo Randle talking—"you'd better get out of this."

"Leave me alone!" Judith exclaimed and, twisting about, struck at Randle's face. "This is your doing!"

"My doing?" Randle stepped back. "Why, Judith—"

Applejack closed in between the two and swept

Judith back, out of the line of fire. "I'll take care of her," he said shortly to Randle. Then to the girl, "How many are up in that building?"

"Just one—Jake Tracy—I think."

Another shot, fired from deep in the room with the shattered window, ripped into the hotel building at Peaceful's back. Peaceful started at a run across the roadway, reloading as he went, knowing the man in that upper story would be reloading as well. His head was clearing fast now.

He reached the stairway scaling the side of the building and bounded up the steps three at a time, Colt gun in hand. Reaching the top, he flung open the door to the narrow hallway, then glanced quickly at the closed doors that opened on the empty rooms. Yes, it would be that middle door.

"Better come out, hombre," Peaceful snapped.

From within the room came the roar of a forty-five, and a leaden slug ripped through the door panel, not far from Peaceful's body. He jumped quickly to one side and tried the doorknob. The knob turned easily. Apparently the man within hadn't the key. The door was unlocked.

A second slug tore viciously through the door and embedded itself in the hall wall.

"You coming out," Peaceful called, "or have I got to come in after you?"

"You'll have to come and get me if you want me!" Tracy snarled back.

In one swift movement Peaceful turned the knob and flung open the door, leaping back as he did so. A hail of lead swept through the open doorway. Instantly Peaceful leaped into the room. Jake Tracy was backed against the open window, just raising his six-shooter for another shot. Peaceful threw one swift slug from the vicinity of his hip, again shooting by instinct rather than careful aim.

Through the room, swirling with powder smoke, Peaceful saw Tracy stagger back under the impact of the shot. Even as he was hit, Tracy's gun roared, the bullet burying itself in the ceiling above. Peaceful thumbed another shot from his gun barrel. Tracy was still falling back, his legs giving way beneath him.

With a startled yell Peaceful jumped to reach the man, but he was too late: the next instant Tracy's swiftly retreating form had vanished through the open window. A moment later Peaceful heard the man's body strike the sidewalk below as a great yell went up in the street.

Peaceful methodically plugged empty shells from his gun and reloaded. He mopped perspiration from his forehead and breathed a long sigh of relief. "Danged if I thought he'd have the guts to fight like that," he muttered. "But even a cornered rat will fight, I reckon."

He left the room and started down the narrow stairway that ran along the side of the building.

At the bottom, just starting up, was Applejack Peters.

Applejack said worriedly, "You all right, pard?"

"I'm all right," Peaceful said. "Where's Judith?"

"She's all right. I rushed her into the hotel. That girl's got nerve. She spurred her horse in between you and Tracy's second shot. Only for that—"

"Cripes! I didn't know that. She must have saved my life. I was a heap groggy for a minute."

"I'll tell the world she did! I saw it all from the sidewalk as I was running to get here. She said you were shot. Where'd Tracy get you?"

"I don't think he did, unless I was just grazed. Something struck me on the side of the head. It was sure a wallop. See—here?"

Applejack examined a bruised spot above Peaceful's left ear. "That's odd," he muttered. "No bullet ever left that kind of a mark. Maybe somebody flung a stone."

By this time they had reached the front of the bank building. A crowd had gathered around Tracy's body. Uhlmann had come from his bank.

He looked up and met Peaceful's eyes.

Peaceful said quietly, "It might be a good idea to keep those doors upstairs locked, Uhlmann."

"You're certainly right," Uhlmann said nervously. "I'm glad to see you're not hurt, Jenkins."

"Are you?" Peaceful said. "Thanks." He pushed through the crowd and knelt at Tracy's side. After a moment he stood up. "This man is still breathing. Somebody run for the doctor."

Three men started off at once. Peaceful and Applejack crossed the street to the spot where Cubera's body was sprawled. No doubt about Cubera: he was dead. Peaceful saw his hat (Peaceful's) lying on the sidewalk. He stooped and retrieved it, put it on his head. In doing so he touched the bruised spot above his left ear. A bit of splintered wood was stuck to the hat. Peaceful examined it. "I'd sure like to know what hit me," he said to Applejack. "There was a splinter stuck to my hat."

"What's this?" Applejack stooped down and picked up a wedge-shaped chunk of wood, round on one side. Tiny particles of lead clung to the wood. Applejack said, "I reckon this explains it." He went to the end of the tie rail and fitted the loose bit of wood to the end of the pole which had been cleanly split off.

"You've explained it." Peaceful nodded. "Tracy's first bullet struck the tie rail, splitting off the end. The end flew through the air and clipped me alongside the head. Boy! That nearly spelled my finish. If it hadn't been for Judith—"

Without finishing what he had to say he turned and hurried into the hotel. In the lobby he saw Judith. The girl's face was white, but she forced a wan smile. "You're all right, Peaceful?"

"All right." He nodded. "I'm sorry this had to be—"

"Oh, I was so frightened!"

"I reckon I owe you my life, Judith. Applejack told me how you spurred your horse between me and Tracy's shots. I'll have to buy you a new horse. But I won't be forgetting what you did. You've got nerve, girl."

Judith smiled faintly. "I didn't see any yellow streak in the man who went into that building after Jake Tracy."

Peaceful flushed. "You still willing to take me out to your ranch and meet your dad?"

"That's what I'm waiting for, Peaceful."

He nodded. "That's good. I've got to go outside for a spell, but I'll get back as soon as I can."

He went back to the street. By this time Doc Hamilton, an elderly physician of the frontier type, had arrived and was kneeling near Jake Tracy. Applejack was standing near the doctor, when Peaceful pushed through the crowd.

Peaceful said, "Any hope for him, Applejack?"

Applejack replied, "We don't know yet."

Doc Hamilton glanced back over his shoulder. "He's unconscious, but I might pull him through. He's got two slugs in him that don't look too good. He broke an arm and a leg in the fall. There might be internal injuries as well. I'll have to get him over to my place and see what I can do for him."

"I'll appreciate that, Doc," Peaceful said. "If

there's a chance of his talking before he passes out I want to hear what he says."

"Why you so interested?" a sneering voice asked. It was Hugo Randle.

Peaceful faced Randle. "I'd just like to know, Randle, what your part in this little affair was," Peaceful said steadily. "Somebody worked out a plan to get me. The plan went wrong. I'd like to hear what Tracy has to say about it when he regains consciousness, if he does. He's the type that will talk when he finds himself in a jam.

Randle looked startled. "You ain't figuring I had anything to do with this?"

"I haven't figured anything else," Peaceful said quietly.

"You're crazy, man!"

"You're the crazy one," Peaceful said, "if you think you can continue to get away with your game much longer."

Randle turned and walked away. Peaceful looked after him and saw him in conversation with Deputy Vaughn, a short distance away. The street was milling with people. Peaceful turned back to Doc Hamilton. "How long do you think it will be, Doc, before Tracy can do any talking—if he does at all?"

"Not to-day, anyway," Hamilton snapped. "And maybe not ever if those men don't arrive with that stretcher right soon. I've got to get this man to my place where I can make a thorough examination."

Peaceful nodded and, with Applejack at his side, started back toward the hotel. As he passed Randle and Herb Vaughn, Vaughn took a step forward as though about to speak. Peaceful said sharply, "You want to see me, Vaughn?"

Vaughn fell back, muttering, "No, I reckon not."

Peaceful continued on toward the hotel.

19

RANGE PIRATES

IT was getting along toward three in the afternoon before Peaceful and Judith managed to get away from Spanish Wells. Luckily it was only twelve miles to the JD Ranch, and the ride, even at the gait the two were travelling, could be made in less than two hours. They were riding through rolling hill country. On either side were to be seen clumps of prickly pear, mesquite, and niggerhead cacti, varied with an occasional paloverde tree. A few miles out from town there was more grass to be seen, and still farther on Peaceful spied small bunches of white-faced cattle, burned with the JD emblem, strung along a cottonwood-lined stream. He asked the name of the stream.

"That's the Geronimo River," Judith told him, her lithe form moving easily to the gait of her pony—a pony, incidentally, which Peaceful had procured at the Red Star Livery to take the place of the one killed. However, Judith had refused to accept it as a gift, with the remark that there were numerous horses at the JD. So far the argument hadn't been settled to Peaceful's satisfaction, and he still held an option with the liveryman on the pony.

"The Geronimo," Judith was saying, "heads up in the Los Padres Range and flows across our holdings. It's always furnished us plenty of water, even in the driest seasons. It flows southeast and commences to sink into the earth as it nears Spanish Wells. I imagine the town gets its water from underground reservoirs fed by the Geronimo."

"Does Randle's Wolf Head outfit use the Geronimo too?" Peaceful asked.

The girl shook her head. "He'd like to though. We used to let him run his cattle across our line and drink from the Geronimo, but the last year or so Father thought it best, under the circumstances, to call a halt on that. Randle didn't like that a bit, either, but there was nothing he could do about it. His water holes are none too plentiful, either. You see, the ranches around here sort of spread out fanlike from Spanish Wells. Our place lies practically due west, clear to Los Padres Range. Conejo Canyon, which is one of the few passes through the Los Padres—the others are much farther north—lies on our property. Northwest of Spanish Wells, with the ranch building about twenty miles from town, is the Wolf Head. Then directly north of town is the Rafter-H. The Crossed Keys outfit stretches out in a northeasterly direction, and adjoining the

Crossed Keys is Bigelow's 8-Bar Ranch. There are a few other small spreads scattered around here and there, but I've said enough to give you an idea of the layout hereabouts."

"With ranches on either side of his," Peaceful commented shrewdly, "Randle should have easy picking when it comes to rustling cattle. But where does he dispose of them?"

"Remember," Judith pointed out, "we haven't any actual proof of his rustling. As for disposal— well, he'd simply have to drive north over the county line. There are a few good-sized towns up that way, not to mention several outfits that might be interested in getting cattle cheap. Oh, Randle would sell 'em all right. He's too smart to try and induct stolen cattle into his own herds. Or he might trade cows with some unscrupulous ranch owner. But we do know Randle's herds increased faster than they should. He and his gang are just a crew of range pirates, as old Tarp would say."

They rode on, following the well-defined trail that ran to the JD Ranch. Overhead there wasn't a cloud in the sky, though the sun was swinging to the west by this time and picking out brilliant high lights on the towering, jagged peaks of the Los Padres Range that lay dead ahead and stretched as far north as the eye could follow. Peaceful stole a look at the girl riding at his side. In her white dress, her singing costume she had worn the previous night, Peaceful had thought her decidedly pretty. Now, he mused, she looked even more attractive in a trim riding skirt of tan corduroy, high-heeled boots, mannish flannel shirt, and wide-brimmed sombrero pulled tightly down on her blonde head.

Suddenly, topping a rise of ground, Judith said, "There's the JD—that's home, cowboy."

Peaceful's eyes followed the girl's gaze down a long grassy slope where a clump of cotton-woods sheltered a rock-and-adobe ranch house of long, rambling construction. There were other buildings and corrals scattered about near by. A windmill poked its whirring fans above one of the smaller trees.

"Come on, let's hurry!" Judith exclaimed, touching spurs to her pony.

They raced down the long slope and finally stopped the ponies beneath the overhanging boughs of an ancient cottonwood tree, not far from the front of the house. A cheerful hail reached them from the long gallery fronting the house. On the gallery sat Tarp Thompson, while beside him, swathed in blankets in an easy chair, was Jabez Drake. Drake was thin and eldery, with iron-grey hair. An invalid's pallor showed through the tan of his lined features. The left half of his body was bandaged from the shoulder down. Blankets covered the lower part of his body.

Judith ran to the gallery, bent over the invalid,

and kissed him, leaving Peaceful to come more slowly behind. "Dad, how do you feel?" she asked.

Jabez Drake's eyes twinkled. "Just about well enough to spank a certain portion of your anatomy until it's pink," he chuckled.

"Dad!" Judith crimsoned. She turned on Tarp. "You told him!" she said accusingly.

"Reckon the captain of a ship has the right to know of imminent mutiny among his crew," Tarp defended himself. "You knowed you'd be goin' against his wishes, Judy."

"But," Drake laughed, "Tarp neglected to tell me until after you had quit that job in the Spanish Dagger. Judy! I don't know what I'm going to do with you."

"We had to have some money and I got it," Judith said defiantly. "While you're at it, you might just as well bawl me out for being in a shooting scrape—right in the centre of it—and get my call-down over all at the same time."

"Shooting scrape!" Drake exclaimed. Tarp's jaw dropped.

At that moment Peaceful arrived at the gallery. Judith said, "Dad, this is Peaceful Jenkins. He's really turned Spanish Wells upside down since his arrival. Maybe he'll help us too."

Drake shook hands firmly. "Tarp—he told me a heap about you, son," the elderly man greeted. "It all sounded good. Drag up a chair and sit down."

212

Tarp had already pushed a chair in Peaceful's direction. Judith sat down on the edge of the gallery and let her feet dangle. Drake's eyes again sought Judith's. "What's this you were saying about a shooting scrape?"

"I reckon that was my fault, sir," Peaceful started to explain. "I had a bit of trouble in town with a couple of hombres just before we left. One of them had drawn a bead on me, when Judith drove her horse in between us. Well, I owe her a horse—and a lot more for saving my life—but so far she refuses to allow me to replace her pony."

"Shiver my timbers!" Tarp exclaimed indignantly. "If you call that an explanation of a shooting scrape I'm a barnacle-bottomed old scow! Let's have what happened."

Thus urged, Peaceful furnished details, with Judith putting in additional words from time to time. When he had finished Drake said, "That's a mighty good piece of work, Peaceful. I'm more than glad Judith was able to help out. Maybe"—his eyes twinkled—"she's justified her existence at last."

"Dad!" Judith exclaimed indignantly.

Tarp eyed Peaceful admiringly. "So you downed both Tracy and Fred Cubera. That's the kind of shooting that can be writ down in the log with pride. They're tough scuts, them two." He glanced at Drake. "How about it, Jabez, don't you think a round of grog is indicated for all hands, including the captain?"

Drake nodded. "I could stand a wee touch."

Tarp vanished within the house to reappear shortly with a bottle and glasses. For Judith he had a small glass of wine. Peaceful rolled a cigarette and sat there sipping his liquor. It was really pleasant here. He liked the JD almost as well as the ranch he and Applejack owned back in Texas. Looking at Judith, he commenced to wonder if he didn't like this outfit even better. Now if Judith were only in Texas . . . Right then Peaceful Jenkins came to certain definite conclusions.

Conversation rambled a bit until Peaceful said, "Mr. Drake, what I'm going to say should be kept secret, but the fact of the matter is, it was your being shot and robbed that brought me to Spanish Wells."

"I just felt it," Judith said.

"Keep still, Judy," Drake cut in. "We're waiting to hear."

"In the first place," Peaceful said, "Louie Dawes, who is responsible for your misfortune, Mr. Drake, is a brother to Steve Dawes, a wealthy and well-thought-of citizen of Montana. Louie is much younger and was pretty wild as a boy. He was always getting into scrapes. He got to running with some cow rustlers up there, and when the gang was chased down, Louie was one

214

of three sent to the penitentiary. The rest escaped out of the country, though it was known who they were. One of them was Jake Tracy, who had already served three short sentences for cow thieving—"

"Well, blow me down!" Tarp exclaimed. "How do you know all this?"

"I made it my business to get Louie Dawes's history, who he had been running with, and so on, before I took this case."

"Are you a detective?" Judith's eyes widened.

Peaceful smiled. "Not a regular detective. I used to be with the Texas Rangers and I had some luck solving one or two murder mysteries down there. Later Applejack and I resigned and got us an outfit. When Steve Dawes heard of Louie's death he wanted the whole business investigated. He was sure Louie had been living honest. Steve's an old friend of mine, and when he wanted an investigator I couldn't refuse his request and—well, that's what brought Applejack and me to Spanish Wells."

"What I want to know," Jabez Drake put in, "how did Steve Wells hear of his brother's death? So far as we know, the body just disappeared—if Deputy Vaughn really shot Dawes as he claimed to have done."

"Vaughn shot him all right—at least somebody did. Dawes was shot twice. Either wound was fatal. I'll get to what happened in a minute.

You see, Louie Dawes had been sent to the Montana penitentiary. While there he contracted tuberculosis. He didn't want to die in prison, so when the opportunity came he made his escape. He went at once to his brother Steve's home, and Steve, seeing his condition, hadn't the heart to return him to the prison authorities. Figuring the boy hadn't long to live, anyway, Steve gave him money to get out of the country. Louie Dawes eventually landed in Spanish Wells and secured work in Sam Purdy's store. In this climate he regained his health and became a respected citizen of the community. He wrote his brother Steve that he intended to stay here and lead an honest life. No one here, of course, knew Louie was an escaped convict. It was just his bad luck to have picked a town where his old crony, Jake Tracy, was due to appear. What passed between Tracy and Dawes we don't know. We can only surmise. One thing is certain: Tracy didn't report Dawes' whereabouts to the Montana authorities, though it is quite likely he threatened to do so if Dawes didn't do his bidding."

"In what way?" Drake asked.

"We come now to your part of the affair," Peaceful said. "You owed money to Randle. You wanted to pay it off. You arranged to borrow the money from the bank for that purpose. As you left the bank you were shot and Louie Dawes seized your sack of money. Deputy Vaughn followed, overtook and shot Dawes, so he claims. I reckon that part is true. But somewhere along the line an exchange of money sacks was effected, and Vaughn brought back only packages of newspaper, cut to resemble the size of bills. This he hasn't yet explained to the satisfaction of any honest man, but as there is no actual proof against him, there is little can be done about it right now."

"Or ever, I fear," Drake sighed.

"Don't be too sure." Peaceful smiled. "We may have some luck yet. Meanwhile, Vaughn has shot Dawes and left him for dead. That night two Mexican woodcutters, on their way to the county seat of Surcingle, ran across Dawes's body. Discovering the man still breathed, they took him in to Surcingle's hospital, where the doctors did what they could to save his life. Dawes regained consciousness long enough to ask them to send for his brother Steve in Montana, then became unconscious again. Steve got there too late. Louie had died. But the doctors reported that an hour or so before he died he kept up a continual delirious muttering about a letter he had written to Steve and placed in a pack of cards. The doctors couldn't make head nor tail of that, and it was all they could tell Steve when he arrived after his brother's death. Steve got in touch with me and asked me to see what I could learn."

"That first day I saw you in the Spanish

Dagger," Judith said, "you took out a deck of cards, and I saw you get a folded piece of paper from within the deck."

"You saw more than you were intended to." Peaceful smiled. "But I got the letter sure enough." He told them how he had secured it, then took the letter from his pocket and passed it to Jabez Drake. Judith went to her father's shoulder to read it, as did Tarp. Drake looked up. "This isn't signed."

Peaceful nodded. "There's no doubt of its being written by Louie Dawes though. I have the word of a fellow who saw Dawes write it and place it in the deck of cards. Had his signature only been there, it would have given me proof I needed to apprehend Tracy. Or if Dawes had had time to write more we'd have had further names involved, I imagine. That was written on the morning you were shot and robbed, Mr. Drake."

Judith said, frowning, "This letter sounds as though Dawes had been forced into doing what he did."

Peaceful nodded. "It's my guess that Tracy was going to inform the Montana authorities where Dawes could be found unless Dawes went through with the robbery. It was wrong, of course, but I suppose Dawes preferred to go through with it rather than be returned to the Montana penitentiary where he'd probably contract his old illness and die." Peaceful paused as Drake returned the letter, then said, "Just where did the bullet strike you, Mr. Drake?"

Drake frowned. "That's the funniest thing about the whole business, There I was, standing on the sidewalk facing Dawes. I was watching his gun, trying to get my own weapon out. Then I felt the bullet strike. I can't remember seeing any flame or smoke or anything come from Dawes's gun. What's queerer still, that slug entered the top of my shoulder and ranged down past my heart, narrowly missing it. Only for Doc Hamilton getting to me quick, I'd have been dead.

"You probably don't believe it, but I can still show you the wound. It ain't entirely healed. Maybe you think I'm crazy."

Peaceful shook his head. "It's exactly what I wanted to hear. It bears out my own suspicions. Mr. Drake, Louie Dawes never intended to shoot you. His brother Steve told me he'd always hated guns and had a horror of bloodshed. Does that sound as though Dawes was the killer type? No! He didn't know you were going to be shot. He figured to bluff you out by brandishing his gun. As a matter of fact, he didn't shoot you."

"Well, by the tarnation, who did then?" Drake demanded.

"The man who shot you," Peaceful said slowly, "was stationed at the open window of one of those empty offices over the bank. I'd suspicioned that much before; after the same thing was tried on me to-day I feel certain of it."

"You mean," Judith asked, "that it was Tracy who shot Dad?"

"I don't reckon so. Until I'm sure I won't mention any names. Funny thing about those offices over Uhlmann's bank—until this past week Uhlmann always kept them locked, so Sam Purdy told me shortly before you and I left to-day, Judith. A few days back Purdy had a prospective tenant for one of those offices, thinking to help Uhlmann rent 'em. But Uhlmann had the keys and couldn't be located at the time. The tenant rented another place. When Purdy told Uhlmann, Uhlmann swore he'd leave the doors to the vacant offices unlocked from then on. They were unlocked the day I went up to look at them—"

"By gosh!" Drake broke in. "Those offices must have been locked the day I was shot then. Whoever did the shooting must have got the key from Uhlmann."

Peaceful nodded. "I reckon that's how it was."

"Say! Say!" Amazement spread over Drake's features. "That places the job squarely in Fletch Uhlmann's lap."

"I reckon." Peaceful nodded.

"But why, dang it why?" Drake puzzled. "I never did anything to Uhlmann. Never took to him much, either; just figured he was the banker to do business with, that's all."

Peaceful said, "Look at it this way: both Uhlmann and Randle now hold notes secured by your ranch. Suppose they got together? The JD is a valuable property—"

"But there's lots of other range land open," Drake protested. "They wouldn't go to all the trouble of shooting and robbing just to get my buildings."

"Maybe they want your water—Geronimo River."

"Could be," Drake acknowledged, puzzled. "But water isn't so scarce as all that, hereabouts."

Judith said, "You men figure it out; I'm going in and start supper. I figure the boys are pretty tired of eating Tarp's cooking by this time. You'll be staying, of course, Peaceful?"

"I'll be darned glad to, but I've got to get back to town right after."

At suppertime Peaceful met the three JD cowpunchers who ate in the dining room of the ranch house during the absence of a cook in the mess shanty. Their names were Post-Hole Quinn, a grizzled, bow-legged veteran of the range who had worked for the JD for years; Ed Larrabee, young, smiling, and loyal; and Lennie Owen, a freckled-faced youngster who worked at any odd job that was given him about the ranch.

Before departing that night Peaceful told Judith he was going to leave the pony to see if she wouldn't change her mind about accepting it. "In

221

that way"—he grinned—"I'll have an excuse to ride out here again. You see, I can't take no for an answer. You really should keep that pony, but don't decide too soon."

"All right, I won't." Judith laughed. "But, cowboy, you don't ever need an excuse to ride to the JD. You're always welcome."

"You mean that?"

Judith extended one hand. "On my honour. And I know the same goes for Dad and the boys."

Peaceful took her hand, held it a trifle longer than he should have. Then somewhat confusedly he released it and mounted his horse before he spoke too much. After all, he'd only known this girl a short time. He didn't want her to think he was completely crazy. Rather stiffly, to cover his feelings, he said "Good night" and spurred his pony out to the trail. A soft breeze was lifting across the range. It smelled good. "By golly," Peaceful muttered as he rolled a cigarette, "if I don't watch out I'll be liking this country better than Texas."

20

"HE'S BRINGING TROUBLE"

THE following noon Hugo Randle and one of his gamblers, Ace Hodkins, were sitting on the veranda of the Spanish Wells Hotel, awaiting the arrival of the daily stagecoach from Surcingle. They sat in tilted-back wooden chairs, their booted feet resting against the veranda railing. This was a daily occurrence for Hodkins, who lived at the hotel; it was unusual to see Randle here. Hodkins commented on the fact.

"No, I ain't usual interested in who arrives," Randle said, taking a long, thin black cigar from between his lips. "Some of the boys generally tip me off if anybody that looks like money comes in. To-day is different. The Drake girl quit me, you know."

"I heard a rumour to that effect," Hodkins confessed, "but as you didn't say anything, I thought maybe there wasn't nothing in it. What was wrong with her?"

"We had a few words," Randle said noncommittally. "I reckon maybe she didn't like the atmosphere of the Spanish Dagger. She's the goody-goody sort. It was probably a mistake to hire her in the first place."

Hodkins looked dubious. "I dunno, Hugo. Judy Drake drew a lot of folks to the place. People liked to hear her sing."

"That's mighty true." Randle scowled. "Her stepping off that way, without any notice, sort of left me in the lurch. I haven't let it be known yet; I want the same crowd as always. I sent a man riding to Surcingle yesterday afternoon with instructions to hire a girl that's been singing over there in the Golden Bird dance hall. The feller got back this morning with word that this girl—Lottie Lamere—will arrive on the noon stage. I figured it might be a good idea to meet her when she arrives. Dammit! I had to pay her twenty more a week to get her away from the Golden Bird. Figure she'll be worth it though. I heard her in Surcingle one time. She don't sing these wishy-washy, old-fashioned songs like Judy Drake did. This Lamere female sings 'em real snappy—what folks call risqué—but I reckon my crowd will go for that. If it don't I stand to lose money."

Hodkins nodded. "And if things don't change around right soon, Hugo, you stand to lose still more money."

"How you meaning?"

Hodkins explained, "That Applejack Peters watching our games last night didn't help matters any. That hombre can sure spot a rigged game in a hurry. Course with me it was just a matter of changing over to square dice, so he didn't catch me at anything. But, hell, I was just lucky to break even last night. And it was the same way with some of the other fellers."

"I'd like to bust that Peters wide open." Randle growled.

"Sure, so would all of us, but what we'd like to do and what is actually done is two different things entire. Look how quick Peters spotted those lead frets in Hubbell's roulette wheel. I reckon you heard him tell Hubbell to stop the game until he could replace those leads with the standard steel frets."

"Yeah, I know. Hubbell told Peters he'd make the change before he opened for play again."

"That's what he told him, yes. But Hubbell is plenty sore. I don't figure he'll make any change-over. To my way of thinking, Hubbell is figuring to pull up stakes for some other town where the law isn't so strict."

Randle swore. "He's crazy. I don't reckon the change from steel to lead and vice versa would make that much difference."

"T'ell it won't," Hodkins contradicted. "That shows how much you know about roulette wheels. Remove those steel frets and substitute lead and when your wheel is spinning, that ball ain't so inclined to bounce when it hits a lead fret. Instead it will land on—"

"I know, I know," Randle snapped impatiently. "If Hubbell just has the sense to stall along he'll get back in the money again. Same with the rest of you fellers. You call yourselves gamblers, but you lack the guts to take a chance. Just play along with me; we'll get rid of Jenkins and Peters before long."

"Like Cubera and Tracy got rid of Jenkins yesterday, I suppose."

"No use getting sarcastic, Ace. I was hoping for a break there. I didn't get it, that's all. We'll do better next time."

"You planned that job, didn't you, Hugo?"

"What do you think? Anyway, Ace, what you don't know won't hurt you. I'll tell you this much, if that fool Cubera hadn't tried to plug Jenkins the story would have been different."

"Well, he paid for his folly. How's Tracy; have you heard?"

"He was still unconscious when I talked to Doc Hamilton this morning. Hamilton thinks he may pull through though."

At that moment Deputy Vaughn stepped up on the hotel veranda. "Morning, Hugo—Ace. Hugo, is that new songbird of yours due to arrive on the noon stage?"

"That's what I was given to understand. Stage is late, ain't it?"

"Might be a minute or so. Howsomever,

Ribbons Riley is generally on time. There it comes now!"

There came a thundering of galloping hoofs as the stagecoach swung into view around the bend at the far end of Main Street. Clouds of dust plumed up from its rear. People commenced to gather about the hotel corner as they always did for the daily arrival of the stage. There were several yells of greeting as Ribbons Riley footed the brake of the rocking vehicle and brought his horses to a wild, plunging stop in a scattering of sand and gravel before the Spanish Wells Hotel. Riley's shotgun guard dropped the strongbox to the earth and jumped down after it, then picked up the box, which probably contained nothing but mail this day, and disappeared in the direction of the hotel bar. Ribbons Riley climbed down and went around to the rear end of the stage coach with a view to opening the luggage boot. A couple of men came running from the Red Star Livery across the street and started to unhitch the panting sweat- and dust-streaked horses.

Randle rose to his feet and from the hotel veranda stood looking at the passengers alighting from the stage. A salesman for a grain-and-feed company alighted, followed by a whisky salesman. The whisky salesman gallantly turned and assisted a brunette girl with a hard mouth and painted cheeks to get down.

"There's your songbird, I'll bet," Deputy Vaughn said.

"That's her." Randle nodded. He started toward the steps at the end of the hotel porch, then stopped, his eyes falling on the fourth and last passenger to alight from the stage. Randle paused, saying to Deputy Vaughn, "Who's that hombre? His face looks familiar."

"Damned if it doesn't." Vaughn frowned.

The man in question was middle-aged, dressed in citizens' clothing and a broad-brimmed Stetson. He was somewhat chunky in build with blue eyes and a florid complexion. A gold watch chain stretched across his vest. He appeared well-to-do.

Ace Hodkins said, "Wait! I know that hombre. I've seen him somewheres." His brow furrowed, then cleared. "I got it. Remember him from the time I spent in Montana a few years back. Lemme see, what's his name? Davis? No. Something like that though. Dawes! That's it—Steve Dawes! He's pretty well fixed, well thought of up Montana way."

"Dawes!" Randle exclaimed.

"Dawes!" Vaughn echoed. He looked quickly at Randle. "No wonder he looked familiar to us. Except for being older, his features are a heap like Louie Dawes's. Seems like I remember Jake Tracy saying that Louie Dawes had a brother up in Montana. Hugo, I don't like this."

"No more do I," Randle frowned. "Look, Herb, I've got to go pick up that Lamere girl. You keep an eye on this Dawes hombre. See if you can learn what he's here for."

Ace Hodkins looked curiously at the two. "Say, do you suppose that this Steve Dawes is related to Louie Dawes, that bandit Herb killed a month or so back?"

"Let's not talk about that," Randle snapped. "I already told you once to-day, Ace, that what you don't know won't hurt you. That still goes. You run your dice game and I'll take care of the rest of the town."

Hodkins shrugged. "Just as you say, Hugo."

Steve Dawes followed the two salesmen into the hotel lobby. The Lamere girl stood on the corner, a pair of valises at her feet, glancing impatiently in both directions along Main Street. Randle came up to her, doffing his sombrero. The girl smiled. They talked a few moments; then Randle took her arm and one of the valises and escorted her off in the direction of the Spanish Dagger.

Ten minutes later, after Randle had shown the Lamere girl to her dressing-room, Deputy Herb Vaughn came hurrying into the big honky-tonk. He met Hugo Randle just inside the entrance.

Randle said, "What's up, Herb?"

"Steve Dawes," Vaughn said, "registered at the hotel under the name of Dave Stephens. He gave it out that he was down here to look around for mining properties. The clerk at the hotel offered to bring in a couple of mining men to talk to him, but Stephens—or Dawes—vetoed that—told the clerk he wanted to rest a few days before looking into any business deals. He's got room 28 on the second floor."

"Where'd you learn all this?" Randle asked.

"Talked to the clerk after Dawes had gone up to his room. You know, I didn't ask particularly about Dawes. I just went into the lobby and glanced at the register. Told the clerk that, being deputy, I liked to know who was arriving in the town."

"Good work, Herb. Maybe the man isn't Dawes, then."

"No doubt about it, Hugo. He's Dawes all right. Ace Hodkins recognized him. We both know he looks a heap like Louie Dawes. To clinch the fact, Dawes started to write his real name in the register—got as far as putting down the 'Ste,' then scratched it out and wrote down Dave Stephens. Yep, there ain't no doubt he's Steve Dawes. The Dave Stephens is a fake name; Dawes didn't even have enough sense to choose a name completely different from his own."

Randle frowned. "I don't like it, Herb. I've got a hunch that Steve Dawes is bringing trouble. He looked like he had money. Maybe he wants an investigation of his brother's death."

Vaughn looked uneasy. "I don't want that business reopened. Y'know, maybe it was him told Ike Kimball about that letter in Louie's pack of cards. I've been wondering about that. Ike didn't say in his letter—"

"I wish we knew what was in Louie Dawes's letter. Damn that Jenkins!"

"Look, Hugo, if that matter is reopened you've got to back me up if things get to looking bad."

"Hell! I'll back you up—like always."

"You'd better," Vaughn growled. "If I go down I won't be alone in this."

"I don't like the way you say that, Herb."

"I'm stating a fact. I ain't going to be the fall guy for anybody. You might as well know that now, Hugo."

Randle forced a thin smile. "I never let you down yet, did I? All right! You do as I say and we'll come out all right. Right now you'd better get back and hang around the hotel. See what else you can learn about Steve Dawes. If you pick up anything that sounds bad—well, we'll just have to forget Jenkins for the time being and get Dawes out of the way."

"How do you mean," Vaughn asked dumbly, " 'out of the way'?"

Randle laughed coolly. "How do we put anybody out of the way that butts in on our business? Don't be a fool, Herb."

"It's a job I don't want," Vaughn said flatly.

"Did I ask you to take it?" Randle growled. "Now go on back to the hotel and keep your eyes peeled."

21

DUE FOR A SHOWDOWN

IT was nearing one o'clock when Peaceful stepped into the Bon-Ton Restaurant. The place was filled with midday diners; every stool and chair was occupied. Applejack was seated about halfway along the counter, just commencing his dinner. He turned and saw Peaceful standing at his shoulder. "Haven't you eaten yet?" The clatter of dishes and voices nearly drowned out his voice.

Peaceful shook his head. "I was talking to Sam Purdy."

"What about?"

"Nothing in particular. Kind of late yourself, aren't you?"

Applejack grinned. "I got tangled in a scuttle of suds over to the Demijohn. Say"—he lowered his voice a trifle—"maybe something is up."

"What do you mean?"

"I was sitting on the Demijohn porch, enjoying my beer in the shade, when I saw Hugo Randle arriving at the Spanish Dagger with a black-haired cutie and a couple of valises."

"I thought you weren't interested in women. Probably it's some new girl that Randle hired to take Judith's place."

"Did I say I was interested in the girl? You didn't give me time to finish. About five minutes after Hugo and the girl had gone in Deputy Vaughn came hurrying along and popped into the Spanish Dagger. I could tell by his manner that he must have discovered something important."

"What way did he come from?"

"From the direction of the hotel."

Peaceful's eyes narrowed thoughtfully. "Let's see, Randle must have been at the hotel to meet the stage when it arrived. Yet Vaughn shows up later from the same direction. Like as not he was there when the stage arrived too. He must have learned something after Randle left. Hmmm! I wonder who was on the stage besides the new girl of Randle's."

"I haven't any idea. It might be sensible for us to check up, because Vaughn only stayed in the Spanish Dagger three or four minutes before heading back toward the hotel again. And he wasn't walking slow."

Peaceful nodded. "I reckon I'll go to the hotel dining room for my dinner. It doesn't look as though there'd be any empty seats here for a spell. I'll see you later, Applejack."

Peaceful left the Bon-Ton and headed toward the hotel. As he drew near the building he saw

Steve Dawes standing uncertainly on the hotel porch, glancing along the street. Peaceful mounted the steps. Dawes saw him and turned with a smile of welcome.

"Danged if I'm not glad to see you, Peaceful."

"What are you doing here, Steve?"

"Shh!" Dawes looked quickly around. "My name is Dave Stephens. I'm here looking for mining properties. Going to rest up a few days before starting out though. I was just wondering where I could find you. I didn't want to ask any questions for fear I might be questioning the wrong people."

Peaceful's gaze flitted both ways along Main Street. Across the street, in the entrance to the Red Star Livery, Deputy Herb Vaughn stood lounging lazily just inside the opening.

Peaceful said, "Steve, have you had your dinner yet? . . . Neither have I. Let's go in the hotel dining-room." They left the porch and made their way into the building.

As they disappeared inside Deputy Vaughn left his post, strolled across the street, and entered the hotel bar, whose entrance was around the corner on Saddlehorn Street. In the bar-room, which also had an entrance to the dining-room, Vaughn called for a bottle of beer and took up a stance at the long counter that enabled him, through the process of peering around a corner of the entrance, to see Peaceful and Dawes just sitting

235

down at one of the dining-room tables. Vaughn smiled inwardly and settled back to see what could be learned.

After a waitress had taken their order Dawes said to Peaceful, "You don't seem overjoyed to see me, cowboy."

"I'm always glad to see you, Steve, but not right now. You asked me to come here and make a secret investigation. Now I'm afraid you've tipped yourself off. Oh, you probably haven't done any great harm, but—well, I just wish you hadn't turned up at this time."

"But, Peaceful," Dawes said earnestly, "that's why I registered under another name."

"I reckon that won't do any good, Steve. Somebody here must know you."

"What makes you think so?"

"There was a man spying on you from across the street when I came up on the hotel porch. He saw us together. He was the hombre who shot your brother Louie."

Dawes's face flamed angrily. He started to rise from the table. "Where is he?"

"Sit down," Peaceful said quietly. "You gave me a job to do here. Either I'm working on the case or you're taking over to do it your way."

Dawes dropped reluctantly back into his chair. At that moment their waitress came with several steaming plates of food. It gave Dawes time to regain his composure. He sat back, biting his lip. When the waitress had departed he said, "I'm sorry, Peaceful. Maybe I've gummed up the whole business. I didn't stop to think. It's just that I thought so much of that boy—why, I practically raised him—and then to learn that his murderer was so near—" His voice broke on the words.

Peaceful said, "Take it easy, Steve, and eat your dinner. And don't forget the man that did that shooting was legally empowered, under the circumstances, to do what he did—whether we like it or not. Exactly what brought you here?"

Dawes said, "Hell, I haven't been able to eat or sleep decently since it happened. I just had to do something. I got to thinking that maybe if I came to Spanish Wells I might be able to help you in some way. I'd at least be here when you learned what was at the bottom of the whole dirty business. I know that Louie wouldn't shoot anybody. I don't care what anybody says—"

"All right, I agree. I think I'm on the way to finding the proof of your words."

"You are? What have you learned?"

"I'll tell you in a minute. First, Steve, did you mention to anybody but me what the doctors told you about Louie's delirious words regarding that letter in the pack of cards?"

Dawes shook his head. "No—" Then he hesitated. "That is, not until recently."

"Who'd you tell?"

"Sheriff Kimball—over to Surcingle—I stopped there on business on my way through. Also, I wanted to ask Kimball to do what he could toward an investigation of the case."

Peaceful smiled wryly. "It's too bad we can't pull the whole U.S. army into this too."

"I am sorry, Peaceful. I've acted like a fool. But I've been so wrought up."

"Forget it, Steve; we'll make out," Peaceful said sympathetically. "What did you tell Kimball?"

"Just that Louie had said something about a letter for me in a deck of cards. Kimball said he'd write to Deputy Vaughn and see if he could find anything of the sort."

Peaceful said, "That explains how Vaughn knew about that letter. What sort of hombre is Sheriff Kimball?"

"I figure him as square. He's well thought of in Surcingle. I had quite a talk with him. He doesn't like Vaughn, but certain politicians made him place Vaughn in office in the first place. He didn't say that Vaughn was dishonest or anything of the sort. Kimball just figures him as incompetent. There was that money he failed to bring back, of course. By the way, did you ever find anything of that letter?"

Peaceful nodded. "I'll give it to you in a minute. It's addressed to you and should be yours. But first I want to tell you just how I got it and what's been done here so far by Applejack and me."

Peaceful sketched briefly his operations since arriving in Spanish Wells, only telling Dawes so much as was already known to the general public.

"All you've got so far, then, is the letter?"

"Here it is." Peaceful produced the folded sheet of paper and handed it to Dawes, then went on eating while Dawes read it. The man's eyes looked moist when he looked up. "I can keep this?"

"It's your letter from Louie. It's told me all I could get out of it."

"This letter proves that Louie was forced to do what he did."

"I reckon it does. But with one exception, it names no names. Nor is it signed."

"Where's this Tracy my brother mentioned?"

"He's the fellow I just told you about. I shot him yesterday. He's at Doc Hamilton's now. If he ever regains consciousness maybe we can get him to talk."

"And if he doesn't?"

Peaceful shrugged. "We'll just have to get what we want some other way."

"I'm relying on you, Peaceful. Don't spare expense. By the way, speaking of money, you say you've talked to this Jabez Drake who was robbed by Louie?"

Peaceful nodded. "He's all right. Square as they come. Got a nice daughter too." Peaceful coloured a trifle as the words slipped out and rushed on, "Losing that money put him in a bad hole. Now he owes ten thousand dollars instead of the original five."

"That's something I wanted to talk to you about. I stand ready to make good Mr. Drake's loss. It's the least I can do."

"That's mighty square of you, Steve. Howsomever, it wouldn't surprise me none if Drake refused your offer. I figure him as being plumb independent, and naturally he don't hold you responsible for what Louie did."

"That's as may be. At any rate, I want to square matters if possible, and if worst came to worst it would take a worry off his mind. Suppose you take me out to see him tomorrow. I want to do everything possible to even things for Louie's doings."

"Well," Peaceful said, "we can ride out and see what Mr. Drake thinks of the idea. We might go see him tomorrow, like you say. Meanwhile, what you going to do?"

"I reckon that's up to you, Peaceful. I realize I've sort of put my foot in it by coming here. You tell me what to do and I'll do it."

Peaceful considered. "Now you're here, you might as well stay, I reckon. There's a showdown due one of these days, and I don't figure it as too far off. Keep up the pretence of being here for the purpose of looking into mining properties. That won't do any harm. Just rest up for a few days. I'll drop around now and then and keep you posted if I learn anything new. If you want a drink the hotel bar is okay. The Demijohn Saloon has good beer, according to Applejack. Keep away from the Spanish Dagger. Its liquor isn't too good and the games are crooked."

They finished dinner after a time, and Peaceful rose to take his departure.

Steve Dawes said "So long" and settled down on the hotel porch with a newspaper and a thick cigar.

A short time later Deputy Herb Vaughn was talking to Hugo Randle, standing at the Spanish Dagger's long bar. Randle listened intently until Vaughn had finished. He didn't say anything for a minute as he meditatively drew on the long, thin black cigar clenched between his teeth.

Finally, "You say you saw Jenkins pass this Dave Stephens—or Steve Dawes—a folded sheet of paper?"

"That's what." Vaughn nodded.

Randle frowned. "I don't like it, Herb. I'm commencing to think that Dawes sent Jenkins here to investigate Louie's death. We know that Louie wrote a letter to his brother just before he pulled that hold-up on Drake. We also know that Louie didn't want to do that job. He wouldn't have done it if Jake hadn't put pressure on him. All right. What names did Louie mention in that letter to his brother? Nick Corvall told us Jake's name was mentioned. Maybe yours is in there, too, and mine."

"That's what I'm afraid of," Vaughn said.

Randle did some more speculating. "I figure it was just luck, Jenkins getting himself made town marshal here. Outside of town his word wouldn't have much weight. I'm betting that he had Steve Dawes come here. He's given that letter to Dawes. Now Dawes can take it to a higher authority. Vaughn, we've got to get that letter."

Vaughn shivered. "But how, Hugo, how? I've gone as far as I dast. I can't—"

"You'll do a hell of a lot," Randle said harshly, "if your neck looks like it's headed toward a noose. You listen to me and we'll get that letter. I'm not asking anything from you I wouldn't do myself. Maybe neither of us will run chances. But we've got to have that letter. If Steve Dawes won't give it up—well, maybe that's just too bad for Steve Dawes. We're in too deep now to baulk at trifles!"

22

A SHOT IN THE NIGHT

PEACEFUL was sleeping quietly in his bed at the hotel when he awakened suddenly, every sense alert. He came to a sitting position, listening. Through his window he could see a section of star-studded sky. The street below appeared quiet. Peaceful frowned. Was it a shot he had heard, or had he been dreaming? Everything appeared quiet now. He strained his ears. Nope, not a sound to be heard. Peaceful waited a moment longer. Gradually a sense of uneasiness crept over him.

"Maybe I'm just a danged fool," he muttered, "but that sure sounded like a shot." He reached to his pants hanging on the edge of the bed, found a match and his watch. Blinking in the sudden light of the flame, he made out the time on his dial. It was a few minutes after three. He was wide awake now. Rising from the bed, he pulled on his pants and boots, strapped on his cartridge belt and holster. Then he opened his door to the hallway and stepped out.

At the same instant the door to the next room

opened and Applejack appeared in the hall. Applejack said, "What you doing up?"

"You heard it too, eh?" Peaceful said.

Applejack said sheepishly, "I thought I heard a shot, if that's what you mean, though I wa'nt sure if I really heard it or was just dreaming."

"Same here. I reckon we must have heard it all right. To me it sounded like it came from the rear of the building."

"Who's staying in the back rooms, do you know?"

Peaceful shook his head. "Maybe we're just getting excited over nothing, but I reckon we better wake up the clerk and make an investigation."

They went quietly downstairs to the clerk's room, which was located just off the lobby. The hotel closed at one o'clock; anyone arriving after that time used a night bell. The clerk emerged from his room, rubbing his eyes. He looked startled when he'd listened to the reason for his awakening. "You're sure you're not mistaken, Mr. Jenkins?"

"Sure, I could be," Peaceful admitted. "But both my pard and me thought we heard the shot and we both figured it was at the back of your building. Who's in your backrooms?"

"There's only three of them occupied at present. There's a feed salesman, a salesman from a whisky house, and a gentleman here looking at mining properties, Mr. Dave Stephens. He's in 28."

Peaceful's brow furrowed. "I reckon we'd better check into it," he said. "If those three are all right we'll check on the other rooms. I know Mr. Stephens; I'll go up and see if I can rouse him. Get your pants on and bring your keys."

Peaceful turned and raced back up the stairs, followed by Applejack. In the narrow corridor at the back of the building they scratched matches and knocked at the door of 28, softly at first, and then more loudly. After a moment Peaceful called "Steve! Are you there?"

No answer.

Peaceful turned the doorknob. The door was bolted from within. Peaceful said again, louder, "Steve!"

From the two other occupied rooms on the hall came angry mutterings and drowsy orders to keep quiet and shut up and the like. Applejack said, "The shot didn't come from either of those rooms, anyway."

The hotel clerk came shuffling around the corner, bearing an oil lamp and a key. "Learn anything, Mr. Jenkins?" he asked.

"I can't get any answer from the man who registered as Dave Stephens."

"Is that right?" the clerk said. "Maybe Mr. Stephens isn't in there. He may have stayed out late some place."

"I don't reckon so," Peaceful said, frowning. "I know him. I think he'd have told me if he was going out. Let's open this door."

"Here's the key," the clerk replied. "The same key opens all the rooms."

"I reckon your key won't do much good," Peaceful cut in. "This door is bolted from the inside."

"Mr. Stephens *must* be in there then," the clerk insisted.

"That's what I'm commencing to be afraid of," Peaceful said grimly. "We'll have to bust down this door."

Ignoring the clerk's protestations, Peaceful hurled his weight against the door. At the second blow there came a sharp splintering sound as the bolt was wrenched from the wood. The door swung back into the darkened room. The instant Peaceful stepped inside his nose picked up the odour of burned gunpowder. "Let me have that lamp," he said.

But the clerk was already in the room, holding the lamp aloft. He gave a sudden startled cry; the lamp wavered in his hand. Applejack took the lamp from him and set it on a bureau.

"But—but—God! This is awful!" the clerk chattered. "Mr. Stephens has killed himself!"

Steve Dawes lay slumped to one side in the bed, his nightshirt-clothed form only half covered by the blankets. His pillow was stained with blood which still trickled from an ugly hole just below his right cheekbone. A nickel-plated revolver was clutched in Dawe's stiffening fingers.

Peaceful straightened from an examination of the body. Dawes hadn't been dead long, but he had died almost instantly after the fatal shot had left the gun barrel. Peaceful glanced around the room. It was furnished similarly to his own. It had one window, now closed, that overlooked the alley back of the hotel. Dawes's coat hung over the back of the chair; his other clothing was draped on the end of the bed. Peaceful's gaze swept quickly across the floor; then he spoke to the clerk: "I hear some of your other tenants. Reckon this noise we made woke 'em up. You'd better go tell 'em what's up before they come pouring in here on us."

"That's a good idea." The clerk nodded nervously and scurried out into the hall. The instant he was gone Peaceful stooped and retrieved a wallet that lay on the floor under the chair that held Dawes's coat. He glanced quickly through the contents of the wallet, then turned back to the stiffening figure on the bed. Applejack said, "What do you think, pard?"

Peaceful replied, "I don't like this a bit. Applejack, you'd better slip down and wake up Deputy Vaughn. Tell him what's happened. After all, he's the county deputy; he'll have to handle this."

Applejack nodded and departed.

The clerk came back into the room, followed

by the whisky salesman. Sounds of further commotion came from the other rooms. The clerk was saying. "Yes—suicide. His door was bolted. We had to break it down."

Peaceful said, "I note you don't have locks on your windows."

"No, we've never put them on on the second floor," the clerk replied, stealing another nervous look at the still form on the bed.

"You'd better take care of his wallet," Peaceful suggested, handing the well-filled billfold to the clerk. "There's quite a sum of money there. Put it in your safe. And while we're at it, we might as well go through his pockets to see if he had any other valuables."

"That's a good idea." The clerk nodded, without thinking, though he left the searching of Dawes's pockets to Peaceful. Nothing else of value was discovered.

The whisky salesman said, "The fact that the wallet contains money proves that this wasn't a matter of robbery and murder."

"Who said anything about robbery and murder?" Peaceful asked.

"Well, you mentioned that the window wasn't locked shut," the whisky man said. "I thought maybe you figured that somebody might have entered that window and—"

"That's ridiculous," the clerk broke in. "This is plain suicide. We've all seen the gun in Mr.

Stephens's right hand. That's his own gun, no doubt. You don't see those nickel-plated weapons here in this cow country. As for anybody entering the window, well, that window is 'round eighteen feet from the ground."

A few more men crowded into the room, asking questions. Peaceful left the replies to the clerk and once more returned to the bed to study the dead man.

"What do you suppose ever made him kill himself?" The clerk frowned. "Apparently he was wealthy and—"

"May be sorrow," Peaceful suggested. "Like I told you, I know Mr. Stephens. He recently lost a brother. That broke him up right bad. That may be the reason for the suicide."

"Who's this feller what killed himself?" Deputy Vaughn's voice broke in as he shouldered his way into the room. "All you hombres get out of here. Jenkins, you stay. I want to talk to you." Vaughn's eyes still looked heavy with sleep.

The room cleared gradually. Vaughn said, "Jenkins, tell me what you know about this."

Peaceful said quietly, "There's not much to tell, Vaughn. My pard and I both thought we heard a shot. We awakened the hotel clerk, busted down the door, and found things as you see 'em."

"No suicide note left or anything of that kind?" Vaughn asked.

"I haven't found any," Peaceful replied quietly.

"You can give a look around. I figured this was more your job than mine; that's why I sent my pard to get you. You'd better notify the undertaker."

"I know my business," Vaughn growled. "What do you know about this hombre, Jenkins? I saw you eating dinner with him to-day."

"Yeah," Peaceful drawled, "we had dinner together. He's registered here as Dave Stephens—looking for mining properties."

"What did you talk about?" Vaughn snapped.

"About an hour, I should judge," Peaceful replied.

"Don't get funny, Jenkins," Vaughn growled. "I asked you a question."

"You'll get an answer," Peaceful replied coolly, "if I'm called as a witness at the coroner's inquest."

Vaughn looked startled. "Who said anything about an inquest?"

"It's the customary procedure," Peaceful pointed out. "Vaughn, sometimes a good inquest can produce a heap of fresh facts. I suppose you'll report this to Doc Hamilton right off?"

"I'll report the facts," Vaughn snapped. "I don't reckon an inquest is necessary. It's plain as anything that this hombre killed himself. The gun is still in his hand."

Peaceful nodded. "It's your case, Vaughn. I'm going to bed."

23

MURDER!

PEACEFUL left the room, followed by Applejack and the hotel clerk. Men were crowding back into Dawes's room by this time. The clerk followed Applejack and Peaceful downstairs to the lobby where he lighted a lamp, then asked timorously, "Mr. Jenkins, should I have told Deputy Vaughn I have Mr. Stephens's wallet?"

"You keep that wallet in your safe," Peaceful said. "If Vaughn had been on his job he'd have asked if you found anything of the sort. Now keep this under your hat—Dave Stephens's real name was Steve Dawes."

"You don't tell me!"

"He's a brother to that bandit, Louie Dawes, that was killed here a spell back," Peaceful said. "You'll find identification cards in Dawes's wallet. If there's an inquest held this will all come out, of course, and you can tell the truth about the matter. Otherwise I wouldn't say anything to anybody. Now can you let me have a lantern?"

"Got one right under my desk," the clerk replied promptly. He produced it and touched a lighted match to the wick. "What are you intending to do?"

"Applejack and I are going to take a walk around town," Peaceful replied. "I can't sleep after a thing like this. Streets are pretty dark this time of the morning, and a lantern will save us stumbling some."

The clerk looked rather dubious, but he didn't ask any more questions. Applejack and Peaceful made their way outside. Applejack said, "That clerk doesn't exactly believe you, pard."

"I reckon not. But he's got too much sense to get too curious. And he's the type that will keep his mouth shut."

"You don't think it's a matter of suicide, then?"

"Murder," Peaceful said quietly. "The sign is plain."

"I figured it might be, pard. Who did it?"

"I don't know yet. How did Vaughn act when you went to get him?"

"I'd swear he didn't do it. If he did he's sure got steady nerves. I watched him close. He was asleep in his office when I got there. Hey! Where we going with this lantern?"

"Around back of the hotel building. As soon as Vaughn gets away I want to look the ground over under Dawes's window."

They made their way around to the rear of the building. On the second floor a light still burned in Dawes's room. Peaceful extinguished the light of the lantern. "Just in case Vaughn happens to look out," he explained. "He might get to wondering what I was doing down here."

They stood in the shadow of the building, in the alleyway, puffing on cigarettes, talking in lowered voices. Applejack said, "What makes you so sure it was murder?"

"Steve Dawes isn't the type that commits suicide."

"Aside from that?"

"Well, he was in bed, in his nightshirt. Would a fellow that figured to kill himself go to the trouble of getting undressed and in bed? Did you ever hear of a suicide doing that?"

"You're right, pard."

Peaceful continued, "Somebody killed him to get that letter of Louie Dawes's."

"How do you know?"

"I gave Steve that letter to-day. I saw him put it in his wallet. When I looked through his wallet after I found it on the floor the letter wasn't there. It wasn't in any of his pockets, either."

Applejack said grimly, "That puts it squarely up to Randle and some of his gang. Maybe we'd better start down there right now and bust that Spanish Dagger wide open."

"Wait!" Peaceful placed one restraining hand on Applejack's arm. "I've already thought of that, but it wouldn't do any good. If Randle or one of his gang did this they'll have an alibi. Every one of 'em would perjure himself if the case came up in court. We've got to get more proof before we move. Let folks think it's suicide—better yet, let Randle and his crew think that I believe that it's suicide."

"You may have a tough time proving otherwise, pard. There's the bullet hole under Dawes's right cheekbone. His own gun—I reckon it's his own gun—was held in his right hand."

Peaceful said, "I'll give you more facts. A suicide usually shoots himself in the temple. Now here's the clincher. I've known Steve Dawes quite a few years and I happen to know that Steve was left-handed. Would he be likely to shoot himself in the right side of the head?"

Applejack whistled softly. "No wonder you were so sure it was murder!"

Peaceful said suddenly, "Hush!" Applejack fell quiet.

Booted footsteps clumped hollowly along the plank walk. They came nearer. Peaccful and Applejack hugged the shadows back of the hotel. In the dim light they saw a man's form stride along Saddlehorn Street, pass the alley and out of view. After the footsteps had commenced to die away Peaceful said, "That was Vaughn. He's gone to get Doc Hamilton. It'll be fifteen minutes before Hamilton gets dressed and over here. Let's work fast."

Overhead, light still shone from Dawes's

window, but they had to take a chance on anyone glancing out. Swiftly Peaceful relighted the lantern, and the two bent close beneath the window to scrutinize the earth. After a moment Applejack swore disgustedly. "This ground is packed too hard to leave any footprints."

"Here's something," Peaceful said, holding the light closer to the earth. They both stooped to examine two rectangular notches in the earth, placed about two feet apart. The imprint of each notch was deeper on the side closest to the building.

Peaceful said quietly, "Looks to me like somebody had placed a ladder here recently. The earth is too hard to show boot marks, but the ends of a ladder are sharper."

"Wait! Let me have that lantern." Applejack took the lantern and hurried across the alley to the rear of a building that fronted on the next street. He disappeared around the building, but returned inside a minute. "I thought so," he said triumphantly.

"What?"

"I know where the ladder came from. Thought I remembered that a painter and carpenter lived in that house across the alley. I've seen the sign on his house. His ladder is there, standing against the front of his barn. That's where your murderer got a ladder. When he was through he replaced it."

"Good work, Applejack. The picture is coming clearer now. Let's have another look at the earth." They held the lantern closer to the ground. Suddenly Peaceful stooped and picked up something.

"What you got?" Applejack asked.

"A piece of a button."

"Piece of a button?"

Peaceful nodded. "Like a man has on his vest. It's been broken. We'll examine it later."

Further search revealed nothing more. Peaceful put out the lantern and they returned to the hotel lobby. The lantern was left under the clerk's desk. Voices drifted faintly down from the second floor, one of them belonging to the clerk. Peaceful and Applejack made their way softly up the staircase, turned into the narrow corridor where their own rooms were located, and slipped into Peaceful's room without being seen by any of the men in Dawes's room.

Once inside his room, Peaceful lighted his lamp and he and Applejack examined the broken bit of button they'd found. It was brown in colour, manufactured from bone, of the type that had four holes for thread to pass through. The button had split off across one of the holes. Peaceful said, "That's a fresh break all right. Too clean to have been laying on the ground very long. Probably the thread in the three holes left is holding the rest of this button to some hombre's vest."

Applejack didn't say anything. They rolled cigarettes, puffing in silence, and sat on Peaceful's bed to think it over. Finally Peaceful stirred. "I reckon I've got it doped out, pard."

"You mean who did it?"

"How it was done. It looks this way to me. Randle or one of his gang did it. They wanted that letter I gave Steve. And here's how: the murderer got that ladder and climbed up to Steve's window after Steve was asleep, pushed up the window, and then crawled into the room. His first move was to locate Steve's gun after he got into the room. Nowadays a heap of fellers sleep with a gun under their pillow. I happen to know Steve did that. Once the murderer had the gun he'd feel freer to search. It probably wouldn't be any trick for him to slip the gun from under the pillow while Steve slept. Right so far?"

"Right." Applejack nodded interestedly.

"So," Peaceful continued, "after getting the gun he starts going through Steve's pockets. He finds the wallet and gets the letter out. Probably had to scratch a match to see what he was doing. I noticed a burned matchstick on the floor, though Steve might have dropped that himself. About that time Steve suddenly wakes up. He sits up in bed. Remember—the blankets were back part way from his chest as he lay there. The murderer may have been recognized by Steve. We don't know that, of course. Anyway, when Steve woke up the killer plugged him with Steve's gun. Steve fell back on the pillow, and the murderer put the gun in Steve's hand to make it look like suicide. Then he went out the window again, closed the window after him, climbed back down the ladder, and returned the ladder to where you found it."

"By cripes, pard!" Applejack said enthusiastically. "You've hit it! But who is the killer?"

"The hombre who broke the button off his vest climbing down the ladder. I figure he was hurrying. The button caught on one of the rungs; there was a weak spot where one hole had been drilled, and this piece we found snapped off. Ordinarily that wouldn't happen to a feller, but remember the murderer was climbing down fast and hugging the ladder close, so nobody would be likely to notice him should they pass the alleyway."

"Pard, you've doped it out plumb elegant. Now all you've got to do is find a hombre with part of a button dangling from his vest. Or maybe it wouldn't dangle; maybe the rest would come loose."

"Whatever happens"—Peaceful scowled—"I'll find the scut."

"And when you do?"

Peaceful said, "Steve Dawes was a friend of mine. He hired me to do a job down here." Now a grimmer tone entered the words. "Finding Steve's murderer and settling with him has become part of that job. And that settling will have to be done with hot lead, I reckon."

24

"MAKE YOUR PLAY!"

DOC HAMILTON, in his official capacity of town coroner, decided an inquest should be held. The time set was for ten o'clock, the morning following the discovery of Steve Dawes's body, and the inquest was staged at Hamilton's office, the size of which prevented a crowd of the curious from attending. As nothing had been produced to prove otherwise, it was practically assumed at the beginning that the verdict from the jury of six would be suicide. More than anything else the inquiry was a matter of form to satisfy Hamilton's sense of what was just and legal.

Peaceful and Applejack were called and told how they'd heard a shot and had awakened the hotel clerk to investigate. Next Deputy Vaughn testified and added but little to what Peaceful and Applejack had related, beyond stating definitely that in his opinion it was a clear case of suicide. The hotel clerk's testimony regarding the closed window to augment the suicide idea. In his testimony, however, the clerk brought out that the name of the deceased was, in reality, Steve Dawes and that Dawes was a friend of Peaceful's.

Doc Hamilton called on Peaceful for further testimony. Was this true? It was. Did Peaceful have any idea what had brought Dawes to Spanish Wells?

Peaceful said quietly, "Steve was a brother of that bandit, Louie Dawes. Steve may have come here to see what he could learn of Louie's death."

This caused some small stir in the room. Vaughn frowned and leaned forward eagerly as Hamilton put his next question: "Did you send for Dawes to come here?"

Peaceful said, "No. I had no idea he was coming, nor that he was here, until I ran into him on the hotel porch." There was no doubting the sincerity in Peaceful's tones. Vaughn appeared relieved at the answer, a fact that Peaceful didn't fail to note.

Hamilton asked next, "Have you any idea of why Dawes should commit suicide?"

"Not the slightest," Peaceful replied.

"Was this, in your opinion, suicide?"

Peaceful said truthfully, "It sure looked like suicide. Dawes held his own thirty-two in his hand. I couldn't say definitely, however, without making a thorough investigation. I haven't been asked to do that. Deputy Vaughn is in charge of the case."

At this point Vaughn growled, "I made all the investigation necessary. It was suicide. There ain't no doubt."

Hamilton said icily, "I'm not questioning you at present, Deputy Vaughn." Then to Peaceful, "Suppose you were asked to make an investigation, do you think you could turn up any more evidence than has already been found?"

Again Peaceful answered truthfully, "I don't know."

That settled it. The jury was taken to the hotel to view Dawes's body, which still lay as it had been found, then once more returned to the doctor's house. It took but a short time for the six men to arrive at a verdict of suicide. Vaughn seemed to breathe easier. Arrangements were made for the local undertaker to ship the body to Surcingle, where it would lay until definite instructions had been had from Dawes's home in Montana. The inquiry was over.

On the way back from the inquest Peaceful and Applejack stopped at the Demijohn a minute. Peaceful joined Applejack in a bottle of beer, then announced he was going to drift across the street to visit Sam Purdy's General Store a minute. "I suppose you'll be here for a spell," Peaceful added.

Applejack turned gravely to Johnny. "How many bottles of beer you got cooling, Johnny?"

Johnny said, "Three or four cases anyway."

Applejack turned back to Peaceful. "I'll be here," he said.

Peaceful smiled and left the saloon. Crossing the street, he entered the store and found Willie Horton in charge. Sam Purdy was out somewhere. Peaceful said, "Willie, a spell back you said you'd like to help me with my detecting. Still feeling the same way?"

"Gosh, yes, Marshal Jenkins."

"And you can keep your mouth shut?"

"I wouldn't say a peep to nobody," the boy said earnestly.

"Good, Willie. I trust you. Now there's just a slim chance you may be able to help me. It's a slim chance, as I say, but I can't afford to overlook any bets."

Willie broke in, flushing with pride at being an assistant, "Anything you say, Marshal Jenkins. You want somebody shadowed?"

"It's simpler than that, Willie. I want you to keep an eye out for folks buying buttons."

"Buttons?" blankly. "What kind of buttons?"

"Like folks wear on their clothes. Vest buttons I'm interested in. Sam Purdy stocks buttons, doesn't he?"

"Sure. We got all kinds of buttons here, pants buttons, coat buttons, vest buttons, dress buttons, shirt buttons—well, we got a complete stock. Much completer than Cal Perkins's General Store. Folks always come here for their buttons."

"Anybody come in for buttons this morning?"

Willie tried to remember. "Sure, but I can't say who. We sell buttons every day. Mr. Purdy probably sold some too."

Peaceful drew from his pocket the piece of button that he had found the night before. "There's a slim chance, Willie," he said, "that some hombre may come here trying to match this piece of button with a new one. If he does will you let me know?"

Willie examined the bit of broken bone. He frowned. Suddenly his face lighted. "Somebody already did, first thing this morning."

Peaceful's heart leaped. "Who was it?"

"Flora Fanning."

"Who's Flora Fanning?"

"One of the girls that works in the Spanish Dagger. She's—she's—" Willie blushed. "Well, she's sort of Scott Heffner's sweetie, kind of, if you know what I mean."

"I reckon I do," Peaceful said dryly. "You're sure it was this same kind of a button she was after?"

Willie nodded. "I remember perfectly now. First I looked among the ladies' buttons, but I couldn't find anything of this kind. Then I looked in the men's stock and I found her a right good match."

"You're *sure* it was a button like this she wanted?"

264

Willie said, "Wait a minute." He crossed the big room and opened a showcase displaying buttons on cards. He searched on the bottom of the case, then held up for Peaceful's inspection a second piece of broken button. "Here's what she brought in to be matched. When she left I just tossed it into the case, thinking she might come back later and claim I didn't sell her a good match. Now here's what I sold her. See? Practically the same thing."

But Peaceful wasn't listening now. He had snatched the piece of button from Willie's fingers and was engaged in matching it against the broken bit he had found the previous night.

The two pieces fitted perfectly.

Peaceful looked up, smiling. "I'm going to keep this, Willie. You've already done a good piece of work. You'll learn why later. Meanwhile, keep your eyes peeled, and if you learn anything you think I might be interested in let me know." He drew a silver dollar from his pocket and placed it on the case. "A good detective deserves to be paid."

"Gee, golly! Thanks, Marshal Jenkins."

On his way out of the store Peaceful nearly collided with Sam Purdy. Purdy said, "Mornin', Peaceful. You're certain raisin' hell with the Spanish Dagger."

"What do you mean?"

"I just come from the hotel. There's four of

Randle's gamblers there waiting for the stage to Surcingle. They're quitting. Seems you and Applejack have cramped their style. And that new songbird of Randle's didn't please the crowd near so much as Miss Drake. I reckon Randle's business is due for a falling off right soon."

"I hope so," Peaceful said and brushed past to the street. Across the road, seated on the Demijohn porch with a bottle of beer, sat Applejack. As Peaceful came up Applejack said, "You look plumb pleased about something."

"I am. I've just found that other piece of button."

"T'hell you say! That's fast work. Tell it."

Peaceful related briefly how he had found the missing bit of broken button.

"I'll be damned!" Applejack said. "What's your next move?"

"I'm aiming to visit the Spanish Dagger and talk to this Flora Fanning girl. If I find she really intended the button for Heffner's vest—well, I'm going after Scott Heffner."

"Now's a good time to talk to the Fanning gal. Heffner and Randle just left the Spanish Dagger on their way to the hotel. It seems a lot of Randle's tinhorns quit him. I suppose he and Heffner are going to try and persuade them to stay."

"Yeah, I heard about that. Well, I'll go see that girl."

"Want I should come with you?"

"It won't be necessary."

Peaceful crossed the street and entered the Spanish Dagger. The big room was empty of customers. There weren't so many covered games in the place as formerly. Two bartenders stood behind the bar, polishing glasses and refilling empty bottles from a small keg. The bartender named Mike glanced up and saw Peaceful. He forced a smile. "What's yours, Marshal?"

"There's a girl working here named Flora Fanning."

"Is there? Well, ain't that news!"

Peaceful snapped, "There'll be more news than that if you get lippy, Mike—and said news will be in the obituary column."

Mike said sullenly, "What you want with Flora?"

"I want to talk to her."

"You ain't got nothing on her. She's a good girl."

"I haven't said she wasn't. Get her down here."

Mike shrugged. Then he turned to the other bartender. A signal, unseen by Peaceful, passed between them. "Give Flora a hail, Joe."

Joe rounded the end of the bar and called up to the balcony. "Hey, Flora!" After a moment a door opened up there and a strident female voice called down, "Whatcherwant?" Joe replied, "There's a gent down here to see you—I mean the town marshal." Silence, then the girl's voice, reluctantly, "What for?" Joe replied, "He'll tell you when you get here." Another silence, then, "All right, I'll be down in a minute." Joe turned to Peaceful. "She'll be down pronto."

Peaceful said thanks. Joe nodded and instead of returning to his place behind the bar he picked up a case of empty beer bottles, opened the rear door of the building, and stepped out to the alley.

Mike said genially, "Have a drink on the house, Marshal?"

"Much obliged—no." He looked around. Joe was engaged in carrying out a second case of empties.

Peaceful waited five minutes. Just as he was commencing to wonder when Joe was going to return for another case of empties he heard a step on the staircase leading from the balcony, and Flora Fanning hove into view. The girl wore a cheap calico wrapper; in the harsh light of day her face looked white and lined, though Peaceful could see she had just applied fresh rouge to her cheeks. Her hair had been dyed a vivid auburn. She left the stairs and came around to the other side of Peaceful, causing him to face the front of the building.

"You're Flora Fanning?" Peaceful said.

"What about it?" the girl said defiantly. "You haven't got anything on me, lawman. I don't roll drunks. I'm an honest working girl. I know too much to tangle with the law. What do you want, anyway?"

Peaceful said, "You went to Purdy's General Store this morning to buy a button."

The girl stared uncomprehending. "So I bought a button," she said, somewhat puzzled. "It's no crime." Peaceful could see she looked relieved, as though fearing to be questioned on some other shady matter. "Sure I bought a button. What about it?"

Back of him Peaceful could hear Joe removing cases of empty bottles again. Those cases must be heavy, judging from the way the man was panting.

"You sewed that button on Heffner's vest?" Peaceful asked.

"Sure. Why not?" the girl replied readily. A simpering smile crossed her thin lips. "Scott and me's good friends. I'd sew on a button for him any time."

"Particularly if he asked you, eh?" Peaceful smiled.

"Scott don't have to ask me," the girl bragged. "I do things for him 'thout being asked. I happened to see the vest in his room with the broken button on it and I took care of the matter."

"Do you know how he broke that button?"

The girl shrugged. "How should I know how buttons get busted? Maybe he drank too much. I know I didn't hear him come up to his room last night."

"That's enough, Flora," a new voice broke in

269

harshly. "Go on up to your room." Instantly the girl headed for the balcony.

Peaceful turned to see that Scott Heffner, with Randle at his back, had entered softly by the rear door. Peaceful smiled lazily. Now he knew why Joe had been breathing so heavily: Joe had run out the back way to get Heffner.

Peaceful said, "Howdy, Heffner. I reckon the jig is up. We found a piece of button under Dawes's window last night. It matches the broken piece Flora had to replace this morning."

"I don't know what you're talking about, Jenkins," Heffner said, backing away a trifle.

Randle said, "What you hinting at, Jenkins?" He left Heffner's side and came around to Peaceful's left. Now Peaceful was between the two. Neither had made a move toward guns, however. Unseen by Peaceful, the two bartenders had by now gone to watch the front entrance.

"I'm not hinting," Peaceful said quietly. "I'm stating a fact. I've got all the proof I need to convict. Heffner, you murdered Steve Dawes. I'm arresting you! Are you coming peaceful, or do you want it the other way?"

Heffner backed another step, eyes hard on Peaceful's. This was a show down? He realized he was cornered at last. His hands commenced to edge slowly toward the guns at his hips.

He backed still another step; then his voice came hoarsely, decisively, "All right, Jenkins. I killed him! But you'll never take me alive. It's up to you, Texas man. Make your play!"

As the words left his lips his clenched fingers closed suddenly on the twin gun butts!

25

FAST GUNWORK

IT was Heffner's twin weapons against Peaceful's single Colt forty-five!

Peaceful's right hand darted down—came up—stopped in a savage burst of smoke and white fire, the detonation of the heavy weapon shaking the rafters of the building. Instantly he knew he'd missed, but that single swift shot, coming even before Heffner's gun barrels had cleared leather, momentarily disconcerted the gunman's aim when he triggered his first shot.

Peaceful heard the slug thud into the wooden bar at his back, even as he leaped to one side, colliding with Hugo Randle, who was standing close, undecided whether to draw or not. Randle, thrown off balance, staggered back, his arms flying into the air.

With his left hand Peaceful reached out and jerked the six-shooter from Randle's holster; at the same moment he thumbed another shot from his own weapon. The report blended with that of Heffner's left-hand gun. Again Heffner had missed, but Peaceful saw him sway back as a leaden slug ripped across the gunman's ribs.

Upstairs on the balcony a girl screamed suddenly. There were loud female voices. Hugo Randle had thrown himself flat on the floor to get out of range of the flying bullets. Heffner fired again, missed aim again. He cursed hoarsely and set himself for the next shot.

By this time Peaceful's swift steps had carried him out to the centre of the room. He threw one swift shot from Randle's weapon in his left hand, followed it with another shot from his own weapon. Two bullets flew harmlessly from Heffner's six-shooters. The man was already falling; he broke into a stumbling run; then his legs seemed to turn to jelly and he fell awkwardly in a clumsy heap on the floor, convulsive muscular action triggering still another shot that ripped into the baseboard across the room, even after he had pitched to the floor. A long breath of air was expelled from his lungs; then he was quiet.

The room was swimming with powder smoke. On the balcony above a girl was sobbing. There came a sudden commotion at the front entrance, and Applejack Peters rushed in, drawn six-shooter in one hand, a half-filled bottle of beer in the other. The two bartenders, Joe and Mike, retreated swiftly before Applejack's menacing six-shooter. Applejack's eyes bulged as he gazed around the room. Hugo Randle was just climbing from the floor, white and shaken.

"You hurt, pard?" Applejack exclaimed.

"Not any," Peaceful replied calmly.

"I was sitting on the porch enjoying my beer," Applejack said, "when I heard the shots. How in the devil did Randle and Heffner—?"

"They came around by the rear," Peaceful interrupted. "That's why you didn't see 'em. It was Heffner killed Dawes. He admitted it."

Applejack set the half-filled beer bottle on the bar and went to examine the gunman on the floor. After a moment he glanced up at Peaceful and nodded. "Dead as a doornail—Hey! What you doing with two guns?"

Peaceful still held his own weapon and Randle's. Peaceful said, "I had to borrow Randle's hawgleg to make sure he wouldn't get any ideas." He turned to Randle now. "You got a hankering to continue this fight, Randle?"

Randle shook his head, his usually dark features ashen. "It's not my fight," he said nervously. "If Heffner killed Steve Dawes that's the first I've heard of it. It was a surprise to me—"

Peaceful said, "You can't lie out of it, Randle. If I'm not sadly mistaken you ordered the killing."

"I ordered the killing? You're crazy, Jenkins! Why should I want Dawes killed?"

"To get a certain letter his brother wrote him. It's probably in your pocket right now, or in Heffner's, unless you've already destroyed it, which you probably have. Much good may it do you; I got all the information I wanted from it."

"I still think you're crazy," Randle said unconvincingly, then changed the subject. "You aiming to keep my six-shooter?"

Peaceful smiled thinly. "On the contrary, Randle. I'm much obliged for the loan of your weapon. Reckon I owe you a ca'tridge though." He slipped his own weapon into holster, then plugged out the empty shell in Randle's gun. Picking a cartridge from his belt, he slipped it into the empty chamber, closed the loading gate, and handed the weapon back to Randle. "I'm sure obliged," he said dryly.

Randle growled something unintelligible under his breath and slammed the weapon angrily into his holster. By this time a crowd of curious men had poured into the Spanish Dagger. Deputy Herb Vaughn suddenly came barging in, exclaiming, "What in hell is going on here?" He paused, eyes widening, "Kerist! Scott Heffner! Who killed him?"

"I did, Vaughn," Peaceful said, level-voiced. "You'd better tell Doc Hamilton that his coroner's jury can reverse its verdict. Heffner admitted killing Steve Dawes. I tried to arrest him, but he preferred to fight. There's your killer, Vaughn— in case you didn't already know it."

"Hell! How should I know it?" Vaughn growled, but his eyes didn't meet Peaceful's.

"Oh, cripes!" Peaceful said disgustedly. "Come on, Applejack, let's get out of here."

They turned and shouldered their way through the crowd of curious men who had streamed into the big room.

Once Peaceful and his pardner had departed Hugo Randle seemed to recover his confidence and started giving orders. He spoke to the crowd: "All right, you hombres, there's nothing more to be seen. Clear out!" Then to his bartenders, "Joe, you and Mike throw a tarpaulin over Heffner's body; then one of you go down to the undertaker's and tell him that there's some more business for him. And, Mike, before you leave, for Gawd's sake, tell that girl up there to cut out her caterwauling. There's nothing gets on my nerves like a woman blubbering and snivelling around the place. Tell her I'll buy her a complete outfit of widow's weeds if she ain't found herself another soft guy inside a week." The thought seemed to put Randle in good humour. "These women," he chuckled to Herb Vaughn, "they can cry all over the place, but buy 'em a trinket and they forget all their troubles. I'll lay you two to one, Herb, that by to-night Flora has her hooks in some new range Johnny."

Vaughn shook his head troubledly. "You're sure taking Scott's death easy," he reprimanded. "I don't see how you can do it, Hugo. I thought a heap of Scott."

276

"Sure, I did too," Randle replied, "but there's no use crying over spilt milk—not with cows all over the range. Hell! I paid Scott good money. He knew the chances he run when he accepted my pay. He gambled and lost, so what the hell!"

Vaughn said stubbornly, "What we got out of that letter, Hugo, wasn't worth it."

"How was I to know?" Randle said testily. "I just had to see that letter. Knowing only Tracy's name was mentioned has relieved my mind a lot. And yours, too, I'm betting."

By this time the room had cleared. Heffner's body lay covered on the floor. The sobbing on the balcony above had ceased.

Though there was no one near, Vaughn lowered his voice. "Did Scott really admit to killing Steve Dawes?"

Randle nodded. "Yeah. The damned fool got tough and figured he could beat Jenkins to the shot. I still don't know why he didn't. He had his hands on his guns before Jenkins even started his draw. Then Jenkins seemed to sort of explode into action. Damn nigh knocked me down, grabbed my gun, and moved so fast around this room Scott couldn't get set for a decent shot. Oh well"—philosophically—"the woods are full of good gunmen. I'll get a line on somebody to take Scott's place. It might be a good idea to get three or four lead slingers while I'm at it. We've been whittled down some, with Nick

Corvall, Cubera, and Jake Tracy out of the way."

"Speaking of Tracy"—Vaughn scowled—"I was talking to Doc Hamilton a spell back. He thinks he can pull Jake through. Jake's recovered consciousness."

"Has he talked any?" Randle asked sharply.

Vaughn shook his head.

"He's able to talk some, but Doc wanted him kept quiet to-day. He said Tracy might be strong enough to have a visitor this evening some-time—"

"I don't like that a-tall," Randle cut in. "Jake's all right so long as things are coming his way, but put pressure on him and he might crack. Herb, you've got to keep a good watch to see what's going on every minute, or we'll both be in the soup. If Jenkins ever got Jake to talking, Jake would spill his guts to save his own hide."

"Well, you got any ideas as to how we can stop it?" Vaughn asked nervously.

"I've been thinking about that, Herb. We've got to stop Jenkins. Once we get Jenkins out of the way we can handle his pard easier, but Jenkins comes first. Now listen close: nobody but me and Jenkins actually heard Heffner admit to killing Dawes. I can deny that Heffner ever made such an admission. That puts only Jenkins's word against mine."

"Yeah, but"—Vaughn looked dubious—"I'm afraid folks will be li'ble to take Jenkins's word."

"Not if we put Jenkins out of the way. Look, Herb, you're the deputy sheriff here. Jenkins is town marshal. A deputy sheriff outranks in authority a town marshal any time. So you're going to arrest Jenkins for the murder of Scott Heffner. I'll swear that Jenkins came in here and plugged Scott without giving Scott a chance to draw his guns. So get busy and arrest Jenkins."

"You're crazy, Hugo! Have you blowed your top complete? How long do you think that I could keep Jenkins in gaol?"

"Long enough."

Vaughn paused, staring, then asked slowly, "What do you mean by that?"

"I'll explain. As deputy sheriff you carry more authority than a town marshal. Correct?"

"Correct. I haven't said I couldn't make an arrest, but—"

"All right. You make the arrest. What happens."

"We-ell, Jenkins will probably get bail."

"Yes, but when you make the arrest you disarm him. He won't buck your authority on that point. While he's waiting in gaol for his bail an accident happens to him. In short, he gets shot while trying to escape. That's the story you tell, anyway."

"Oh no, Hugo, I don't run a risk like that!"

"Why not? You'll be within your legal rights. Nobody can prove otherwise. It's our only chance, Herb. Jenkins has to be rubbed out."

"I don't like it."

"You fool!" Randle said harshly. "I don't either, but it's our only chance. If you're too yellow I'll do the actual shooting myself once you get him, unarmed, in a cell. But you've got to make the arrest. Now get going!"

Vaughn protested some more, but in the end he weakened and gave in. The two men talked earnestly for several minutes; then the deputy departed. As he left a triumphant smile crossed Randle's dark features. He drew out a long, thin black cigar, lighted it, and puffed the smoke airily toward the ceiling. He chuckled to himself, "They may stop Hugo Randle now and then, but he always gets going again. I'm just too sharp for these law fellers, I reckon; I just outsmart 'em. That's what it is to have brains."

26

SHOOTING OFF EVIDENCE

PEACEFUL and Applejack were in the middle of their noonday meal—though it was after one o'clock—at the Bon-Ton Restaurant, when Peaceful happened to glance out of the window. Instantly he hastily bolted his coffee and slid from his stool at the counter.

Applejack looked up in surprise. "What bit you? You jumped like a chigger had reached a vital spot in your carcass."

Peaceful grinned. "Judith and Tarp Thompson just loped past. I wanted to see Tarp about something."

Applejack grunted sceptically. "Uh-huh, you're probably aiming to persuade Tarp to run away to sea with you, I reckon. Don't forget to say hello to Judith when you catch up to 'em. It wouldn't be polite to ignore her while you're talking to Tarp."

"You go to hell," Peaceful said good-naturedly and started toward the door. He heard Applejack's derisive snicker as he left.

A block away Peaceful saw Judith and Tarp

directing their ponies toward the hitch rail of the Spanish Wells Hotel. He hurried his steps and got there just as they were dismounting.

"Hi-yuh, folks," he greeted, smiling. "What brings you to town?"

"Blow me down if it ain't the town marshall," Tarp chuckled.

"Hello, Peaceful." Judith smiled. "We didn't expect to see you."

Tarp snorted, "I'll be a salty son of a sea cook if that shouldn't go down in the log as a soo-blime exaggeration."

Judith coloured. "Well, naturally, we expected to see you, Peaceful, but not so soon. Tarp, you can say the darnedest things!"

"Yessum, Judy," Tarp said lamely. "What we meant was we didn't expect to see you the instant we dropped anchor, Peaceful."

"So long as I see you"—Peaceful laughed, and he was looking directly at Judith—"that's what counts. But what brings you in?"

They were standing on the sidewalk by this time. Judith explained, "One of our boys—Lennie Owen—came in town yesterday for the mail. While he was here Lennie heard there was a man staying at the hotel looking for mining properties. Dad has always thought there was silver to be found in the hills back of us. We thought we might get this mining man interested and lease to him. You see, we've got to get some money in, and we'd lease cheap. Do you happen to know who the man is, Peaceful?"

"Yes, I knew him," Peaceful said soberly, "though he didn't really come here for the purpose of looking for mining property. At any rate, it doesn't matter. He was murdered last night. I—well, I apprehended his murderer this morning."

"How horrible!" Judith exclaimed. Peaceful related briefly what had happened. The girl paled slightly as she listened.

Tarp said, "That was a fast bit of action, Peaceful, but shootin's too good for such swabs. They should be keelhauled and strung up to the yardarm!"

Judith said ruefully, "Well, we've had our ride for nothing, I guess."

"Let's hope it's not that bad." Peaceful smiled. "Why don't you and Tarp stay over and eat supper with me? My duties sort of keep me around town most of the time, but if you'll wait I'll ride back to the ranch with you to-night. . . . I see you're still riding the pony. Decided to keep him yet?"

"I'm not sure." Judith smiled.

Tarp said, "Well, Judy, you and Peaceful decide what you're going to do. I miss my sea air. Throat gets mighty parched in this desert atmosphere. Reckon I'll go in the hotel bar and wet my whistle." He departed in the direction of the building.

"I wanted to talk to your father, anyway, when

I got a chance," Peaceful continued. "This Steve Dawes that was killed said he was going to make good your dad's loss. Of course he's dead now, but I think Jabez could collect from the estate."

"I don't think Dad would want that," Judith said promptly. "After all, Steve Dawes wasn't responsible for what his brother Louie did. However, it might be a good idea for you to talk to Dad. I think we'll wait and have supper with you, Peaceful."

Peaceful said gravely, "That's a good idea. There'll be a new moon to-night, I think. It'll give you a chance to see how that pony acts before you decide to accept him. You know, some ponies are mighty susceptible to new moons and get loco. It would be best if I was along."

"It might be at that." Judith smiled.

"And," Peaceful continued, "we could sort of send Tarp on ahead, maybe; in case the pony ran away with you, Tarp could be there to stop him."

Judith laughed, flushing prettily. "You certainly do have original ideas—" She broke off suddenly, her face sobering. "Here comes Deputy Vaughn. He looks as though he were coming to see you."

Peaceful turned and saw Herb Vaughn just coming up behind him. Vaughn looked nervous; he already had one hand on his gun butt. Peaceful said, "You want to see me, Vaughn?"

Vaughn said, "Howdy, Miss Judy," and then

faced Peaceful. "I reckon I'm going to have to put you under arrest, Jenkins," he said somewhat apologetically. "I hope you're not going to make trouble."

Peaceful said quietly, "What's the charge, Vaughn?"

"Murder. You killed Scott Heffner."

Peaceful smiled coolly. "That was a fair fight. Heffner killed Steve Dawes—"

"There's no proof of that," Vaughn said.

"He admitted it to me," Peaceful pointed out.

"Nobody else heard it," Vaughn said. "Now are you coming or ain't you? I don't want trouble. You can probably get bail until this matter is settled, but I've got to do my duty as I see it. I was going to let the matter drop, but several citizens insisted I make this arrest. I hope you won't hold it against me." Vaughn was growing more nervous as he talked under Peaceful's penetrating gaze. Small dots of perspiration stood out on the deputy's forehead.

"But look here, Deputy Vaughn"—Judith's voice was almost a wail—"you can't arrest Peaceful. He's a law officer himself. He's the town marshal."

"A deputy sheriff's authority outranks a town marshal's, miss," Vaughn said. "Jenkins will admit that himself."

"That's right, Judith"—Peaceful smiled— "but—it doesn't outrank this." Putting one hand in his pocket, he drew out a gold badge and held it before the astonished deputy's gaze. "Deputy Vaughn will admit that himself," Peaceful paraphrased Vaughn's words of a minute before.

Vaughn's eyes widened as he gazed at the badge in Peaceful's hand. Then he seemed to wilt. "You—you a deputy United States marshal?" he stammered.

Peaceful nodded. "Can't believe your eyes, can you, Vaughn? Well, you ready to give up this idea of arresting me? Do you admit that my authority is the stronger?"

"Cripes, yes," Vaughn mumbled, commencing to back away. "Forget it, Jenkins. You outrank me." He turned so fast he stumbled and almost broke into a run as he headed hurriedly off in the direction of the Spanish Dagger.

Peaceful looked after the man, chuckling: "And that's sure something when you outrank a man like Vaughn." He grinned. "He's pretty rank himself."

"Peaceful," Judith accused, "you never told me you were a deputy United States marshal."

"I've been going to tell you ever since I knew you"—Peaceful smiled—"along with some other things I want to tell you."

"Save them for later," Judith said hastily.

Peaceful went on, "When Steve Dawes had me come down here to investigate his brother's death he thought it might be well for me to have legal authority. He fixed it up with the United States marshal for this district. I didn't let it be known when I arrived here. Didn't know what I might run into. Thought it best to see what I could learn as a private citizen first."

They talked a few minutes longer before Peaceful escorted her into the hotel, after promising to come back later in the afternoon and take her and Tarp to supper.

Ten minutes later Peaceful walked into the Demijohn, wearing the gold badge on his vest. Applejack put down his glass of beer and said, "Decided to come into the open, eh, pard?"

Johnny and two or three other customers in the place stared at Peaceful's gold badge; then the customers hurried out to spread the news. Johnny said shrewdly, "I kind of had you figured as being more important than you acted."

Peaceful told them what had happened, then unpinned the townmarshal's badge from his vest and passed it over to Applejack. "Here, you're promoted." He smiled. "I reckon my authority is good enough to make you town marshal, pard."

"Your authority is good enough to tear this town wide open right now," Applejack snorted. "The idea of you being arrested for Heffner's murder. They probably figured to get you into a cell and then shoot you for an attempted escape or some such stunt. The sidewinders! When you going to close down on 'em, pard? You probably got Randle worried sick right this minute, to say nothing of that louse Vaughn."

"I'll close down right soon," Peaceful said quietly. I've got nearly all the evidence I need, but there's one or two things I want to know first."

"How about a beer?" Applejack said.

"It's a good idea." Peaceful grinned. "We'll drift down later and see how the gang in the Spanish Dagger is taking the news."

But by the time they reached the Spanish Dagger there was nothing to be seen of Hugo Randle. Nobody in the place knew where he was, or so they claimed. Passing Vaughn's office, they saw the deputy seated at his desk, looking worried.

The afternoon passed swiftly. At sundown Peaceful met Judith and Tarp at the hotel and took them into the dining room for supper. Tarp insisted on ordering salt beef and hardtack and fish for his supper—which he knew the hotel didn't have—and then grumbled at the lack of "seagoin' rations." He finally contented himself with a thick juicy steak instead.

They were just finishing supper when Applejack entered the dining room and came directly to their table.

"What is it, pard?" Peaceful asked.

"Doc Hamilton wants you to come right over to his place. Jake Tracy is conscious and wants to see you. I've got a hunch that Tracy is ready to do some talking to save his own skin."

Peaceful rose and excused himself with a "Take care of Judith until I return, Tarp. I don't reckon to be too long."

It was dark when Peaceful and Applejack stepped out to the street. They turned the corner at Saddlehorn Street and swiftly walked the block's distance to Doc Hamilton's house, which stood on the corner of Trail Street and Saddlehorn. The doctor's wife let them in and showed the way to the room where Jake Tracy lay in bed. Doc Hamilton sat at the bedside. A lighted oil lamp, covered with a shade, stood on a table near by. The doctor rose as the two men entered. The bed stood next to a window in the side wall.

Tracy's face was almost as white as the pillow beneath his head. One white hand plucked feebly at the bedspread. He spoke weakly as Peaceful entered. "Hello, Jenkins."

Peaceful sat on the side of the bed. "Doc says you want to see me, Tracy."

"Yeah . . . got a few things on my mind. . . . Figure mebbe you'll give . . . me a chance . . . when I get out . . . bed."

"I'll do what I can for you, of course," Peaceful said. "You're wise to make a clean breast of things. Randle is back of everything that's happened here, I suppose."

"Yeah," Tracy said, weak-voiced, "but Uhlmann is . . . back of him and—"

Peaceful saw the livid hole appear in Tracy's face, under one eye, even before he heard the sharp report of the rifle. Tracy gave one agonized moan and died. Peaceful leaped to his feet. Back in the house, the doctor's wife called sharply to see what was wrong. Hamilton swore with excitement. Applejack snapped, "By God! They tried to get you, pard!"

"I don't reckon so," Peaceful said calmly, noting the angle at which the bullet had entered and the small hole in the windowpane, near the top. "That shot was meant for Jake Tracy. Someone was just shooting off evidence. I sat too far over to be in line for a clean shot, or I might have got mine too. C'mon, pard!"

With Applejack close behind, Peaceful rushed outside, while Doc Hamilton hurried to quiet his wife's fears.

27

CAUGHT RED-HANDED

IN the middle of Saddlehorn Street, Peaceful and his pardner paused, hoping to hear running footsteps, but they were too late. Applejack said, "I don't reckon that scut—whoever he is—would stick around after firing that shot."

"Not if he was as smart as I figure him to be," Peaceful said. "At the same time, he wouldn't want to appear on Main Street carrying a rifle. I figure it was a rifle did the work, don't you?"

"No doubt. Too sharp for a six-shooter."

They stood looking at Doc Hamilton's house on the corner, considering the matter. Three windows showed along the side of the house. The first, nearest Trail Street, was dark. The third showed a light from behind a shade. It was the middle window beyond which the dead body of Jake Tracy was situated.

Applejack said, "I don't see how the devil anybody could see to plug Tracy from the street. I can't even see the bed from here."

"I don't figure it was done from street level,"

Peaceful said. "Remember that hole in the windowpane was fairly high up."

He glanced around. On the corner across from Hamilton's house, on the same side of the street, a big cottonwood tree spread its branches wide. Peaceful turned and strode across the street to stand beneath the tree. Reaching up to one of the lower boughs, he exerted the strength of his muscular arms and hauled himself up to a crotch located between two big limbs. A sudden exclamation of triumph left his lips.

Applejack, standing below, asked, "What's up, pard?"

"I am," Peaceful replied. "Up here, where the rifleman fired from. Yep, this is the spot—no doubt of it. I figured it must be something like this after I looked at the angle between the hole in the windowpane and the wound in Tracy's head. Gosh, there's even a convenient bough here where a man could rest his rifle barrel. I can see right into Tracy's room; even with that lamp in there shaded it's quite plain. Yes, from here I could draw a bead on Tracy's head if I had to."

Below Applejack was scratching matches and examining the earth. Peaceful dropped down beside him. Applejack said, "Here's sign where a hombre dropped out of the tree. I reckon he was waiting up here quite a spell, maybe. Long enough to smoke a cigarette, leastwise. Here's a dead butt, with one end still moist."

"Good going, pard. Likely enough the killer ran for the alley that runs back of Main Street. From there he could duck into any one of a number of buildings without appearing on Main. Well, there's no use of looking for more sign now. That's just wasting time. We'll have to move fast."

"In what direction, Peaceful?"

"Anyway you look at it, that was dang fine shooting. Who's the best rifle shot you've heard of around here?"

"Deputy Herb Vaughn," Applejack said promptly. "I've heard a heap of folks tell about how Vaughn could shoot rings around anybody in these parts with his thirty-thirty Winchester."

Peaceful nodded. "Deputy Herb Vaughn is nominated for arrest," he said grimly. "You go get him, pard. Hold him until I see you again. We'll grill him plenty."

"I'll do it with pleasure. Where you heading?"

"Tracy implicated Fletcher Uhlmann. I'm going to find Uhlmann and put some pressure on him. Let's hurry!"

They walked swiftly along Saddlehorn Street. Ahead the lights of Main showed against the darkness. As they neared the corner Applejack said, "I'll try the Spanish Dagger first, then Vaughn's office, if he's not there."

They separated, with Peaceful swinging over toward the Spanish Wells Hotel, where he saw

Tarp Thompson, standing in the broad light of the hotel window, on the sidewalk. Tarp spied Peaceful hurrying toward him. "Where away, cowboy?" he hailed.

"What you doing out here?" Peaceful asked. "Where's Judith?"

"In the hotel lobby reading a newspaper and some magazines. Somebody came in the hotel and said they thought they heard a rifleshot a spell back, but I reckon they were mistaken. There doesn't seem to be any excitement around."

"There was a rifleshot all right," Peaceful said. "Back on the next street, in the residential section. I reckon nobody paid any attention to it though. There's always some wild shooting going on in this town." He explained briefly what had happened; then before Tarp had a chance to do any talking he concluded, "Come on with me. I'm going to see Fletcher Uhlmann. I might want you as a witness to what he says. Hurry up!"

Tarp fell in beside Peaceful. "I got full sail on, cowboy. If there's a squall due I want to led a hand on the lines."

They crossed Main Street diagonally toward the bank building on the other corner. The bank windows were dark, but a light showed from behind blinds in Uhlmann's living quarters on the second floor. Leading the way, Peaceful started towards the wooden stairway that scaled the side of the building. As he drew near he saw a horse and buggy waiting, tethered to a short tie rail at the side of the bank building. He swerved direction and glanced inside the darkened interior of the buggy. The seat was empty.

"Looks like Uhlmann might be planning a trip," Peaceful said. "C'mon, we'll go see."

He hurried up the staircase, opened the door at the top. Tarp followed him into the darkened hall. At the first door Peaceful paused and listened. From within the room he could hear rapid movements. "Uhlmann's in there," he whispered and knocked on the door. Instantly there was silence from within. Peaceful knocked again. A none too steady voice replied, "Who's there?"

Peaceful nudged Tarp. Tarp answered, "It's me, Fletch—Tarp Thompson."

"I can't see you now, Thompson," came the irritated reply. "I'm busy. Come around to-morrow."

"Stow that," Tarp snapped. "I want to see you now. It won't take but a minute."

There was some muttered cursing from behind the door; then a key turned in the lock and the door opened a few inches. Peaceful inserted his foot in the opening and shoved open the door. Uhlmann staggered back, his face going ashen as he recognized his visitor. "You! Jenkins!" he gasped.

"That's my name," Peaceful said quietly. Tarp came in behind him and closed the door.

Uhlmann sat weakly down on the bed at one side. Peaceful glanced around the room. It was scantily furnished with the bed, a couple of chairs, and a dresser. At one side was a tall screen, behind which Peaceful could see clothing hanging on hooks. A bureau held a pitcher and a washbasin. Near by on the wall hung a fly-specked mirror. A lamp burned on a table.

"What do you want?" Uhlmann found courage to ask.

Peaceful laughed and pointed to the open suitcase in the middle of the floor in which Uhlmann had been packing clothing. "Going away, Uhlmann?" he asked. "We saw you had a rig waiting down on the street and figured you might be leaving on a vacation."

Uhlmann nodded. "Not a regular vacation. I'm just driving to Surcingle for overnight. I'll be back in the morning."

"You're a fast driver," Peaceful drawled. "And you sure take a lot of clothes for an overnight stay. What else you taking?"

Uhlmann looked startled. "Why-why, nothing."

"Don't lie to me, Uhlmann," Peaceful said. He approached the bed and pushed Uhlmann to one side, then stooped down and drew from beneath the bed two well-filled valises. Despite his protest Peaceful made Uhlmann deliver the keys to the two bags. Uhlmann finally surrendered them, then fell back with a moan of fear.

Peaceful opened the bags and found them stuffed with money—bills, gold, and silver.

Tarp gasped. "Well, blow me down for a water-soaked swab!"

Peaceful said grimly, "Uhlmann, I reckon we just got here in time to catch you red-handed. Running off with the bank's funds, eh? You blasted embezzler! Only a dirty crook would run off with the money entrusted to him by his neighbours. You're pretty low, Uhlmann."

Tarp said angrily, "You should be put in irons and thrun down in the hold."

Uhlmann didn't say anything, only stared at Peaceful with fear-stricken eyes. "Wha-what you going to do with me?" he gasped after a long silence.

"It depends on how fast you talk up and tell what you know about the skulduggery in these parts," Peaceful snapped. "What was back of the move to rob Jabez Drake?"

"I swear I don't know anything about that," Uhlmann said hoarsely. "That was Randle's doings."

"Don't lie to me, Uhlmann," Peaceful said grimly. "Jake Tracy was killed to-night, but before he died he talked. He mentioned your name as being behind everything."

"Oh, my God!" Uhlmann gasped, clutching at his throat as though he already felt a hangman's noose there.

"Talk, damn you!" Tarp growled.

Peaceful said, hard-voiced, "I've got the dead-wood on every one of you crooks, Uhlmann. I know it wasn't Louie Dawes that shot Drake. That was done with your permission."

"Don't say that," Uhlmann fairly screeched.

"Talk up, then. It's the only way you'll save your skin. Otherwise it's the gallows."

"Talk fast, you butt-scuttlin' swab!" Tarp threatened. "A few lashes of the cat would make you talk."

"Talk!" Peaceful snapped. "And talk quick. Either that or off you go to gaol with your pards!"

Together they finally broke Uhlmann's yellow nerve. Cowering, he promised to tell all he knew if Peaceful would put in a good word at his trial. Peaceful said, "I'll promise nothing now. Let's see how you behave first. What was the idea of robbing Drake?"

"We wanted to get his ranch."

"Who's we?"

"Randle and me. Heffner and Tracy were in it too. We wanted to fix matters so we could take the ranch away from him. If he couldn't pay off his loans he'd lose the JD. Louie Dawes didn't want to pull that hold-up, but Tracy forced him into it. He had a hold on Louie. We told Louie he could have half the money he got from Drake. Vaughn put on an act, pretending to miss when he shot at Louie. Then he followed Louie out into

298

the country and really shot him. Vaughn had a fake money sack fixed up, which he switched for the sack of cash. Vaughn got that five thousand for his part in the deal. Randle wanted Drake killed that day, but Louie refused to do any shooting. He just brandished that revolver to scare Drake."

"It was Randle that shot Drake, wasn't it?" Peaceful asked.

Uhlmann's eyes widened. "How did you know that?"

Peaceful said, "That day I came up to look at the offices you had for rent I found this." Taking a wrapped bandanna out of his pocket, he unrolled it and produced an empty forty-five shell and the stub of a thin black cigar such as Randle always smoked. "To-day," he went on, "I fired a shot from Randle's six-shooter and kept the empty shell. The mark of the hammer firing pin is identical on both shells, and as no two firing pins leave exactly the same impression, it proves both shells came from the same six-shooter. And Randle's cigar butt clinches the proof. This sort of evidence will stand up in any court—and it is going to!"

"Shiver my timbers, if that ain't smart deduction," Tarp said admiringly.

Uhlmann slumped weakly. "You're right, Jenkins. It was Randle who shot Jabez Drake. He meant to kill Drake, I guess. I was against murder, of course, but—but—well, once we got into the thing I couldn't back out. Then you arrived. Things went bad from that minute. You got that letter of Louie Dawes's. I was scared then. You shot Cubera and Tracy. To-day you finished Heffner. Somehow we haven't had any luck since you arrived. I warned Randle against his highhanded actions. He's been rustling cattle right and left from all the outfits and running them over into Sombrero County, where he trades herds with another rustling gang headed by a man named Dennis Amber."

"We'll get Amber." Peaceful nodded.

"Anyway, that's how Randle's Wolf Head herds grew so fast and why no local cattle were ever found in a Wolf Head herd. Amber and Randle exchanged bills of sale for the cattle, so everything appeared legal. But I've still got money—money of my own—and I'll square everything for folks who have lost cows. Drake needn't fear losing his ranch. I promise. I'll give him money—anything I—I—"

"Quit your snivelling," Peaceful said disgustedly. "You gambled for big stakes. Now don't start whimpering when you lose. For gosh sake, be a man. I still don't understand why you hombres wanted Drake's JD so bad. There are other ranches! There's lots of good land hereabouts."

"Conejo Canyon lies on the JD," Uhlmann

explained. "It's the only pass through the Los Padres Range, until you go north about four hundred miles."

"What's that got to do with it?" Peaceful asked.

Uhlmann said, "Bankers sometimes get word of happenings long before other people. You know the T.N.&A.S. Railroad that is building to Spanish Wells?"

Peaceful said, "I saw 'em laying track when I came through. The end of the line will be at Spanish Wells."

Uhlmann shook his head. "That was what was first decided, but I happened to learn that now the T.N.&A.S. figures to lay rails straight through the Los Padres, eventually reaching to the west coast of California. The only way to get through the mountains, without going to a prohibitive expense, is through Conejo Canyon. The T.N.&A.S. will pay big money for a right of way through that canyon. Whoever owns it can get nearly any price they name. Now you know why we wanted to get the JD Ranch. Had our plans gone through, we could have held the railroad up for hundreds of thousands of dollars. The railroad expects to start negotiations next week."

"You mean"—Tarp's eyes bugged out of his head—"that Jabez will be rich?"

"There's no doubt of it," Uhlmann said brokenly, "and with a bit of luck it could have been me. But I'm licked. Jenkins, to-day when I learned you were a deputy United States marshal I realized our game was up. I tried to convince Randle, but he thought we still had a chance. I knew he was wrong, so I decided to get out and take the bank's money with me. I know it was wrong. I've been a miserable sinner—" A sob racked his body, and he commenced to weep copiously. Peaceful turned away in disgust.

At that moment a soft knock sounded at the door. Peaceful stiffened and drew his gun. Tarp did likewise.

Peaceful said softly, "Uhlmann, whoever that is, tell them to come in."

Hope lighted Uhlmann's teary eyes. He cleared his throat and called strongly, "Come on in! Is that you, Randle?"

28

CONCLUSION

THE door swung open. Peaceful lowered his gun. A hopeless moan left Uhlmann's lips. Tarp exclaimed, "May I be a son of a sea cook, if it ain't Applejack! What happened to you, feller?"

Applejack and Willie Horton entered the room and closed the door behind them. Applejack was indeed a sight. One eye was nearly swollen shut; his nose was skinned; a bruised spot showed greenish-purple over one cheekbone. The front of his shirt was blood-soaked.

Peaceful said, "Judas! What happened to you, pard?"

Applejack forced a grin from split lips. "I got caught between a couple of sidewinders, the same being named Randle and Vaughn. If it wasn't for Willie, here, I reckon I'd still be out of the picture."

Willie grinned at Peaceful. Peaceful said, "Good work, Willie. Applejack, tell us what you've been doing."

Applejack cast a quick look at Uhlmann

sprawled hopelessly on the bed. "How about him?"

Peaceful said, "He's through. Spilled everything he knew. I'll tell you later."

Applejack caught sight of the bags filled with money. "Cripes! Look at the *dinero*!"

Peaceful nodded. "Yeah, we got here just before Uhlmann left with the bank's funds. But go ahead and talk."

"I started out to look for Vaughn like you told me to," Applejack commenced. "Looked all over town; couldn't sight hide nor hair of the scut. I went in the Spanish Dagger. It's running, as usual, but he wasn't there. Randle wasn't in sight either."

"You tried Vaughn's office, of course?" Peaceful said.

"Tried that first," Applejack replied. "It was dark, so I figured he wasn't there. Like I say, I looked all over town. There ain't a saloon I haven't been in—besides a lot of other places. And I didn't even stop for one beer. Finally I got tired looking, so I figured he'd have to come back to his office sometime. I went back there to look for him. The office was still dark. I tried his door. It wasn't locked. I stepped inside and closed it again, figuring to surprise Vaughn when he showed up." Applejack paused.

"Well?" Peaceful said impatiently.

"That's when I found Vaughn." Applejack

grinned. "Him and Randle had been hiding out in that office all the time. They hit me over the head with something that wasn't a feather, and down I went. Geez! I felt foolish walking into a trap like that. I went out cold for a few minutes. Then they started working on me with their fists. It was the pain of their wallops that brought me back to consciousness. Finally they let up. I pretended I was still out. Randle wanted to shoot me, but Vaughn vetoed that. He was afraid the noise of a shot might bring an investigation. Meanwhile they'd tied me up with ropes until I could hardly wriggle. There I was, lying on the floor and listening to 'em talk. They talked plenty, figuring I wouldn't regain consciousness until morning."

"But where are they now?" Peaceful asked.

"I don't know."

"You don't know?"

"Not right at the moment. I know they're due back in town at ten o'clock. What time is it now?"

Peaceful consulted his watch. "Nine-fifteen."

Applejack went on, "We got plenty of time then. Like I say, I lay quiet there in the darkness and listened to 'em making plans. It was Vaughn that did the rifle work from that tree to-night, by the way. They mentioned that in their talk."

Peaceful asked, "What's Randle and Vaughn planning for ten o'clock?"

"You got 'em scared, pard. They don't like that

305

gold badge of yours. They're skipping town. But first they're coming back here at ten o'clock, when there won't be so many folks around town, except at the Spanish Dagger. They're planning to clean out the bank and skip to Mexico."

"What!" Indignantly Uhlmann leaped from the bed, his eyes flashing. "They're planning to rob my bank—*my* bank! Why, the dirty crooks!"

"Yes, ain't they?" Applejack grinned. "And you don't fit into their plans, Uhlmann, except to have your throat cut if you make a disturbance. They got an idea you're yellow and don't deserve any consideration anyway."

Uhlmann groaned. "After all I've done for Randle too. I never figured he would cross me up this way. Why, if it wasn't for me he'd never have found a place to pass the marked bills he got in a robbery—bills he used to buy the Wolf Head. He's the dirtiest crook I ever met!"

Applejack grinned. "The kettle is calling the pot black."

Peaceful said, "But you don't know where they are now?"

"Not exactly," Applejack shook his head. "Out on the edge of town somewhere, where two of the Wolf Head cow hands are holding horses for 'em. The two are named Lippy Leonard and Gus Clark. The four of 'em will be here at ten o'clock to clean the bank. This Gus Clark used to work for a safe-and-vault company; I heard 'em say he

306

was a whiz at working out a combination. That's why he's being taken in. And Lippy Leonard because he is a friend of Clark's. Besides, they need an extra man to take care of Uhlmann should he wake up and start anything. They figure he'll be asleep at ten o'clock."

"But how did you get loose?" Peaceful asked.

"That's to Willie's credit. I lay there listening to 'em make plans. Finally they left to walk out to the edge of town where the two cow hands are holding the horses. They locked the door after them, leaving me to die, for all they cared. Now, Willie, you tell your part."

"Well, Marshal Jenkins," Willie said pridefully, "you know how you told me to keep my eyes peeled if I wanted to be a good detective and let you know if anything unusual turned up? Well, I knowed you were out to get Randle's scalp, so ever since then I've been sort of trailing him—what detectives call shadowing, you know—thinking I might learn something you'd be interested in."

"I understand, Willie." Peaceful nodded.

The boy continued, "To-night I was sort of spying from the porch of Mr. Purdy's store—you know it's right across from the Spanish Dagger, on the same side of the street, right where Alamo crosses Main, you know. The store porch is right dark in the shadow at night, and I could see fine from there if anybody left the Spanish Dagger.

At the same time, looking across Main, I could see Deputy Vaughn's office. Well, earlier in the evening I saw Vaughn run into the Spanish Dagger. A few minutes later he and Randle came out and crossed over to Vaughn's office—"

Peaceful broke in, "Did Vaughn have a rifle with him at the time?"

Willie shook his head. "No, but as they passed the store porch I scrunched down in the shadow and I heard Vaughn say something about throwing his rifle away in the alley. Then Randle said, "It's too damn bad you couldn't have plugged Jenkins at the same time you got Tracy. With Jenkins alive we don't dare stay longer. We'll go through with the bank job as planned."

Willie paused and then continued, "I knowed something was up when I heard that. I watched them cross over and go in Vaughn's office. They didn't light up and they didn't come out again. I thought that was dang funny. Pretty soon I see Applejack come down the street. Then he went in Vaughn's office. Still no lights. I snuk across the street and listened close at the side of the building. It sounded like a commotion in there."

Applejack said, "If that was just a commotion I'd hate to really get beat up sometime."

The boy nodded seriously and went on, "After a time things quieted down; I could hear Vaughn and Randle talking but couldn't make out what they were saying. I commenced to get real worried about Applejack. Finally Vaughn and Randle stepped outside and locked the door. I heard Randle say, 'The lousy lawman can rot in there, for all I care.' I was sure feared they'd killed Applejack."

"I was damn nigh sure of it." Applejack grinned ruefully, feeling of his swollen jaw. "Anyway, they left my gun in my holster, so I'll get another chance at 'em."

"There ain't much more to tell," Willie concluded. "As soon as Randle and Vaughn left I busted a window in the place and got inside. I found Applejack tied up and I cut him free. And—and here we are."

"By cripes, boy!" Peaceful said warmly. "You've really earned a good fee for this piece of detective work, and I'll see that you get it. If you ever go to Texas I'll gladly recommend you for the Rangers."

"Gee, golly, that's great, Marshal Jenkins."

Peaceful considered a minute. "Well, Applejack, we better slip down inside the bank and get ready for the robbers when they show up. Tarp, you and Willie stay up here and guard Uhlmann. Willie, there's a gun in Uhlmann's suitcase. Get it out. If he makes one solitary peep you bat him over the head with it."

"Too bad it ain't a belayin' pin," Tarp growled. "While Willie watches Uhlmann I'll stay ready for that Lippy Leonard should he come in here."

"You don't need to watch me," Uhlmann said broken-spiritedly. "I hope you catch those crooks. Jenkins, here's the key to the front door of my bank. From now on I want to help all I can."

Peaceful accepted the key, saying, "You should have got wise sooner, Uhlmann." Then to his pardner, "C'mon, Applejack, let's get moving. Tarp, put out this light after we leave. We want to make it look like Uhlmann's in bed."

Together Peaceful and Applejack descended the staircase that ran down the side of the building. At the bottom Applejack said, "That horse and buggy?"

"Uhlmann intended to make a getaway with it. Reckon we'd better lead the horse around in the alley, so Randle and his crowd won't notice it."

They put the horse and rig around back of the bank building, then retraced their steps to the front. Peaceful inserted the key in the front door, and a moment later they stepped inside the darkened bank.

The shades were drawn across the windows, and no light seeped in. Peaceful relocked the door after them, and the two squatted down in the pitch-blackness to wait inside the front doorway.

While they waited Peaceful outlined briefly Uhlmann's confession. When he had finished Applejack whistled softly. "Whew! Drake stands to clean up at the T.N.&A.S. Railroad's expense. I'm glad. It's about time he got a break of luck. Uhlmann sure came clean, didn't he?"

"I never saw anybody turn so yellow," Peaceful said.

"Did you ever notice how bad a feller wants a cigarette at a time like this?" Applejack whispered.

"We wouldn't dare. They might sniff smoke when they came in. That would give everything away."

"I know, but it doesn't stop me wanting."

The minutes drifted slowly past. Now and then footsteps were heard on the sidewalk outside, but they quickly receded into distance. There weren't many people abroad this far from the centre of things, which at night was the vicinity of the Spanish Dagger.

Applejack shifted uncomfortably and said, "Dang it, I keep thinking about that cool beer of Johnny's. I'd give a fortune for a scuttle of suds right now."

Peaceful laughed softly. "If Tarp was here he'd insist on you calling it a schooner."

"I wonder if Tarp ever would have made a sailor."

Peaceful said, "Jabez Drake told me the only time Tarp ever put to sea he was seasick from the time the boat started until it returned."

Applejack snickered softly. "Damn if he won't

like to talk about it though. I'll bet—" He stopped suddenly.

Both men straightened up, hugging the front wall. Hoofbeats sounded rapidly along the street. They stopped out in front of the bank. There came the creaking of saddle leather, then soft steps on the porch before the bank door. A metal tool clanked against the edge of the door. A man grunted. There came a sharp, splintering sound as the lock gave way before violent force.

Then the door swung open. Cool night air swept into the bank.

Three shadowy forms passed inside within reach of Applejack and Peaceful. The two held their breath. Somebody paused to close the door. The steps went on. Randle's whispered voice came through the silence: "Uhlmann was asleep, I reckon. There wasn't any light up there. All right, Gus, get busy and let's see you open that vault."

"And hurry it up," Vaughn growled nervously. "We've got to work fast."

Gus Clark said, "Scratch a match, you hombres. Once I've located that vault I can work in the dark, but I don't want to go stumbling around until I find it."

Both Vaughn and Randle scratched matches. The two flames lighted the room but feebly, but Peaceful could see the three men, their backs to him and Applejack, peering through the cashier's wicket toward the rear of the room.

Suddenly a curse was ripped from Randle's mouth. At the same instant Vaughn fell to swearing, and Gus Clark said, "Hell's bells! I won't have to open that vault! The door is standing wide open. Even from here I can see it's empty. Somebody's beat us to it, damn the luck!"

"It's that damned Uhlmann!" Randle raged. "The dirty crook has double-crossed us! He ain't upstairs a-tall!"

Peaceful's voice came quietly through the room: "You'd better stick 'em up, hombres. You're covered!"

There was an instant's silence while the lighted matches flickered out. Darkness again. A sudden shifting of feet. Then the crashing detonation of a forty-five! At that point hell seemed to break loose. Peaceful and Applejack had thrown themselves apart, shooting as they moved.

Vivid crimson lances of flame crossed and crisscrossed in the intense gloom as the three bandits scattered and pulled triggers. The room shook with the savage reverberations. Someone groaned and fell heavily. In the momentary light from gun flashes Peaceful saw only two men standing. He thumbed another shot. A man crashed down, cursing as he fell.

The shooting stopped as abruptly as it started. There came a moment of silence, broken only by heavy breathing. Suddenly from near the floor a six-shooter roared violently, Peaceful instantly replied to the shot, thumbed another shot.

Silence again. He wasn't sure where Applejack was. The room was thick with the odour of burned powder, stinging eyes and throat and nostrils. Peaceful started to plug out empty shells, reloading as he kept moving continually, eyes straining to penetrate the gloom. The room was swimming with smoke. Across the room he caught the sound of empty shells being plugged out to drop on the floor. He said quietly, "You all right, pard?"

"All right," came Applejack's voice. "Lord, that beer is going to taste good."

"I reckon it's all over," Peaceful said.

"I reckon," Applejack's voice came back through the darkness.

From above, outside, came a sudden fusillade of shooting, then old Tarp's strident tones: "I reckon that weighed your anchor for you, you wind-jammin', barnacle-bottomed son of a salt swab!"

Applejack laughed softly. "Sounds like the ancient mariner settled the hash of one Lippy Leonard."

"Sounds like," Peaceful agreed. "Let's light up and take toll." They scratched matches, glancing quickly at the still figures on the floor. Three men lay dead. Now, from the street, they could hear loud excited cries and the sound of running feet approaching the bank.

Peaceful and Applejack flung open the door and stepped outside. A crowd was already gathering. Lights were springing up along the street. A man rushed up and confronted Peaceful, then stepped back. "Oh, it's you, Marshal Jenkins. What happened? Somebody try to rob the bank?"

"Tried but didn't succeed," Peaceful said quietly. "You're going to need a new banker here though. My nomination is Jabez Drake. He'll be situated right for that job before long."

Leaving Applejack to answer further questions, Peaceful rounded the corner of the building where he found Tarp Thompson bending over a sprawled form on the earth.

Tarp glanced up at Peaceful's approach, saying calmly, "It's Lippy Leonard. I heard him waitin' outside Uhlmann's door until the shootin' broke out; then he made a dash to get away. I set full sail after him. The instant he saw me he cut loose with his Colt gun, so I unlimbered my starboard weapon. I sure scuttled his ship for him. Applejack all right?"

"Right as a trivet. You'd better get back and see that Uhlmann doesn't escape."

"Willie's settin' a dogwatch on him."

Peaceful shouldered his way through the crowd that had followed him around the corner, then broke into a run toward the hotel. Half-way there he saw Judith hurrying to meet him. An instant later she was in his arms, her lips soft and warm on his. After a time she spoke, a sob in her throat: "Oh, Peaceful, I was so frightened for you when the shooting started. And yet I knew, somehow, you'd keep your promise. I was so sure I had the liveryman saddle our horses."

"My promise?"

"You promised to take me home to-night."

"You still want to go—to-night?"

"I want to see that new moon you spoke of— and learn how the pony reacts. I've decided to keep him, you know."

"I forgot to tell you before—you have to take me with the pony."

"I intend to. Oh, let's hurry and get started."

They hurried, but, somehow, they were only half-way to the JD Ranch by the time the new moon started to drop. . . .

Books are produced in the United States using U.S.-based materials

Books are printed using a revolutionary new process called THINKtech™ that lowers energy usage by 70% and increases overall quality

Books are durable and flexible because of Smyth-sewing

Paper is sourced using environmentally responsible foresting methods and the paper is acid-free

Center Point Large Print

600 Brooks Road / PO Box 1
Thorndike, ME 04986-0001 USA

(207) 568-3717

US & Canada:
1 800 929-9108
www.centerpointlargeprint.com